Hear Me Now

Hear Me Now
By
Melyssa Winchester

Copyright | 2014 Melyssa Winchester

Cover Image Copyright Sivilla @ Shutterstock.
Cover Image Design by Melyssa Winchester

This story in these pages is dedicated to my second family. Linda, my mother, Mallory, my sister and Zach; the little man, the best little brother on the block. I love you all more than words can say and these stories would not be written without you.

Prologue

Dillon

I am going to kill that son of a bitch. Everything was fine until he got involved.

Kayden Walker. The guy that thinks just because he fell in love with a retard, it somehow makes him better than the rest of us. He's so full of shit his eyes should be brown.

He looks down on me, going out of his way to make my life a living hell when he's the one that started all of this four years ago.

When I moved here about halfway through freshman year, he'd been the first person to give me the time of day. He saw my size and the scowl I always seem to wear and that's all it took. We hit it off and never looked back. Within six months, we started picking people we saw as weaker than us and tortured them until soon, everyone knew not to mess with us.

Calling the rat squad on me was a dickhead move, but one I should've seen coming. It's not like he didn't warn me he was gonna do it. A few months ago, he made sure I knew that the way things have always been wasn't gonna fly anymore, which is why being here now shouldn't come as a shock.

I don't know what the big deal is honestly. So I grabbed one of the stupid kids, pulled him into the locker room and wailed on him. I've been doing that shit for years and even though I've been warned a couple times, nothing's ever been done before. All of a sudden it's this big fucking deal and I'm having to sit here, my mom by my side and listen as the principal lays down his pathetic version of the law.

Daniels has been gunning for me since Homecoming. I knew it was only a matter of time before I ended up here. Kayden didn't have to tell him what he caught me doing, I would've landed here for some other reason. The guy's got a hard on for me and quite frankly, it's pissing me off. Maybe the next person I go after should be him instead of the special needs moron he's defending.

"You don't seem to get it. The way Dillon is behaving is because of his father leaving. He's a good boy, Principal Daniels. I think you're making a mountain out of a molehill."

There she is.

My mother, Rebecca Murphy; clueless as ever.

It doesn't matter how many times she sits in this chair, she still spouts off the same garbage. My problems are never my own, they're always because of my father leaving or her addiction to pain medication. Maybe that's half the reason I'm such an asshole. She never taught me to own my own shit. Whatever the reason for her excuses now, I'm tired of it.

"That may be, Mrs. Murphy, but it does not excuse his behavior. After what happened at Homecoming, we have implemented a zero tolerance policy for bullying and inappropriate contact of any kind. Despite knowing this, he still refuses to comply and as such needs to be punished."

Here's where she begs him not to suspend me. If he does, I'm going to have to be home alone since because of her job she can't watch over me. It's always the same damn thing with her. I'm eighteen, yet she's about to make me sound like I'm twelve.

"It's not that I don't think he should be punished for what he did, but have you even spoken to the other student? Dillon is not like this when he's home with me. He's a good boy. Maybe this other boy said something to get him riled up."

"Eric Carmen did nothing but attempt to go home for the day. What your son did, he made the conscious decision to do. I am not sure how he appears to you at home, but the way he behaves in the academic setting leaves something to be desired."

I've heard enough of this shit. They're only gonna go back and forth for the next hour debating this. Mom won't believe I'm a bad seed or whatever and he's gonna act like he gives a shit about what goes on here and not back down. I'm ending it.

"Can you just suspend me so we can get this over with?" I interject, making both of them turn to me, finally acknowledging that they aren't the only two people in the room. They might want to talk about me like I'm not even here, but I'm not having any part of it.

"He will do nothing of the sort!" She shouts, which makes me wanna scream back at her. She's nothing but a doped out moron and if she managed to stay clean for five damn minutes, she might be able to see that the guy's telling her the truth.

I'm a first class douchebag. I've always been one and if she would pull her head out of her ass, she'd see it and maybe do some actual parenting for once, instead of always sweeping my shit under the rug.

"I did it, Mom! I took that stupid retard, slammed him against the lockers and beat the living piss out of him!"

"Dillon, Mommy is handling the situation. There's no need for you to do this."

Holy shit. She just doesn't get it. It doesn't even matter who's telling her, she refuses to believe any of it.

"Look man," I say, turning toward Daniels, hoping I'll have better luck with him so we can get this whole stupid charade over with and I can get out of here. "You know I did it, I know I did it, so let's just end it. Tell me how long I'm suspended for, so I can get the fuck out of here."

His body tenses at my language and I laugh. He's gonna sit here all calm knowing I beat on some retarded kid, but is gonna act shocked that I swear. Adults make no damn sense.

"Suspending you may have been the way we dealt with situations like this in the past, but that is not the approach we're going to take this time around. In order for you to truly learn from what you've done, I do believe you need to experience it firsthand."

What the hell is that supposed to mean?

"What did you have in mind?" My mom asks, putting her two cents back into the conversation and leaving me wishing again that she'd just butt out. Being eighteen has to mean I deal with the stuff I do on my own; right? Isn't that what being an adult is all about?

"Your son has spent the last six months picking out students and bullying them excessively. Sending him home is not going to teach him how wrong his actions are. Only when he has experienced time with the very people he's been bullying will he truly grasp the gravity of the situation."

This isn't good. I know what he's getting at, even though he's using way too many words to get his point across. He's not going to give me the easy way out this time; the way he did with Ames and the others months ago. This time he's going to hit me right where it hurts.

"Effective immediately, I am pulling Dillon from his regular classes. From this moment on, he will report to Ms. Taylor's class every day and it is there he will remain until such time as I have seen a change in him."

Son of a bitch!

What the hell am I going to do now?

Chapter One

Cadence

I can't believe I've got to do this for the next two weeks.

Being stuck at Wexfield High School is not my idea of a good time and I'm pretty sure my mom knows it. It's the whole reason she moved me out of the regular elementary school years ago. She knew what being in the regular school atmosphere would bring down on me and I agreed. I should be spending my sophomore year at my school, not dealing with this.

The reason she wanted me in a different school, it's because I'm deaf.

I've been deaf since birth, though no matter how many times I ask my mom to explain just what that means or even ask my doctor, I never get a straight answer for. I've taken to Google in order to get answers to how I ended up this way, but I'm starting to think there's no answer to be found. It's just a freak of nature kind of thing. I wasn't born prematurely, my mom wasn't diagnosed with anything when she was pregnant that would have caused it and there's no family members on either side that are remotely hard of hearing.

So basically, I'm a freak of nature.

A deaf freak that up until this morning, attended Wexfield School for the Deaf and was more than happy about it.

Stupid pipes. If they hadn't burst in the middle of the night, causing the entire second floor of the school to flood, I wouldn't be here right now.

It figures my mom has to be one mother in the entire town that doesn't want to leave me home alone for the two weeks it's going to take them to sort the mess out. Things would be too simple if she did that.

When she got the call in the early hours of the morning, she started planning and by the time I woke up, she informed me of exactly what would be happening.

So here I am; standing in the hall just outside her classroom giving myself the mother of all pep talks in order to gather up the nerve to walk through the door.

It's not that I'm afraid to be here, but when I've been in a place surrounded by people that are like me for so long, being thrust into a situation that's the complete opposite, it throws me off. I might be in my mom's class and it might be with a bunch of kids that have their own struggles and difficulties, but it doesn't mean they'll be accepting of mine.

It's something I would have expected the special education teacher to know or at least sympathize with. Guess I was wrong.

As I prepare to take the steps needed in order to make my way completely into the class, I feel a squeeze on my shoulder. It doesn't take me long to figure out that it's my mom. Even though she'd driven me to school, I've gone out of my way to avoid her since. It was only a matter of time before she found me.

Walking around until she's able to give me a once over, the world's brightest smile on her face, she lifts her hands and starts signing. I dart my eyes around the room as she's doing it, making sure no one is watching. It's my first day here. I don't want a bunch of eyes focused on me; pitying me because I'm the deaf kid.

When I'm secure no one is paying attention, I turn back and see that she's caught me looking away. She knows that half of what she said, I didn't even catch. Where most parents might get annoyed with having to repeat themselves, she just smiles at me and starts again.

She knows she doesn't have to sign. Dealing with this my entire life with the help of speech therapy and spending so much time with her, I've learned to read lips easily. Well, easily if the person talking does it at an even pace.

Signing back as quickly as possible, letting her know that from now on, it would be easier if she would just speak to me like normal, I motion to my seat and turn away from her. There's a few minutes before the final bell so the sooner I get seated and focused, the faster I can get the first day in my two weeks of hell over with.

Accepting my response, she heads to the front of the room and I head for the first available seat I see, as far in the back as I can possibly get. It's only when I get myself settled, pulling my book from my bag, preparing to read that the whole dynamic of the room changes.

Not being able to hear, I'm hyper sensitive in every other way. My sense of smell is more powerful, my sight unmatched and touch, well let's just say that if it's something I've experienced before, I can recognize it instantly. It's that hypersensitivity that causes me to look up as the shadow makes its way through the door.

The guy that my eyes lock on looks about as thrilled to be here as I am and I start to wonder if he's another kid from my school that somehow got forced into showing up today the same as I did. It's only when he scowls as he scans the room that I realize he's not someone from my school at all, but another garden variety jerk. Not just any one either, but the worst one.

Dillon Murphy.

That's another thing my mom told me this morning before practically forcing me in the car to come here. Not only was I going to be a new student in her class, but it seems this guy is too.

The way she explained it to me, Dillon is not a special needs kid, but he's in desperate need of an intervention as far as his attitude goes and apparently this is the way the school is choosing to go about it. Making him a part of the very class full of students that he picks on so frequently.

I don't see that working out well, but that's because I've got experience with people like him. If anything, all putting him in here is gonna do is give him a bigger list of people to pick on.

We're close, my mom and me. She shares her days with me and it's because of this that I know all about this guy. I've never laid eyes on him before today though. So taking him in while he stands there looking like he wants to be anywhere else, I try and figure out what it is about him that makes him such a jerk.

He's about average for a football player, standing a little bit taller than my mom and since I know she's five ten, I figure he's gotta be about six feet. His hair is shaggier than I would expect for a ball player, but not so long that I can see it causing a problem on the field. He's kind of built, again, not a real surprise because of his position on the team, but not so much that he looks like the bodybuilders I've seen on TV.

Nothing about him stands out, at least it doesn't until his scan of the room brings his eyes to me. As we lock on each other, it's then I see the one thing about him that stands out more than anything else. Looking at me with a look of pure disgust on his face, are a pair of eyes the same chocolate brown color as my own.

Holy crap.

Shaking off my initial assessment, I lower my head until it appears as though I'm focused on reading; when the reality is, I'm doing all I can not to respond to the eyes that in just a few seconds have managed to pierce straight through me. I don't know what's gotten into me, but with the way I'm reacting, you would think I'd never seen a pair of brown eyes before.

This is crazy. I'm not supposed to find a damn thing about Dillon Murphy attractive. With all the things my mom told me about him, he's the last guy I want to get within a few feet of. His reason for being in this class is supposed to be a punishment, but if the chills I got when he looked at me are any indication, I'm the one that's about to be punished.

This is definitely going to be the longest two weeks of my life.

Dillon

When I got up this morning, I had this idea of how my day was going to go. I'd head to school, meet up with my girlfriend, have a little fun with her, possibly finding another moron to pick on and then head to first period. It's the same routine I've been doing for as long as I can remember and even though it was starting to get boring, I can't deny the security I get from the familiarity of it.

That's not at all what went down. As per his decision on Friday before my mother stormed out of his office, this day wasn't going to turn out like the others. Standing at the front of the building waiting for me after I drive in and park was none other than Principal Daniels and he looked less than pleased to see me.

So much for having a little playtime with Ames before first period.

"Mr. Murphy! So glad you could make it."

Yeah, I'm sure he's real glad I made it today. I have no doubt he's enjoying the hell out of shattering my reputation with this stupid stunt. I'm having to stop myself from telling him that this little plan of his is gonna fail miserably. Best not to piss the guy off before he's even attempted to straighten me out.

"Where else would I be?"

"Heading off to find that girlfriend of yours of course. I'm here to tell you that won't be happening today."

"Of course it's not. I wouldn't have the welcome wagon meeting me out front if it was."

This really blows. I know I gotta go through with this shit, but does he really have to walk me to class like I'm a fucking kid? I'm pretty sure I can find the retard class all on my own. It's not like it's moved since the last time I was here.

"In order to make sure you comply with what I've put in motion, I'm going to be accompanying you to Ms. Taylor's class today. She is eagerly awaiting your presence."

Yeah, I'm pretty sure that's a load of bullshit. I'm sure the last thing she wants to deal with is having me in her class. It's not exactly a secret that her students are the ones that brought all of this down on me. Eric and stupid Isabelle Reagan. Well, her and that asshole boyfriend of hers.

Thinking about Kayden just reminds me that the next time I see him, I don't care if he's ready for it or not, I'm gonna make him pay for this. If it wasn't for him squealing like the little bitch he is, I'd be able to catch up with my girlfriend and actually enjoy my day.

"Fine, whatever. Can we just get on with it already?"

"After you."

Damn. This guy isn't gonna budge. So not only am I getting an escort to the damn class, but he's gonna add insult to injury and follow behind me? All this shit because I threw a retard up against some lockers?

I've got to come up with a way to get out of this. I can't do this for the rest of the year and that's exactly what I'm looking at unless I can talk my way around it. I'm not gonna learn a lesson, let's be completely honest, which means unless I can come up with a way out, I'm stuck here forever.

When we get to the class, I expect him to push me inside with as eager as he was to make sure I got here, but all he does is walk in and around me. I start to see it for the escape it is, but before I turn around and make a run for it, his attention is back on me again and I've missed my shot.

I'm officially stuck here.

"Make yourself comfortable, Mr. Murphy."

If the son of a bitch calls me that again, sticking me in a retard class is gonna be the least of his concerns. I've never taken down an adult before, but with the way I'm feeling about this right now, I'm not against it. There's a first time for everything.

The only Mr. Murphy I know is the sadistic bastard I like to call dear old dad. It's bad enough that I have to be forced to spend actual time with the guy, I don't need to be reminded of him in the one place I've used for the last four years to escape him and his sick idea of parenting.

They say everyone's got a secret; I guess that's mine. I hate my father because for the last six years, his idea of good parenting has been to throw me into fights with people bigger than me and make me work for every breath I take after the fact. The son of a bitch can rot in hell for all I care.

Making my way into the class, I take in everything going on around me. There isn't a whole lot of people here yet, but the few kids I do see, I don't recognize. These are all the ones I haven't gotten around to harassing yet. I take stock of them, making a mental note for the next time I see Tim again; my hatred at being here growing by the second. They can go ahead and think that putting me in here is going to change the way I am all they want. In the end, all they're really doing is giving me an even bigger list of targets.

Morons.

Resigning myself to the fact that there's no way I'm going to get out of here in the foreseeable future, I look for the nearest empty seat. Giving the room another full scan, hoping I can find a seat as far in the back as possible, I notice something that I didn't catch the first time around. There's a person stretched out at a desk in the far left of the room. A girl, and with the way she's looking at me, it appears as though she caught me staring at her.

She's new. I know this because I would definitely remember seeing someone that looks like her around. I might have a girlfriend, but it doesn't mean I'm blind. If this girl went here, I would've noticed and judging by the look on her face, she looks about as thrilled to be here as I am.

Her caramel colored hair might be covering the majority of her face, but there's no mistaking the eyes looking back at me. They're the mirror image of my own and if she didn't look so damn hot, I might find the whole exchange creepy as hell. The way her gaze is trained on me, it's like she knows me, which is impossible since I have no clue who she is.

Before I can look away, I watch her head dip back down toward the desk and following her movements, I see she's now attempting to bury her attention in a book. That's fine, she can look away all she wants. Odds are, even with the look of annoyance I caught on her face, she's like Isabelle anyway and that's the last thing I need to be getting involved with.

No matter how sexy her eyes are.

Shit. I definitely don't need to be going there. If Amy gets wind of me even thinking what I just did, she'd cut my balls off. As long as I'm here, I'm gonna have to ignore the fact that this girl exists.

That gets harder to do as I catch where the only empty seat in the entire class is located. In the back, just the way she is, but instead of being on the other side of the room, as far away from her as possible, it's directly to her right.

Let the death sentence begin.

Cadence

Of course the only empty seat is beside me.

When I looked away it should have been the end of it, but of course that's not how my life works. He threw his body into the seat and I'm doing everything I can not to look over, even though I see his chest rise and fall out of the corner of my eye, making him even more impossible to ignore.

Why does he have to sit by me? Why can't my mom put him up near the front with the others and bring one of them back here? Having him this close is driving me crazy and he's only been here a few seconds. I'm super aware of every movement he's making and when I'm not cursing the fact that I'm here at all, I'm cursing my senses for being so damn good.

I don't want to smell him the way I do. The scent of sweat mixed with tobacco and talcum powder is a lethal combination to my nostrils. I'm frozen watching him rake his fingers through his shaggy brown hair and the way his lips part, letting what I can only assume is a sigh escape through them. I don't want to focus on this. It's bad enough my mom made me come here, the last thing I want to do is spend the entire time caught up in all things school bully.

Turning my head to the front of the room, I see my mom talking, but this time, the old guy is gone and she's speaking to the class. From the few words I pick up reading her lips, I see she's laying out a lesson, but since it's got nothing to do with what I'm learning, I don't attempt to follow along. Instead I look back down toward my book, but not before catching the guy roll his eyes.

Not thinking, I reach my hand across and flick him. I might not want to be here, but that doesn't mean I'm gonna sit idly by and watch some jackass disrespect my mom. The minute my finger connects with his shoulder, his head swerves and his eyes land on mine. At first he looks confused, but that quickly passes as his eyes turn hard, his lips which had been smirking a few seconds ago, now tight and straight.

Probably not the smartest idea to flick the school bully.

His lips move and I follow along easily. He's asking me a question and it's one I've definitely got an answer for, but it's probably not one he's gonna like hearing.

"What the fuck?"

Pulling the pad of sticky notes out of my bag, I scribble across the page and lift it high enough in the air so that he can see it, but I won't get caught by my mom.

Stop being an ass.

As he catches my words, he smirks and I can't help being drawn in even more by his lips. Giving myself a mental shake and a reminder about who it is I'm staring at, I notice his lips moving again, this time a little quicker than before, but not so quick I can't catch it.

"Why didn't you just say that out loud?"

Crumpling the sticky note and tossing it down into my open backpack, I scribble my response on a new one, this time leaning over and sticking it to his desk when I'm done. There. Let's see how he handles that.

Because you're not worth wasting my breath on.

His eyes fall to my words and I smile as they have the desired effect. The smirk he so proudly displayed a couple of seconds ago is gone and in its place is the long thin line again. I pissed him off.

Mission accomplished.

"Bitch."

Reaching over again after I catch the name he called me, I place another sticky note on his desk, this time way ahead of him and expecting the response. That's one thing I know about bullies. When they get put in their place or don't like the way someone reacts to them, they always resort to childish name calling.

Asshole.

The strangest thing happens when he takes in what I said. Instead of getting annoyed or displaying even more of his douchebag personality, he looks over and smiles.

I don't want to admit it, but when he smiles like that, he's actually kind of cute. I know he's king of the assholes here; I mean I just called him one, but right now, smiling at me the way he is, I don't see asshole at all.

Damn him.

If the smile wasn't enough, his lips part and he talks again. As I follow along, I've never been more thankful for the ability to lip read.

"You might be right about that. So, you got a name?"

Don't we all?

He body shakes as he laughs and my eyes dart to the front. After all the warnings I've had about this guy, the last thing I need is for my mom to catch me talking to him. There's no telling what she'll do with that. Right now, being stuck here the way I am, I need something to pass the time; even if it is the quarterback of the football team and the one guy I need to steer clear of.

Content that his laugh has gone unnoticed as she's now standing with her back turned, I look back to him and return his laugh with a smile.

"I'm Dillon."

Even though I've caught what he said, I turn away and focus my attention back on the book in front of me. He's already managed to get me to smile once already; the last thing I want to do is give him the satisfaction of learning my name. Let him stew on that for a while. I may be a lot of things, but easy is not one of them; especially not for this guy.

He taps me on the shoulder and despite my every attempt to ignore it, I fail and look, watching as his lips move again, repeating the question. I completely bail out of the plan and hold the already filled out sticky note in the air.

Cadence.

He doesn't say anything for a few minutes, so turning back to my book, I focus on the story and again do my best to tune him and his annoying scent out. It's only when I feel the brush of skin against my arm that I jump back in my seat. Looking up I see the paper on the edge of the desk and sliding a glance over in his direction, I see he's seated comfortably; his eyes trained ahead, his good student act a completely success.

Well, it's a completely success to him anyway.

Sliding the paper down to the center of the desk, I pull it open slowly and read the words.

Cadence. Thanks. This isn't such a death sentence anymore.

All I can think as I read the words over is how I couldn't agree with him more. Dillon Murphy may be a first class asshole, but at the very least, he's been an entertaining asshole and right now, I appreciate that more than he knows.

Maybe I can survive these two weeks after all.

Chapter Two

Dillon

When I got sentenced this morning, I figured I would end up here and the day would drag on with no end in sight. As the bell rings, it hits me that I didn't focus on the time because I'd been so focused on her.

There's at least twenty blue sticky notes on my desk and even though it's crazy, I make sure and pull them off, tossing them in the back pocket of my jeans before I head out. It's not all that crazy really, I mean I know why I did it.

She didn't take any of my shit.

The way it works around here is pretty simple. Being the quarterback of the football team, it gives me a whole lot of leeway, or at least it did before I got snagged for messing with Eric. I can pretty much do whatever I want, whenever I want and even if the faculty sees, they don't usually say a word because they don't wanna mess with me. What that means is, I don't usually have anyone that questions me at every corner. They're usually all too afraid to say much of anything.

Cadence isn't like that. Not only did she flick me every single time I rolled my eyes or made any sound that came out the slightest bit bored, but she even had a comeback when I insulted her. It's the first time since I got here four years ago where someone isn't letting me get away with shit.

She's not weak; at least she isn't yet, but considering the class she's in, I'm sure that will change and despite taking my mind off being here, I'm going to be the one to change it.

This might be my best plan yet. The moronic principal wants to throw me in a class full of rejects, well I'm gonna make it worth my while. With Cadence looking as hot as she does, this might even be easier than everything I did with Isabelle.

The more I thought about it while we were chatting back and forth, the more I realized it really is the perfect distraction and plan all rolled into one. I can waste my days away in here getting close to this girl and in the end screw her over in the best way possible.

What better way to waste time than to make some retard fall in love with me?

Packing up my stuff and heading out, I can't believe how worked up I am over this. For the first time since the dance, I've got something to look forward to. The only thing I'm not quite set on is what's going to happen when I tell Amy.

Even though she doesn't seem to care about Charlotte and Eve, adding another girl into the mix, even if it is to screw with her; well it might set the queen off and I definitely don't wanna do that.

I've been with Amy for about a year. We've been off and on for a year anyway. In that time, it seems like every time I so much as turn in a girl's general direction, it sets her off and she dumps me. If I didn't enjoy the things she does when we're alone, I would just let her screw off once and for all, but she is definitely good at what she does. She's also a temperamental bitch, but I'm not stupid enough to say that to her face. I enjoy keeping my balls intact.

Truth is, I like being with her because unlike every other chick on the planet, when I choose someone to pick on she's right there with me, wanting to push it as far as we can go. Some people might let their conscience stop them, but Amy doesn't. She's just as sadistic as I am and honestly, if Kayden isn't around to help, the only other person worthy to do it with me is her.

Cadence—shit. We've been looking for a new target since Kayden caught me with Eric and she's the perfect candidate. Amy will see it that way when I mention it to her, I'm sure of it.

Putting the girl out of my head, I make my way into the hall, coming face to face with Tim and as usual, he's grinning at me.

"Don't even think about it." I warn, motioning down the hall, as far away from this class and the people in it as I can get. "I just wanna get the hell out of here."

"Wasn't gonna say a word, bro."

"Since when? You've always got something to say."

Tim seems to think on this because for the first time in weeks, his mouth goes completely shut. I've never been so thankful for quiet in my life. The guy might be my friend, but that doesn't mean he doesn't annoy the hell out of me most of the time. He's definitely the mouth piece of the group.

If Charlotte wasn't so intent on hooking up with Kayden, they'd be a match made in heaven.

"So how long you gonna be stuck in there?"

"No fucking clue, but if I have my way, not long. I'm gonna see if pleading my case to Coach can get me out. In the meantime, I think I found the perfect distraction."

"What's that?" he asks and catching the grin I'm wearing he returns it with one of his own. Tim may be a total moron most of the time, but he definitely catches on quick when I put something in motion. It's half the reason I've kept him around this long.

"There's a new girl in the class, never seen her before. I'm thinking instead of going for the usual retards; we change things up and go after this one."

"How are you gonna do that?"

"Get close to her; make her think we're friends. I'll even bring her around at lunch to make it seem more legit. I mean if she's in the class, I'm sure she'll hear about the shit I've done, so bringing her close will erase anything people may tell her. Then we can all have a little fun."

"Okay man, whatever you wanna do, but when are we doing it?"

"Well, was planning on starting this afternoon." I say quickly, but seeing the look on his face, I realize that's not what he's getting at. "Wait, do what?"

"Deal with Kayden."

Despite how bad I want to get back at that son of a bitch for bringing this whole thing down on me, I'm not a complete moron. Retaliation is something they're gonna be waiting for. I would figure out a way to make Kayden pay, but it's gonna have to wait. If I try anything now, god only knows what the next punishment would be. Knowing Daniels, he'd probably put me on mop duty for Isabelle and her fucking accidents.

"Not happening, at least not yet. They're gonna be expecting that. He'll get his."

"Uhh..."

I know that sound. Tim's gone and done something and odds are because of his association with me, it's gonna end up falling back in my lap.

Fantastic.

"What did you do?"

"Ames told me everything that went down and when he met up with the retard this morning, we got some retribution."

Knowing that Tim and Amy had my back should make me happy, but nothing about what he's saying sparks that in me. If anything, it just pisses me off more. I might act like a complete idiot sometimes, but even I know that doing anything after what just happened to me would only bring more trouble. I would've thought Tim learned that by now, hanging out with me as long as he has.

Apparently not.

"What did you do?" I repeat, annoyed that he won't just spit it out.

"We popped his back tires. Well, I did that. Ames keyed the side of his car."

Shit!

So much for going under the radar for a while. Kayden was gonna catch on to what they did and when that happened they wouldn't be the ones handling it. I would. It was all gonna fall back on me because I'm supposed to keep these idiots under control.

Before I can rip him a new one the way I want to, my phone goes off. It's not the first time Amy's texted when I'm not there to meet her, so as I pull it out that's what I'm expecting to find. Looking at the screen, I see it's not Ames at all, but the very last person I want to talk to right now.

My father.

Bruce Murphy only contacts me for one reason and it's got nothing to do with a father son weekend, at least not in the way most dads are. He wants to get together all right, but it's only because he's got another fight set up for me and he's letting me know so I can prepare for it.

You know how my mom is completely clueless about the shit I cause here at school? Bruce knows all about it. In fact, whenever we do spend any amount of time together where I'm not having a guy's fist shoved in my face, he's the one telling me to do it. He doesn't come right out and say it, but he implies that anyone that displays weakness is in need of a good beating.

So that's how I've been doing things since just after my twelfth birthday.

Anyone who appears weak is wrong and it definitely applies to these so called *'different'* people. They're all weak as hell and it's my job to beat it out of them, breaking them down until there's nothing left.

I don't wanna answer this call. He just saw me last weekend, lined up three fights for me, all of them I somehow managed to win. I need a break. My body is still healing from the beating I went through; putting me back into another fight might be smart for him, but it wasn't for me. If I say no or ignore the call though, it just means I'm weak and that's the last fucking thing I am. So as usual, I break and answer.

"What do you want?"

"Bout damn time you answered the phone. What else you got going on that's so important?"

"I don't know Dad; this thing called school that you and Mom insist on making me deal with?"

"Wednesday night. The abandoned farm. You know where it is right? Be there at seven. Got another three lined up."

So damn predictable. He's going to have these guys beat on me, so as he says, I can turn into the man I'm meant to be instead of the pussy my mom made me and there's not a damn thing I can do about it. Saying no, hanging up the phone, it's not an option. Everything just goes to shit even more when I do that and trust me, I know. I've done it exactly one time before and learned my lesson real quick.

"Yeah, fine. Farm. Wednesday. Seven. Got it."

Pushing the button to end the call, not in the mood to hear any more from him, I slide the phone back in the pocket of my hoodie and I turn my attention back to my very idiotic friend and the mess I'm gonna have to clean up.

"What was that?" he asks and I roll my eyes.

No one knows what my dad's been doing with me and I'm gonna keep it that way. If I want people to know I'll tell them, otherwise it remains my secret. I'm not sure what the hell these guys would do with the information, so for now, I'm gonna keep going about my business and keep my private life exactly that. Private.

"Nothing important. Look, let's just go find Ames and figure out a way out of the shit storm the two of you just brought down on me."

"I thought you'd be happy about it. I mean the asshole had it coming. He wants to play games with us, he deserves it."

"Not denying that he needs to pay, Tim. I fully intend on making him pay, but not like this. All you two did is make Daniels hard on for me that much worse."

God, he's such a moron. When I first met him, the fact that he was such a muppet and followed along with everything I wanted made him an asset, but now he's just messing everything up. If he wasn't on the damn team with me, I'm pretty sure I'd have ditched him by now. Tim actually thinking about anything is a joke.

"Whatever. This morning's been bad enough, I don't wanna think about what's gonna happen next. Let's just find the others and we'll deal with this later."

It hits me as we make our way down the stairs and I round the corner and see my girlfriend and her friends that I just lied to him. The morning might have started off bad, but it hadn't ended up that way at all.

It's all because of those brown eyes that even with all the interruptions from Tim, I still can't get out of my head. Yeah, I've definitely gotta get the others on board with this. This time I'm not taking no for an answer.

Cadence

Going back and forth with Dillon for the entire class, it's easy to see why he's earned the reputation he has. The sheer amount of times he rolled his eyes alone speaks to it. I'm not exactly the biggest fan of school, but damn, this guy literally hates every bit of it and I'm pretty sure it has nothing at all to do with the class he's in now.

I flicked him on the arm every single time he did it and after earning the death glare the first time, he mellowed out and started smirking at me instead. If I didn't know any better, I'd think he was doing it just so he could get a reaction, but having no experience with guys and how they act, I can't be sure. If that is what he was after though, I gave it to him in spades.

He managed to call me a bitch three more times and every single time earned an equally damning response. It was just another thing that seemed to please him. It's like he enjoyed being called an asshole. The thing is, by the end of class, I kind of enjoyed it too.

When the bell rang, I was more than ready to get out of there, even though I didn't exactly have anywhere to go. I've been here before, when Mom's had to come back after picking me up at school, but I never made a point of going around and checking the place out. I was braving a whole new world here and for the first time in ages, I'm thankful I'm deaf.

I'm a new face to these people so the minute I came out of the class, I felt the eyes on me and it turned my stomach inside out. It doesn't matter if you go to a school for the deaf or a regular high school, teenagers act the same way. I'm the new kid, which means I stand out and now everyone is interested in me. In no time at all, they'll start talking about me.

Yes, it's definitely a good thing I can't hear because I would hate to know what people are thinking about me, much less what they're gonna say.

As I escape through the door to the stairs, I practically race down them, eager to find a spot, hopefully somewhere on the first floor that isn't occupied by anyone so that I can stay under the radar. If I want to survive the next two weeks here, putting myself front and center for all of these new eyes is definitely not the way to go about it. I don't call attention to myself at my actual school. I'm not about to start here.

The library.

If I want a place to go unnoticed, there's no better place in the world then there. I can hide away in a corner, pull my book from my bag and settle in to read.

It's only when I turn the corner and head in the direction of my salvation that I see them. They're all sitting with their backs lined in perfect succession to the lockers and they're laughing about something or someone, their smiles and open mouths a dead giveaway. When I see the blonde guy point down the hall toward me, but not directly at me, I notice exactly what it is they're laughing about, or who.

Eric Carmen.

Another kid I know because of the amount of time my mom spends talking about him. He's hunched over, walking down the hall at a snail's pace and of course, these jerks are making fun of him for it. I don't see him doing anything remotely abnormal but it seems that with these guys, even walking is a joke.

I hate popular kids. They think because they're on the football team or friends with the head cheerleader that they're above everyone else. Some of them come from money, and the ones that do are even worse because apparently the money their parent's make means they're untouchable and can buy themselves out of any situation they find themselves in.

There's only one person who that didn't work for and he's the one I lock eyes on the minute I turn back to them.

Dillon.

He's laughing along with his friends, but there's something different about the way he is that sets him apart from the others. His laughter isn't reaching up into his eyes. His are vacant. Like he's only laughing in order to keep them off his back.

Interesting.

Pulling away from my dissection of Wexfield's resident jerk, I turn back in the direction Eric went and decide on a change of plan.

Speeding up until I find myself directly behind the slow moving boy, I tap him on the shoulder and wait until he slows to a complete stop and spins around to face me. Raising my hand in the air, I wave, giving him a small smile and hoping he remembers me or at least realizes that I'm not here to harass him.

"Caddy?"

I smile even brighter at his recognition and he returns it with one of his own. I have never been so thankful for my mother being his teacher. The way he turned around, his shoulders tensed and a look of fear across his face, I can tell he'd been expecting something worse.

That won't be happening today. Today he's about to entertain the new kid.

Holding up my hand, I reach around into my bag, grab out the pen and pad and start writing. Out of all the kids in the school, I know for a fact that he's gonna be cool with waiting. His best friend Isabelle, used to have to do the same thing, which means he's got loads of experience with it. Finishing up what I want to ask, I hold it up for him and the minute he reads it, he smiles again.

"Yeah, sure. You can eat lunch with me."

"Thank you." I answer back, this time choosing to speak instead of using the pad.

This is something not a lot of people know about me. I can speak. For a long time I never spoke anywhere, but after learning sign language, meeting with a speech therapist combining the two and having the world's most supportive mom on my side, I slowly began doing it. I still don't do it often, but when I'm comfortable, I will. With Eric right now, I feel that way. I don't have to fear the looks I get with him. It's the rest of the world that needs to catch on.

The few times I've spoken in public, the reaction alone was enough for me to never want to do it again. So for a really long time I didn't. I might not be afraid of people the way Eric and some of the others are, but reactions, peoples words, they still hurt me and after a while, it's just easier to be silent and write with the pad or signing then it is to speak out loud.

"I was wondering if you were gonna speak."

I smile and grab him by the hand, dragging him down the hall, not sure of my destination, but figuring if he'd been walking this way, then there has to be someplace over here where we can sit and hang out. It's only when he comes to a stop, pulling me back with him, pointing in the opposite direction that I realize he's got another idea.

"I'm supposed to meet Isabelle outside." He says and pointing again toward the front door and looking back down at me, I smile. It wasn't exactly what I wanted to do, but it beat spending it alone in the library.

"Let's go."

Dillon

The plan is a go.

Once we were all sitting around in the hall, I decided to bring it up. If I wanted to put it in motion the minute I got back to class, the sooner I got it out there and got everyone's thoughts, the better. Turns out, they were more on board with it than I was and I'm the one that thought it up.

I expected to have to plead hard with Amy, so when she was one of the first ones to agree, it threw me off. It didn't take me long to recover though. Once everyone agreed, I started to fill them in on what I planned to do when I got back to class, but their attention was quickly taken away when Eric made his way into the hall.

"Now that we screwed up Kayden's car, we need to do something to this kid."

"What did I tell you about that? You see what Daniels did to me right? The last thing any of us needs to do right now is screw with him."

"It sounds like you're going soft on us, D." Tim jokes while I resist the urge to punch him in his throat. After the way things have gone already today, the last thing he wants to do is piss me off.

"In your dreams maybe. I'm just being smart."

"Dillon's right. What we did this morning; it's gonna cause shit."

The last thing I expect Amy to say is that I'm right. It's not like she's never done it before or anything, but with the way she willingly helped Tim screw with Kayden's car, I had to figure I'm the last one she'd agree with.

"You really wanna end up in the retard class with me?" I ask him, though the question could have been to any of them. It's time they remember who the real brains of this whole thing is. Going off on their own was just gonna breed more shit I didn't need.

"Fine, you're right. We'll leave him alone, but the minute the heats off, I swear I'm dealing with that guy."

I'm the one that ends up with the punishment; yet he's the one that wants to take the little moron out. There's definitely something wrong with that.

"I'll leave you a piece when I'm done Tim, I promise." I say, pursing my lips and making kissing noises straight at him, which has the desired effect as everyone cracks up in laughter.

"Whoa! Who's that?" Tim asks completely disregarding my comment and motioning down the hall, the way we just saw Eric go. By the time I follow his line of vision, the person has their back to me, but there's no denying who it is and also who she's chasing after.

"That's the girl I was telling you about. The new retard."

"I might be willing to rethink this whole thing if they all look like her. Shit; even Isabelle was pretty hot for a mute bitch."

"Man, all you can see is her back! How the hell can you think she's hot?" I ask though deep down, I already know the answer. It's the same way I thought the exact same thing this morning. It's because she's gorgeous. Even with a few feet between us, it's impossible to deny.

"I saw her when she came around the corner, D. Shit. Now I see why you wanna screw around with her so bad."

No way. Him admiring Cadence like this, it's not happening. Call me territorial or whatever, but I saw her first, which means she's mine. I don't give a shit what he wants to do. She's off limits.

"Looks to me like she's got a thing for Eric. There goes your shot."

Everyone starts laughing again, but this time, I'm not feeling it. For whatever reason, I don't like the way Tim is looking at this girl, even though a few minutes ago I was putting together a plan to screw with her head.

I know what I've got to do.

I'm not waiting until we get back to class to put the plan in action. I'm gonna do it now. Cadence is chasing after Eric; well it just so happens I've got a few choice words I need to say to the guy and there's no better time than now to do it.

Cadence

I'm not sure what I was so afraid of.

As soon as we make our way outside, Eric practically dragging me to the tree where I could make out a guy and a girl cuddling underneath, I felt completely at ease. Not only did the two lovebirds separate, but the girl reached out to me. It's only after Eric says hello that I realize who they are.

Kayden and Isabelle. I know of Isabelle the same way I do Eric. Mom comes home and talks about them a lot. I probably know a lot more than I should about these three, especially Isabelle. Because of my disability, my mom seems more protective than most teachers and she's protective over no one more than the girl in front of me now.

Isabelle Reagan is autistic and because of that and her inability to speak, she was bullied excessively. I can't even count the number of times my mom came home in tears because of what the people here put this girl through. Like in most cases of bullying, it's easy to see within five seconds of being around her that there's no reason for it.

She's amazing.

The minute we're seated, she surprises me by signing. I know for a fact she's not deaf; so I'm pretty surprised she's doing it, at least I am until I see Eric's face.

"Our moms taught us how to sign when we were little so they could communicate with us."

For the first time since my mom told me I had to come here this morning, I actually feel like I belong.

Turning back to Isabelle, responding to what she asked me, I pull my phone out of my jacket and hand it to her. Watching as she slides her fingers across the screen at a speed I'm pretty jealous of, she adds in her number and hands it back to me. Looking down at the screen, I see she's got the messaging app open and a message for me typed in the box.

Now you don't have to stress over reading lips.

Smiling, I put the phone back in my pocket and I watch the two boys talk back and forth. I can easily keep up with Eric, but it's not the same with Kayden. From the way it looks, he just said something about liking women's underwear. Obviously seeing the confused look on my face, Isabelle taps me on the leg and points to my pocket, her phone visible in her hands, signaling a text message.

Pulling the phone back out, I look down and smile. Maybe keeping up with Kayden wasn't as hard as I thought. He really was talking about women's underwear, just not in the way I thought.

Don't mind Kay, he's just making fun of Eric's My Little Pony underwear.

My Little Pony underwear? Now I definitely need to know more.

Why is he wearing those?

She wastes no time texting me back, which just makes me even more jealous. Is this girl just naturally gifted with everything electronic?

Eric's little sister, Summer dared him to wear them.

Now everything makes sense. It also helps me lighten up considerably. I don't want to admit it, but not being able to read Kayden, at least when I thought I couldn't; it upset me. It's not often I can't keep up.

How do you like it here?
Not really sure yet. I miss my friends.

Instead of texting her response the way I expect, she tips her head to the side and nods, letting me know she gets it. From everything I know about her, the only friends she has are the two people sitting with us now, so I can see how she might sympathize with me. I can't imagine how hard it is being here without them.

Well, you've got three new friends for the next two weeks. If you want them.

The happy face emoticon at the end makes me smile even more than her words do. I definitely don't feel alone now. I might be able to make it through these next two weeks after all.

We stop texting and after a little while, I feel a tap on my shoulder. Having spent the time watching everyone move around outside, enjoying the slight breeze as it passes by, I didn't even realize I zoned out. Looking up, I see Eric smiling at me.

"Time to get you back to class."

I'm about to question what he means when it hits me. He's not in the afternoon class because he takes regular classes. Another tidbit my mom shared with me in one of her many sharing sessions. Looks like I'm about to go it alone.

Raising myself off the ground, rubbing at my knees in an effort to get any dirt and grass stains off, I follow along behind him. When we make our way inside, I start to pull him toward the way we came earlier and I'm met with resistance. I feel myself being pulled back too late to stop it, so bracing myself for the bump I'm going to take as I hit the floor, I feel a pair of arms come around and I'm being pulled up and into a very warm body.

The way he catches me, there can be no mistaking the way it looks to anyone that might be around us. My face is in perfect proportion to his and if I walked in on the way we look, it would look intimate, the very last thing that's happening.

It doesn't take long before I see shadows around us and lips moving. With the way I'm positioned, I'm able to lock on one set of lips and reading them easily, my stomach turns over.

"Looks like the retard got himself a hottie."

Glancing up at Eric and back at the person spouting off the disgusting words, who I thought was just someone random, is not so random after all. The person standing behind us, eyes locked on mine is the very guy I'd been stupid enough to believe I saw something different in.

Dillon; and if looks could kill, I'm pretty sure I'd be dead.

Chapter Three

Dillon

I should have known this was how it would go down. That the hot girl I met in the retard class would turn out to be friends with one of them. With the way she's gripping on to Eric right now, it's pretty obvious they're more than just friends.

First Kayden gets involved with one of them; bailing on his friends and treating us like we're the ones with the problem and now before I have the chance to put the plan in motion, Cadence is doing the same. What the hell is it about these freaks that people seem to flock to? What the hell does Eric Carmen have that I don't?

Why the hell I even care is beyond me. There was this moment in the hall earlier where I felt her eyes on me. It was like we were in class all over again and she was somehow looking straight through me. It was weird as hell. It was that look and the way Tim was acting that made my thoughts go south, which when Amy caught on, didn't go over too well.

That's the one thing she hates more than anything. Being ignored. I need to have my attention on her all the time. God forbid I think about something and take my attention off her; I'll never hear the end of it. As much as I like the girl, her need for constant recognition and attention is annoying as hell.

When I caught Cadence running off down the hall toward Eric, I should have left well enough alone, but that's never been my style. So I wait, hanging out with the others for a little while longer, wasting time until I can go find them.

Of course the minute I stand up and try to get away, Amy and Tim are right on my heels. As much as I hate admitting it, what Isabelle said a couple months ago is true. It's like they're dogs following their master. I think if they had a thought of their own separate from me, I might die of shock. For now though, it works. I can't go wrong having a little backup for what's about to happen.

"Come on Caddy; let's get out of here."

The clear concise way he says it, so sure of himself, proves what he thinks. Now that I've been punished, he's untouchable. Too bad for him I don't give a shit about what Daniels puts me through. I'm not gonna change the way things are for anything. He's just as much a target as he was on Friday when I went after him.

"What's the rush, Eric? We just wanna meet your girlfriend."

Tim moves in on him and I notice Cadence's eyes go wide. I'm pretty sure she knows what's about to happen and despite the fact that I'm gonna allow it, even joining in, I can't help wanting to get her out of here before it does. If I want my plan to work, having her witness this, it will ruin it before I even start.

Eric breaks away from her, leaving her wide open for me to swoop in and get her out of there, or at the very least bring her over with me where she should be, but I don't do it. The look on her face as her friend turns to face us down stops me from going anywhere near her.

She's scowling; not only at me, but Amy and Tim the same way she'd done when she caught me rolling my eyes at the teacher. Yeah, she definitely knows what's about to happen and doesn't like it one bit.

Even if Cadence isn't like Eric and Isabelle, it's obvious she's sympathetic to them, which makes her just like Kayden.

"Caddy; go outside. Get Kayden."

Of course he's gonna call for Kayden. After the threat he leveled on us a couple of months ago, my ex best friend has gone out of his way to make sure he's been everywhere we are. Preventing us at every turn from doing what had come so easily to him only a few months before. He can think he's better than the rest of us all he wants, but I know who started all of this and it wasn't me.

Cadence, hearing what Eric said, turns to go but before she can make it even two steps away, Amy jumps right in her path, blocking her.

"You're not going anywhere retard."

I expect this to be the time she finally speaks and I anticipate hearing her voice for the first time considering how she went the whole two hours earlier drenched in complete silence. As wrong as it is, I'm actually looking forward to hearing her response, wondering if her voice will sound as tough as her attitude toward me.

She doesn't speak though. She just stands there, her eyes frozen on Amy's, the scowl still evident. Watching her like this, I realize she's just like Isabelle. She can't speak. Great. I found another mute girl attractive.

What the hell is going on with me?

Turning my attention away from the girls, I focus on Eric and the minute my eyes lock on his, whatever sense of security he felt drains away and the fear I'm used to seeing is back again. He knows the deal. Kayden isn't coming to his rescue this time.

"I think it's time we have a little chat." I say, moving in until my face is inches away from his. When he backs up in an attempt to get away, he bumps into Tim, who has now taken up residence behind him and I laugh. I would have thought by now he would know that there's no way he can get away from us.

"I—I—I've got nothing to s—s—say to you." He stutters and I inch even closer, the laughter gone, only a smile remaining. A smile that he's seen on more than one occasion and one he knows has nothing to do with happiness.

"That's where you're wrong."

"I—didn't—tell."

"Oh, I know you didn't. Your new best friend did that, but since I can't make Kayden pay; it leaves me with you."

As I move on him again, this time grabbing him by the collar of his shirt and yanking him as close as possible, I hear a guttural sound from the other side of the hall and turning toward it, I'm face to face with Cadence. Before I can reach out to stop her, her hands are flailing and I feel them pushing into me repeatedly, until the lock I've got on Eric's shirt breaks and we've been completely separated.

Yeah, I've definitely pissed her off. Looking her up and down, I see her face is red with rage and her brown eyes, which had been softer in class, are darker and if it's even possible, hard. I've always wondered what hate looks like and I'm getting a front row seat to it now.

She steps toward me, her arms out in front of her, her eyes locked on me, so upset that she's not even blinking. Before her now balled up fists can connect with my body, I put my arms up in an effort to fend off the attack. Her point has been made. She doesn't want me anywhere near Eric. I got it loud and clear.

Before I can say something to get her to stop, Amy appears from behind and grabbing her by the hair, drags her backward. She tosses Cadence easily, everything completely silent until her body hits the floor with a thud so loud it takes even me off guard.

I've always known Amy was strong, but damn. I've never seen her react like this.

"Don't you ever lay your hands on my man; you hear me, you stupid bitch?" she screams down at Cadence's still form. It's seeing the way she's lying there on the floor, her hair completely covering her face and her hands now coming up to meet it that I've seen enough.

This has gone way too far.

"Ames, that's enough. I think she got the point." I call out, turning back to Eric and leveling him with a smirk. "I'm not finished with you. You can think that because you've got the fullback on your side that you're safe, but you're not. I'm coming for you. Consider this your only warning."

Flinching from my words, Eric breaks eye contact and moves toward the girl on the floor, still curled up in herself. It's watching him reach her, bending down until he's on the floor in front of her, moving her hair out of her face in an effort to talk to her that it hits me.

I'm gonna be in so much shit when Daniels gets wind of this.

Cadence

I'm not a violent person. I hate everything about it, but seeing Dillon grab Eric that way, knowing what was coming, there is no way I can just stand there and let it happen. I knew the girl wouldn't let me get far, her disgusted frown proving exactly what she thought about me, but I didn't care.

Eric and the others have been getting bullied for as long as my mom's worked here. She comes home every single day and tells me about it. Knowing him the way I do, at least the little I do know, he's such a nice guy. So he's a little different. It doesn't mean he deserves to be picked on for it. Eric Carmen wouldn't hurt a fly. I'm pretty sure he's as against violence as I am.

The anger I feel inside seeing the look on Dillon's face and then the look of absolute fear on Eric's pushes me forward before I've given it any real thought. I start pushing at him with everything in me until he finally breaks the hold he's got on my friend. There is no way I'm letting this continue. Whatever it was I saw in his eyes in the hall earlier or the way he kept me entertained in class is gone. All I see now is the jerk my mom told me about.

When the girl threw me to the ground, I'd been expecting it, but that doesn't mean I was expecting the pain that came the minute I hit the floor. I'd been expecting it to hurt a little with the way she grabbed and tossed me, but laying here now, I can feel it running all the way through me, from my legs all the way up my arms. I'm definitely gonna bruise from this.

Not even twenty-four hours into my first day here and I'm locked in a battle with the popular kids. It's exactly what I didn't want when my mom dropped the bomb that I'd be coming here. I was supposed to go under the radar and bide my time until my school was up and running again. Not getting involved in situations like this and getting hurt for my trouble.

He doesn't realize it, but after I fell to the floor, I saw his face. He might want to appear as though he's a big badass and that what happened is funny to him, but he wasn't laughing or even smiling when I hit. His eyes went wide and for a split second before he turned back to Eric, he actually looked concerned.

Whether he's concerned because he knows this is gonna come back to bite him or this went a little farther then he intended, I'll never know but there's no erasing the look from my memory. Even as Eric helps me to my feet after the three of them take off, it's the only thing I can focus on. I don't even care about the pain I'm feeling anymore. All I can see is the haunted look in the eyes of the school bully that I should have known better than to go toe to toe with.

Feeling Eric's hand on my chin, lifting my head up in an effort for me to read his lips, I lock eyes with the boy I just inadvertently saved and smile weakly.

"Are you okay?" he asks and I nod, keeping the smile firmly planted on my face. I might feel pain, but that would pass. All I care about now is making sure he's alright. That what Dillon had done to him before I stepped in hadn't caused any damage.

You? I raise my hands and sign to him.

"Caddy, holy crap! I'm the last person you need to be worried about. Do you need go the office? Ice? Anything?"

His words run together so quickly I'm not sure I've read them right, but the ones I am able to pick up on, I answer back with a shake of my head. I don't need the office. I could probably use some ice, but definitely not if it means going there. The last thing I want to do on my first day here is be the poster child for bullying.

"Are you sure?" he asks, not believing the shake of my head as the truth. I can't blame him. I'm pretty sure my reaction is his standard response when he goes through this.

Yes. I sign again with a sigh. I just want this to be over with.

"Okay, well come on. I stopped because taking the other way around is faster."

I allow him to take my hand in his and walk me slowly back the way we came, all the while doing all I can to ignore the pain that's still shooting up my leg into my back. Blocking it out, I think about everything that just happened and I realize my mom was right along.

Dillon Murphy is bad news.

Chapter Four

Dillon

Heading back into Ms. Taylor's class when lunch is over, I'm thankful for two things. One, it looks like Eric and Isabelle aren't here which means if the little retard did run and squeal to his best friend and her boyfriend, I wasn't gonna have to hear about it for the next couple hours. The other thing is who I see the minute I enter the class. True to the way she'd been a couple hours ago, she's in the seat in the back and her head is stuck in a book.

I don't know why I'm thankful for her being there; I just am. The way everything got so out of control in the hall, I need to talk to her about it. She probably won't want to hear anything I've got to say, but even knowing I'm a total asshole, what happened to her was never supposed to happen and I gotta make her understand that.

The idea of this smoking hot girl being pissed at me for what happened is not something I can deal with. Now that she's here and there's no one else around, maybe I can turn this around to something more in my favor. I have to turn it around if I wanna keep going with the plan.

Throwing myself down into the seat, I pull out a notebook and I write out across the page everything I want to say. If the way she acted in the hall means anything, she's like Belle and can't talk. So, writing this way is my first attempt at softening her up. Maybe she'll react the same way Isabelle did and I'll be able to smooth this over quickly.

The last thing I want is her going to Daniels. When Kayden catches what the others did to his car, I'm gonna pay enough. No need to add what happened earlier into it too.

Leaning across the desk when I'm finished, I wait for some sort of reaction to me being in her personal space. When nothing comes, I slide the paper just like I did earlier into the top left corner of her desk and sit back to wait her out. After a few minutes of waiting and her not even flicking her eyes in the direction of the paper, I feel my anger start to rise.

I'm trying to do the right thing here. The least this girl can do is acknowledge that I'm trying. Her ignoring it the way she is, pisses me off. Doesn't she know who I am? Ignoring me isn't the smartest thing to do. What Amy did to her in the hallway is tame compared to the things I could line up for her if she doesn't do what I want her to.

Shit. I can't believe I'm thinking like this. So she isn't looking at the paper. That's not reason enough to go off on her. Shaking the anger off, I put my focus back on the front of the room in a weak attempt to appear as though I'm actually interested in being here. When that gets me nowhere, Ms. Taylor not paying the least bit of attention to it, I lean back in the seat and let my mind wander.

Last fall, I noticed some shit going down and in an attempt to set it right, I put a plan in motion. It wasn't the most thought out plan, but considering who it involved, I figured it would resolve itself quickly and we could get back to normal. Thing is, it didn't resolve itself and over the course of a few weeks, it took on a life of its own. By the end it was so out of control I couldn't even keep up and I was the one running it.

I noticed Kayden acting different. He was pulling away from us, so in an effort to get him to come back around, I decided to switch up the way things are and go after one of the people we swore we'd never go after. It was only supposed to be that one time in the parking lot and after that things would settle back down. Kayden was supposed to see it and help us. Instead he came to the girl's rescue and that's when everything went to shit.

Isabelle Reagan is a Special Ed kid and the entire school knows it. She has these accidents where she pisses herself. She can't handle a lot of lights and movements and for the longest time she didn't even speak. She was such an easy target, I can't believe I didn't try it on her sooner. When he stepped in, laying me out in the process, I decided to kick it up a notch. Watching him take her to class the day after, I decided to make it my life's mission to harass her. If I couldn't get him to come back the normal way, I'd use the girl to do it.

It worked. In his need to protect her, I got him to choose a different victim, figuring that if Isabelle caught us going after one of her friends, she'd look at Kayden and see him as exactly what he's always been. An asshole; just like me. The way she reacted to what we did to Eric put the final nail in the coffin, or at least it was supposed to, until Kayden again went back to her and further away from us.

It got out of control after that and honestly, by the end of it I was just so jealous of the way everything seemed to fall into his lap that I was determined to take him down. My best friend became my mortal enemy.

The day she ran into the bathroom, she didn't realize it, but her phone slipped out of her pocket. I grabbed it and that's when the final stage of my plan to turn his life upside down came about. I installed the tracker app on her phone, knowing she wouldn't realize it was there and I began to hack into her texts, messenger conversations, compiling as much as I could so I could turn it around on Kayden at Homecoming.

What no one knows and I'm never gonna admit to, is that near the end, before the dance, I wanted to back out. I'd been spending a lot of time getting close to Isabelle in an effort to make it look like I missed my best friend and as much as I hate admitting it, I liked her. She was as innocent as Kayden made her out to be and after seeing her in action, I had doubts about hurting her.

Yeah, I know. It sounds insane. Having any sort of attachment to a person like Isabelle is laughable, but it's true. Seeing her when she walked into the dance that night; man, there was another second where I wanted to back out of the stupid plan I put in motion. She looked like a Disney princess for fuck sakes. If I didn't know she had shit wrong with her, she would've appeared like any other girl at the school.

I didn't back out and now I'm paying the price for all of it. Not only did Kayden beat on me that night so bad that I found it hard to breathe hours after, but he's been by her side ever since, stronger than ever. I failed at ripping my best friend apart, but I'd also managed to screw up my position on the football team for a while after it. It's a pretty big miracle that I'm still quarterback at all.

Whatever it was I felt about Isabelle, it fell away after that. I went back to picking on people weaker than me and enjoying every second of it. Bruce is right. There's no place in the world for people that are screwed up, different or weak. They need people like us to eradicate them.

What happened with Cadence earlier, there's nothing right about that. She's not weak. The way she gave me back as good as I gave proves that. A weaker person wouldn't have done it. People like to pretend that they're stronger than I know them to be, but they always falter in the end and go right back to being weak. Cadence didn't. She stood her ground, even knowing that in the end, there was three of us and only one of her because Eric had already backed down.

If she would just look at my note, read it, maybe I could fix it. She didn't deserve what happened to her and I'm sure that if I can just steal a couple minutes of her time, I can explain the way things are here and get her away from Eric and the others before things end up getting a whole lot worse.

Wait. What the hell am I saying? She's one of them. Sure, she might be stronger than the others, but it didn't change the facts. No matter how hot she is, I need to keep my head in the game. I'm apologizing in order to get close to her so I can screw with her head. Nothing more than that.

In the end she'll learn the way things are here and prove herself to be as weak as the rest of them.

The thing is, if that's the truth and what I wrote to her is all an attempt to screw her over, why does what happened a few minutes ago, the way she looked crumpled on the floor bother me so bad?

Cadence

God, I want to look at that paper.

It's been sitting here for the last twenty minutes calling to me, begging me to reach out to grab it and read it, but I've forced myself not to. It's getting harder to do, but after what happened at the end of lunch, the last thing I want is to see anything he's got to say.

You saw the look on his face in the hall. There's more going on.

Crap. I'm gonna end up looking at the paper if I keep thinking stuff like this. Yeah I saw the look when I fell and I saw the way his laughter at Eric earlier didn't quite reach his eyes, but it means nothing. He's an asshole and for Dillon Murphy, that's a stain you can't wash off no matter how hard you scrub at it.

I'm just thankful that so far Eric hasn't said a word about what happened. When I got back to class, I expected him to say something to my mom and for her to question me about it, but she hasn't paid any attention to me at all. It seems like she's going along with what I told her I wanted this morning. She wasn't going to call attention to the fact that I'm her daughter and I've never been as thankful for that then I am right now.

On the way up the stairs we met up with Kayden and Isabelle and while Eric and Kayden stopped to talk once we got to the top, I just stood and watched everyone moving around me. It's only when I saw hands moving that I realized Isabelle was signing. Missing some but able to pick up on what she wanted to know, I wasn't having any part of it. I know she only wanted to help, they both do, but where they might see me as weak because of my disability, that's the last thing I am.

I don't need them worrying or trying to help me out with the hazing problem because they've been through it before. I just need the entire thing forgotten about.

It's only after I completely turned away from her, tired of watching her attempts at getting me to talk that she tried a different approach. I felt the buzzing against my side and pulling my phone out, saw the screen lit up with a text from my new friend.

~*~*~

I didn't want to talk about it either and that's okay, but if you ever do wanna talk, you should do what I did with Kayden.

It's only when she shakes her phone at me that I get it. She's telling me I can text her.

If you're ever in a situation that you can't get out of, text me.

I know she means well, but I'm gonna be here for two weeks, not the next two years, so odds are as long as I keep myself off the radar like I planned on doing from the beginning, I won't find myself in a situation like the one she's getting at. Even if I do, I'll figure my own way out of it. No pity help needed.

~*~*~

Okay, I've waited long enough. The lined paper has drilled a hole through me to the point where thinking about anything else is pointless. Sliding my hand across the desk, I bring the paper toward me slowly, until it's directly in front of me and doing what I've spent at least the last thirty minutes dying to do, I open it up and read the words printed there.

I know you don't even want to look at me right now, but I just want to say I'm sorry for what happened at lunch. It wasn't *supposed to go down that way and I had no idea she was gonna do that to you. Forgive me?*

Damnit.

I never should have opened the stupid paper. Dillon is a jerk. I need to remember that. He's just doing this now to get to me; it's how he operates. All bullies operate the same way. No matter how much I want to believe in the words on the paper, I need to remember exactly who it is that's saying them. As long as I do that, his stupid words can't get to me.

Except they are getting to me.

Crap. Crap. Crap.

Pulling my hair down over my face so he won't catch what I'm about to do, I lift my head slightly and attempt to get a look at him. It's only when my eyes lock on his face that I realize my stupid little plan was a fail. He caught me because he's looking right at me.

Double crap.

Before I can look away, he opens his mouth and zeroing in on his lips, I follow along with every word, dreaming in my head as I do that I'm actually able to hear him speak them and the husky way my brain imagines them sounding. After a couple of seconds pass and I notice he's no longer speaking I realize what I've done. Getting so caught up watching his lips move and my now overactive imagination, I've missed everything.

"Did you hear me?"

I nod even though it's not exactly the truth and the faintest smile appears on his face.

"So?"

He wants to know if now that I've read the note, I forgive him and am willing to talk to him again. He's already forgiven for what happened, but I'm not about to tell him that. He might be a total jerk, but if I hold everything against him, it makes me like him and there's no way I'm going to allow myself to be compared with him. Forgiving him is easy, talking to him isn't.

Taking the paper he used for his note and flipping it over, I write out my response. Passing it across, careful to keep my fingers far enough away from his so we don't have any kind of physical contact, I watch as he takes it and reads what I've said.

I don't talk to complete jerks. You're forgiven for earlier because I'm better than that, but I won't forget it.

Where I'm expecting his lips to curl into a snarl or for him to call me a bitch or some other equally damning word under his breath, he does none of it. Instead, he focuses his attention on the paper, his eyes glued to it and then starts writing. Holding it up in front of him, not even attempting to pass it over, he waits for my eyes to lock on it and read what he's written.

You are better than that. You're better than me.

Looking up from the paper and catching his eyes, again I see they're locked on me and where before it might have made me feel uncomfortable, it's having the opposite effect now. Despite what happened earlier, what is sure to happen every single time I'm around him when we're outside of this classroom; his words, the way he looks, they're getting to me.

No, no, no. This is not happening. He will not do this to me.

He will not get me to talk to him.

Dillon

When you're like me and have people doing whatever they can to get your attention, you pick up on a few things and it's everything I've learned over the last couple of years dealing with girls that I use now with Cadence.

There's no denying the fact that she's different than most girls I've come across since freshman year, but just because she's different doesn't mean there aren't parts of her that are the same. Most girls are suckers for the right combination of words, whether you speak them or write them and that's what I'm banking on when I take to the paper and write out what I do.

The minute her eyes scan over and they soften from the hard shell they were, I know I've nailed it. She wants to hate me, believe everything she's heard about me after spending time with Eric and the others, but I'm not letting her. I'm pretty damn sure that everything she's been told is right and she's better off staying as far away from me as she can get, but I'm not about to let her do it.

Not when the very reason I'm gonna make it through this death sentence from Daniels depends so completely on her.

Even sitting here groveling the way I am is better than it would have been if she hadn't been here when I walked in this morning. I meant what I said. Her being here makes this, what I'm having to deal with because of what I did, easier to handle. If I'm going to be forced into staying in this class for the rest of the year in some misguided attempt to teach me some kind of lesson, having someone else to do it with is preferable to having to go it alone, even if I do have an ulterior motive.

Other than the time spent with Kayden before we turned on each other, I've always been alone. My mother ignores me unless I do something horrendous enough to get her attention and she has to defend me. My father only wants me when he's got a fight lined up that he's sure to win and even my friends; they only want me because of who I am and what I mean to them in the social order.

Cadence is the first person since Kayden that I don't feel alone with and it only took a couple of hours with her to realize it. Now that I've hooked her though, I've got to keep it going and this is the part I'm not all that great at.

Any girl I've ever been interested in has always come easily to me. I could point out into a crowd of girls during an assembly and whatever one my finger lands on, that's how easy they could be mine. I'm not looking to make this girl mine; I mean I've already got a girlfriend and I don't mess around with cheating, but it works the same way. If I want Cadence to keep me occupied while I'm stuck in this class, I've gotta work harder. She's not someone I can just point my finger at and make her come running.

Just as I'm about to speak, I notice her leaning across the desk toward me, another blue sticky note in her hand.

Reaching and helping her out, I take it from her hand and lay it down on the desk in front of me.

You ever get tired of pushing people around?

"No. If it comes down to being weak or strong, I prefer to be the strong one."

Her eyes widen and I know what it means. She doesn't like my answer. That's just too damn bad. She asked me a question and I don't see a reason to lie to her with my answer. It may have taken six years of fighting and going back and forth with my dad to learn it, but I believe in what I said with everything in me.

Though I gotta admit, seeing the scowl on her face, it kind of sucks. At least it sucks until I see the next note she's written for me.

I don't believe that.

"Oh yeah? Well since you know me so well, why don't you tell me what you believe?"

I know I sound like a dick, but there's something about what she's written, so sure about her answer that gets under my skin. She's known me what, a total of five hours? How can she believe or not believe anything about me?

Watching her, bent over the little sticky pad, her focus completely on the small piece of blue paper, whatever she's writing longer than anything she's said to me so far; I can't help wondering what she thinks of me that's taking this long and this much effort to write. Could she have formed an opinion on me this soon? She pulls the one paper off and hands it over to me, going back to writing the minute I've taken it out of her hand.

Well, whatever it is, it's sure to be winded.

I could easily find out what she thinks by reading over the one she handed me, but I'm determined to wait until she's done. I don't normally give two shits what people think about me, but this girl right now, I wanna know every damn thing in her head, even if it ends up being bullshit.

Ripping off the note and handing it to me, I look down at the two slips of paper in front of me, her messy scrawl covering practically every inch of both and that's when I get her full opinion.

I think the way you act when you're here, that's not the real you. I don't think you're an asshole. I think that deep inside, you're really a decent guy but something's happened to you or someone's done something that's changed you. You hate on the weak because they're stronger then you and you're jealous of them. I also think that the reason you're in this class right now instead of screwing off with those friends of yours is because that so called strength you think you have came back around and bit you in the ass.

"Well, you're wrong."

Two pieces of blue paper full of her opinion and in order to throw her off, I lie to her face. There's no way in hell I'm telling this girl just how right she is.

No way in hell.

Chapter Five

Dillon

This is the grossest place he's ever chosen for a fight.

When Bruce told me we'd be doing this in a farm house, I had a different view of what that would be. I expected to see machinery, most of it old and rusted from lack of use but we weren't at a farm at all. It's a broken down barn and the smell alone is enough to make me wanna turn around and head back out the way I came.

There are bales of hay strewn throughout the place, rakes and even a tractor, rusty and old in the far back corner looking like it hasn't seen action in years. I'm not sure how long it's been since animals have been here but the smell of piss and shit is so strong it's a miracle I can even breathe right now.

No matter what way you look at it, when these fights are over, I'm gonna be covered in manure and living in my shower for at least a week.

The guys he's got lined up for me, they're all in their late twenties and just like he warned me in the car, pretty built up on performance enhancers. Yeah, my father chose some real winners this time. I'm gonna have to go head to head with guys, not only older and stronger than me, but ones that are doped up.

This is the way Bruce Murphy makes you into a man. Putting you in a situation there is no fucking way you can come out of, at least not alive anyway.

"Remember what I said boy. Don't let them go for the face. The minute one of them connects with you that way, it's gonna be noticeable and I can't have that."

Of course he can't have that. No way someone can see the bruises and cuts on my face and put two and two together.

That would ruin his entire operation. He's been spouting off the same warning for the last six years. It's not like I can prevent it if it happens. If these guys take me down and get free reign at my body, they're gonna go for the face. I might be able to explain it away after a fight with Kayden or something, but now, with him coming nowhere near me, it's gonna be a lot harder to talk my way out of.

I want them to hit me in the face. I want to go to school and have someone notice that the way I looked the day before is not how I look now. Maybe then I can get the hell away from this once and for all. I can't walk away on my own so someone stepping in would be a godsend.

The guy he's got me lined up to face first is missing his two front teeth and looks like he's ten sheets to the wind. Drinking before a fight would give me a bit of an advantage, unless for some reason, being drunk makes him stronger. If that happened I'm screwed. If anything, being drunk makes you stupid, which means I might be able to steal a win here just thinking smart and moving fast.

Rodney Morris, that's his name. I've seen him around town before. He drinks with Kayden's brother Dean a lot. Shit. I hope this doesn't get back to Dean. If it does, and Kayden finds out, he'll have something to use against me and I can't risk that happening.

Feeling his hand on my shoulder, I tense from the touch but keep all emotion off my face. If my father sees even the slightest look of fear, Rodney is going to be the least of my worries. Bruce will think nothing of dragging me out of here by my hair and beating on me himself until the fear is gone and all that remains is emptiness.

"Do me proud boy. The more damage you do to these three will determine where and who you fight next."

"More like how much money you make next."

My smart mouth as he calls it, is gonna earn me a beating worse than any of these 'roided up losers can give me, but I don't care. I'm only telling the truth. My dad has a top position with a software development company, makes a shitload on a weekly basis, but cares more about the money he makes from my fighting than he does his job. Making a couple of grand watching as his son gets his ass beat on so hard he can barely walk the next day is a real turn on for the sick son of a bitch.

I hate this, but I never complain about it. There's no one I can complain to. No one gives a fuck. I'm alone and I'll always be alone. I would kill to turn around right now and lay this son of a bitch out, even knowing he's my dad, but I can't. I might be strong against the people I go up against at school, but I'm a complete pussy when it comes to him. I won't lay a hand on him, no matter how badly I want to and I think he banks on that. He's secure knowing he controls me and all of this.

Frank Simmons, the ref for this fight, steps forward and calls to both me and Rodney and as I make my way forward, ready to step into a fight for my very life, I focus on the only thing that can possibly help me get through this. The caramel hair and brown chocolate eyes that have haunted me for the past three days since I first laid eyes on them.

Thinking about her might seem like a distraction if I ever told anyone about it, but for me she's more than that. Right now, her attitude, the glassy look in her eye that she gets when I insult her, disrespect the teacher or any of the kids in the class, is going to be the thing to get me through this. I'm gonna focus on her and maybe, just maybe I'll use all the pent up feelings I have about her and take this son of a bitch down before he can do any real damage.

As Frank calls for us to start, I bring every bit of anger I've got to the surface, seeing not Rodney's face as I make my first move, but my fathers and with thoughts of Cadence and the way she's gone out of her way to ignore me pushing me even more ahead, I unload on the beefed up guy in front of me. I unleash everything I've got on him right from the jump, even knowing that in the end it's going to cost me.

It's only when I attempt to block his retaliating fist and come up short, the impact slamming me right in the cheek, hearing my father screaming his anger at me in the background that I realize the mistake I've made.

That one punch is going to cost me and not just when we got out of this smelly screwed up barn. The stinging in my cheek alone from the impact of the hit is going to cause my face to bruise and when it does, there's no way in hell my secret is gonna remain a secret.

I'm about to be found out.

Cadence

The first thing I notice when I get to class Thursday morning, after two days of ignoring Dillon and all his stupid attempts to make conversation, is the limp he has when he walks to the front, handing some paper over to my mom and turning to make his way back to his seat.

It's only when he sits and I really look at his face that I see something even worse than the limp. His cheek is bruised and there's a small piece of medical tape over his right eye, holding a scrap of tissue or toilet paper in place. His lips, the ones I spent so much time watching are cracked and cut open, dried blood resting just on the surface.

If Dillon looks like this, I'm almost afraid to see what the other guy looks like. Talking to Eric for the past two days at lunch, I've got a feeling I know who the other guy is and seeing him this morning as he walked Isabelle to class, he doesn't have a scratch on him, which means whatever went down, Dillon took the majority of.

Sliding into my seat after tossing my backpack on the floor, I unzip it and like I've been doing for the last two days, pull out my book, prepared to spend the entire time reading and doing my best to put Dillon Murphy and his broken body out of my head all together. I'm curious about what happened, but not enough to reach out and ask. Today is going to be like every other day this week. I'm not going to say a word, he'll ignore me the same way and things will be the same as always.

At least that's the plan until he goes and breaks it.

Leaning over, he puts another small lined piece of paper on my desk, but this time, through the gap where my hair isn't entirely covering my face, I see him flinching in pain as he leans back into his seat. Where I would have just ignored the piece of paper for a while, seeing him flinch and the way his eyes roll back up into his head with the pain of the small movement he made, I reach out and flip it open, reading what's written there.

If the guy's gonna hurt himself in order to talk to me, the least I can do is read it. I don't have to respond, but I wouldn't be able to live with myself if I didn't at least acknowledge the words on the page.

Hey.

One word.

With the way he tried so hard on Monday to get me to talk to him, forgive him for what happened with his friends, I thought for sure I would see more than just this one word, but as usual, Dillon is again proving that I know nothing at all about him and any attempt to figure him out is pointless.

Using his paper to respond instead of reaching for my sticky pad, I scribble the same word back to him, hoping it will be enough and he'll go back to ignoring me so that I can pretend to do the same even though the voice in my head is screaming at me to ask what happened to him.

Hey.

Before I know it, he's handing the paper back to me, this time not reaching out around the desk, but holding it out across the space between our desks in order for me take it. After a split second of deliberation on whether or not I should engage with him this way, especially after the way the last two days have gone, I reach my hand out and take it from him.

What are you reading?

A book. You know, those big things with pages that you turn for enjoyment?

Fuck. Are u always such a bitch?

No. Just for people that deserve it.

We continue to go back and forth like this for at least another ten minutes while my mom stands at the front of the room, her back to us, explaining some math lesson to the other six students in the room. After every pass of the now filled paper between us, I scan the front, praying as I do that she doesn't catch me talking to him.

After the conversation we had this morning before coming here, the last thing I want her to see is me going against what she wants and talking to Dillon.

~*~*~

"I had an interesting talk with Eric Carmen yesterday afternoon."

I know where she's going with this. There's only one thing that Eric could talk to her about that she would find interesting, at least enough to tell me about. Anything else he may have said to her, she would have kept to herself, which means she knows what happened on Monday.

Motioning with my hand, not willing to speak up and admit to anything, I try to get her to continue. The sooner we get this over with, the better. It's been two days since it happened and even though I couldn't get it out of my head, the last thing I want to do is talk about it.

"He said that Dillon, Amy and Tim attempted to start something after lunch on Monday and you got knocked down in the scuffle. Is there anything you want to tell me?"

I shake my head and turn back toward my cereal. I don't want to talk about this with her, especially since it happened two days ago and nothing's happened since. So, some girl knocked me down. It's not like there was some big fight or something. She's gonna freak out over nothing.

"Cadence, I know the way it works. When a student gets bullied they keep it to themselves. I don't want you feeling you need to do that. What you tell me here will remain between the two of us. If you are being silenced in some way, it ends now."

Not being silenced, Mom. Don't want to talk about it.

"Who pushed you to the ground?"

The girl. I sign easily.

"If it was Dillon, you can tell me."

It wasn't Dillon. He just watched it happen.

She seems surprised by my answer. My mom is usually pretty understanding when it comes to just about anyone, but I can tell she wants to believe the worst of Dillon. It's not like her at all. Where's the non-judgmental teacher I've been living with for the past sixteen years?

"Well, I suppose it doesn't matter who did it. If it happens again, I don't want to hear about it secondhand from Eric or any other student. I want you to bring it to me, even if you think you can handle it on your own."

Okay. Are you done now?

"Cadence, I'm aware that going to work with me is not something you're happy about and you would like nothing more than to be back at your school with your friends, but this is the situation we've been dealt. I want you to promise me something."

I already agreed to tell her if something happened at school, what else can she possibly want me to promise?

"I want you to promise that you will stay as far away from Dillon as possible. I know that he's in the class and the two of you sit in close proximity to each other, but he is not a person you want to be getting involved with."

Nodding my head in agreement, I put my attention back on my cereal and tune her completely out. We haven't said so much as hello to each other since Monday afternoon when I told him what I thought about him. If she wants me to stay away, that's an easy promise to make since I didn't have any plans on speaking to him again.

"Good. You're such a sweet girl, Caddy. The last thing I want to see happen is for someone like Dillon Murphy to come along and change that."

~*~*~

Focusing my attention back on the paper in front of me, a new one he ripped out of his notebook and taken to writing on, I see the question he has waiting for me and it just reminds me again of how true my mom's words were this morning. Though with the back and forth so far this morning, I'm doing a bang up job of listening to them.

So I gotta ask. Why are u in this class? You don't seem retarded.

I'm not letting him get away with this. It's one thing to roll his eyes at my mom and for me to reach over and flick him repeatedly, but there's no way I'm gonna let him refer to the kids in this class as retards. By all rights, with my disability, I'm one of the so called retards he's talking about. I've never been a fan of that word and that's not going to change now.

I'm not in a retard class. There's no such thing. I'm in this class. If you wanna know why I'm here, I'll tell you as soon as you tell me what truck did that to your face.

His response is immediate and as I read it over, I can easily see its bullshit. I saw Kayden this morning, I know he had nothing to do with what's going on here. Even if Dillon had taken the brunt of an attack, there would still be some kind of marks on Kayden and there just wasn't.

Got into it with someone I used to be friends with. No biggie. So why are you here?

I think you're lying, but I'm here because my school got closed down for a couple weeks.

His eyes raise at my admission or me calling him out on his lying. I can't be sure which one he's doing it to, but it's obvious that he hadn't been expecting that to be my response.

Is this you thinking you know me again?

I don't think I know you; I do know you. I've met a lot of guys just like you and you're all the same.

He attempts to hide it but I catch the eye roll the minute it happens and it's at that point I make up my mind. I've had enough of this back and forth with him. I'm done. When he's ready to stop acting like a brat, I might think about responding again, but for now, I'm just done.

Turning back to my book, I flip back to the page I left off on and go back to ignoring him. When no note comes, either with him reaching painfully across my desk to deliver it or holding it out for me to take, I know I've made the right decision.

Dillon

Jesus Christ; this girl just doesn't let up.

There's a second there where she calls me out for being a liar that I almost tell her what really happened to me, but just as quickly as it comes, I push it down. It doesn't matter how hot this girl is, or how much I enjoy our conversation, there is no way in hell I'm telling her the truth.

When I got to school this morning and people started staring at my face, I thought for sure that shit was about to come falling down around me. People would find out that I hadn't gotten into a fight the way I'd spread around the night before through texting with Amy and my secret would be exposed.

So far, it hasn't happened but it doesn't mean I'm gonna go out of my way to make it reality. Telling this girl would be exposing myself in a way that I'm just not willing to do. So I attempt to flip it around on her, my ability to be a total jerk coming as easily as it always does and within a couple of minutes, she's got her nose back in her book and I'm back to being left alone.

I don't know how it happened, but somehow I managed to get through all three fights last night. Sure, I feel like I've been run over by a truck the way Cadence said but it's been happening for so long now that I'm used to it. In a few days, the cuts and bruises will fade and I'll be back to normal. I just hope that he doesn't schedule another fight before that happens. This time I definitely need time to heal.

Kicking Rodney's ass had been easier than I expected. I let him wail away on me for a while, watching as he became winded quickly due to his size and the amount of liquor and drugs in his system. When that happened, it was easy to take him down. It's only when I got to Mark and Alex that I lost steam and ended up looking the way I do now.

Bruce had not been happy, but considering what he told me while he drove me home, he should have seen it coming. According to him, Mark and Alex are training to become professional fighters, which means they know what the hell they're doing and going up against a kid like me is easy as shit for them. Hearing what he told me, I'd been pretty pissed. It's one thing to throw me against someone my own age or maybe even a few years older like Rodney, but professional fighters?

What dear old dad doesn't know is that by the time I got to Alex, I was prepared to lie down and let him get the win. I actually did lie down at one point, praying for it to end. I had sucked all the blood I could stand off my lips and I could barely see out of my right eye with the blood that was pouring out of the cut Mark left me with. By the time I got home and looked in the mirror, my eyes were completely bloodshot and it had nothing to do with me not sleeping. It was the blood that managed to hole up there.

Most kids, if they went through what I did, would be freaked out going home, afraid their mom would see it and lose her shit on them, but I'm not like that. Between all the fighting I get into at school and then all the shit that went down at Homecoming with Kayden, my mom is used to seeing me like this. She didn't even bat an eyelash when I walked through the door.

She also didn't ask what happened.

That's Rebecca for you. She's so out of it, I'm shocked that she even gets up for work in the morning or knows enough to leave me money for lunch. She's always been a space cadet, but the last couple of years since she kicked my dad out, she's gotten worse. It's the pills. She drowns herself in them so much that the world is completely lost to her. I'm thankful for her being this way though. It means I don't have to answer any questions about what Dad really does with me during our time together.

I bandaged up the wounds as best I could and here I am, back at school, earning some looks but nothing I can't handle. My secret is still intact, my friends doing what they're good for and spreading the perfect amount of lies in order to make it seem as though all I did was get into a fight after school. The only risk to all of that being one of my own making in wanting to tell Cadence the truth.

As long as I can keep my mouth shut with this girl that seems to know more about me than I do, I'll be just fine.

Thing is, I can't do that. She's sitting there reading her book, the pages all bent and worn, like she's read it multiple times and I'm kind of interested in exactly what it's about. I'm so pathetic right now that I'm willing to listen to her tell me about some stupid book I'll never read just so she'll give me the time of day again.

"Can I see what you're reading?" I ask and when she doesn't look up or even acknowledge that she's heard me, I try again.

"Cadence. Can I see your book?"

What the hell is with this girl? Is she still pissed about what happened Monday so she's purposely ignoring me? Considering I got her to talk to me a couple seconds ago, there's no way she can be all that upset. I gotta figure if she hated me she wouldn't have said a word to me this morning, but she did, so what the hell is with her now?

Reaching across and tapping her on the shoulder even though it causes my ribs an enormous amount of pain, I watch as she jumps back in the seat. She must have been more into the book than I thought. It looks like I freaked the hell out of her.

When she settles and her shoulders go from rigid to relaxed, her eyes catch mine and I try one more time to get her to talk to me. Now that she's looking at me, there's no way she can ignore me the way she just did.

"Can I see what you're reading?"

Her eyebrows raise and she smiles weakly, closing the book after bending the top of the page down, marking her location and passing it over to me. Reaching out to take it, my hands brushing softly over hers and my body tenses with the shock that takes place. Shaking it off, believing it to be something related to the amount of times she's run her fingers through her hair since she got here, I look down at the cover of the book and I'm surprised.

I expected to see some kind of romance, since that seems to be what most girls read when I do pay them enough attention to notice, but what's in front of me now is as far from romance as you can get. It's a fantasy novel, science fiction I think, and the very last thing I expected to see someone like her reading.

Shit; I know absolutely nothing about this girl.

I feel her eyes staring a hole into the side of my face as I'm looking at the book so I turn back to her and hold it back out for her to take.

"You like this kind of stuff?

She nods as she takes the book back and I press forward the minute I feel her eyes back on me.

"Didn't think many girls read science fiction."

She pulls the paper out and as much as I don't wanna do it, I feel the frustration growing watching her write on it. I figured she was like Isabelle with the way she always writes everything out, but I'd been hoping I was wrong and she would open her mouth and speak to me. I know I haven't exactly earned it, but she's gotta know by now that anything she did say wouldn't be a waste of breath like she said the first day.

As she reaches up to hand the paper out to me, I decide to go for broke and ask her why she won't speak.

"Are you planning on speaking to me or are we just gonna do this forever?"

Bringing the paper back to the desk, she starts writing on it again, obviously answering my question and after a few minutes of her scribbling away on the paper, I'm getting anxious with how badly I want her to finish so I can read it.

I have no idea what the hell is going on with me lately. I haven't had any contact with this girl for two days, yet she's the first thing that comes to mind before I go into the fight from hell and now I'm sitting here practically dying inside to read what she's writing to me. I shouldn't give two shits but it seems to be all I care about.

Getting to know her, it's supposed to be a game. A way to keep me occupied, but now there's nothing about it that feels like a game. I want her attention because I actually like the way it feels when I have it.

You obviously don't know the right kind of girls.

We can just not talk at all if you prefer. You're the one that talked to me. Truth is, I don't talk much because I don't like the way my voice sounds.

Well, if I didn't already know I was an asshole, her words in response to my question slam the point home. I feel like a dick now. Asking the question was a risk but her answer— damn. She's telling me the truth, I can tell it by the way her eyes look as she watches me reading. She's not aware I can see it and right now, I'm thankful. Let her think that her concern over my reaction is her secret.

I want her to speak even more now. People are always more critical of themselves than they are of other people, so I think in order to know the truth, I need to be the one to hear her. She's probably just being too hard on herself.

That's not what I write back to her though. It should have been what I said because that's the topic we were on, but with the way she chose to be honest with me even though it was none of my business, I feel the need to do the same.

I'm sorry. You were right earlier. I got hit by three pretty big trucks.

Does it hurt?

Like hell. Maybe worse than hell, IDK.

Why did you throw yourself in front of them then?

I can't help it. When I see her response and the way she's still pretending I mean actual trucks and not being pummeled by three very big people, I laugh and it comes out a lot louder than I expect it to.

"Is there something you find funny, Mr. Murphy?"

Shit. I knew the minute the laugh came out it was going to end up causing something like this to happen, but I'd been hoping that Ms. Taylor would be so absorbed in grading papers or whatever that I would go unnoticed. I'm obviously not that lucky.

"No, Ms. T."

"Well alright. Please refrain from outbursts like that in the future."

Nodding my head in acknowledgement, I lower my head back down to the desk again, but not before catching the tiny blue square of paper out of the corner of my eye.

BUSTED.

Chapter Six

Cadence

I don't know what I was thinking agreeing to this, but now that I'm here there's nothing I can do to change it even though I probably should.

After Dillon got busted for laughing and I held up the sticky note in an attempt to be funny, we went back to relative silence with each other again. He kept his head down on his desk, not looking over at me once and believe me, I was watching for it. Accepting it even though I wanted to continue our conversation, I went back to my book until everyone moving around me signaled that the bell rang.

Before I get through the door, I felt a hand on my shoulder and freezing in place at the touch, one I don't recognize, I turn around slowly to find out just who it is that's stopping me. Coming face to face with Dillon, his familiar smirk in place like always, I allow the slight race in my heart to slow to a dull crawl before dipping my head to the side in confusion.

"Come to lunch with me? I know it's probably the last place you want to be, but I think you'll have a good time with us once they get to know you. So will you do it?"

Stuck with no alternative other than to grab the notepad from my bag and tell him no, I just nod my head in acceptance and now I'm stuck.

I've been here with them for almost twenty minutes and it's painfully apparent that none of them, Dillon included, have figured out that I can't hear a word they're saying. I'm doing my best with reading lips, but with the girls, it's hard since they talk so fast. I'm nodding at the right times or at least what I think to be the right times and I'm doing everything I can in order to appear normal, but it's not easy.

It doesn't help that the girl that knocked me to the floor has been shooting looks at me since Dillon and I got here and he introduced me. It's pretty obvious they're together and she sees me as a threat. I'm the last person she needs to worry about. I know what Dillon is about and even though I agreed to be here when he asked me, I'm not going to forget it any time soon.

Watching everyone laughing at something I missed while lost in my own thoughts, my stomach turns over in knots. I should have ignored the touch on my arm earlier and run to meet Eric. Being outside with him, there's no awkwardness. He knows all about me and my disability and I don't have to pretend to be something I'm not. I want that now more than anything because it's obvious I just don't fit in here at all. I'm nothing like these people and once they find out the truth, they'll want to get as far away from me as they can get.

Once the laughing dies down, I watch as Amy starts to speak and this time, she goes slowly enough for me to catch every word she's saying.

"So why did you bring one of them to lunch, Dill? It's pretty obvious she's mute."

Preparing myself to stand and get the hell out of here, not wanting to read any more lips since it's obvious it's all going to be an attack, I pull my knees up, ready to push up and off the floor. It's only when I read Dillon's lips as he answers that I stop myself.

"She can talk, Ames. She just needs to feel comfortable. Considering what you did, can you blame her?"

It's the nicest thing I've heard him say in the last four days and I'm pretty surprised by it. With the way he's answering his girlfriend, I gotta figure I was right about him from the start. There's more to him than just being an asshole. Maybe I'll finally get a chance to see it.

"She earned that shit, attacking you the way she did. No one's allowed to put their hands on you while I'm around, not even some stupid mute bitch that likes retards."

I flinch from the hate in her words and again prepare myself to get the hell out of here. I don't have to listen to this. No one is gonna sit here and disrespect me or my friends. Getting to my feet, I sling my bag back over my shoulder and turn to go, resisting the urge the entire time to turn around and give Amy the finger. I might not want them to hear my voice, but that doesn't mean I can't find other ways to get my point across.

Starting off down the hallway, thankful again that I can't hear any of them, I feel the knot in my stomach start to loosen. No matter what Dillon says, the people he hangs out with will never accept me and I was stupid for even believing for a second that anything he said about them was right.

I am never going near those people ever again.

Dillon

Shit. That didn't go the way I wanted it to.

When I saw her leaving class earlier, another opportunity to ask her to hang out about to pass me by, I jumped out of my seat in an effort to reach her before she ducked out on me again. Despite knowing that she's friends with Eric and she spends her time at lunch with him and the others, I wasn't gonna let the chance to further my plan slip out of my hands.

What better way is there for this girl to warm up to me than having her hang with me and my friends instead of outside under that nasty tree with the others like her?

It's about more than that. Even though I'm going back and forth about what I set out to do, I still wanted to be around her. I've never had this kind of conflict before. Things are usually so cut and dry with me. I either want to screw with this girls head or I genuinely want her to like me. There's no in between.

With Cadence though, it's all just in between and back and forth. Nothing is clear.

I get her to finally agree, bring her around my friends and of course it all has to get blown to shit because my girlfriend can't tame the fucking jealousy. If Amy would just open her eyes, she'd see that this has nothing to do with Cadence having a thing for me. It's about getting her away from the freaks and continuing on with the plan I told them all about the first day.

That's not how it works though. Amy instantly goes on the defensive, not trusting the girl and now Cadence is walking down the hall and I'm doing everything I can not to jump up and go after her.

"Finally! Good riddance." Amy mutters under her breath the minute Cadence is completely out of earshot and I resist the urge to smack her. I know that her attitude is half the reason I like her, but shit, even to me right now she's taking it too far.

"Do you always have to be such a bitch?"

"What the hell did you expect? Bringing one of them to lunch? Was I just supposed to jump up and hug her or something?"

"I expected that you'd at least pretend to be nice."

She laughs and again, I feel the urge to slap her rising to the surface. I hate when people laugh at me, absolutely despise it and even though it's my girlfriend laughing and she's not doing it at me but about what I said, I still wanna unload on her.

"Since when are we nice to retards? I know you got this whole plan thing mapped out about what you want to do to her and I agreed, but that doesn't mean I have to act the same."

"She's not a retard, Ames."

"Says you. She's in that class with you and she didn't say a fucking word the entire time she was here. If she's not one of them, she's trying awfully hard to look like she is."

"Did she not try with all of you while she was here? That's more than a so called retard would do. You didn't have to be such a bitch to her. You running her off isn't gonna make this shit work."

"The only reason the girl came with you is because she's got a thing for you. I saw it in her eyes."

It always comes back to this. Every girl that looks at me has a thing for me. This is the part of being with Amy that I hate. Her jealousy is huge and it makes interacting with her absolutely impossible. I won't get through to her no matter what I say. She's got it in her head that Cadence has a thing for me and nothing will deter her. She's completely lost her mind. If anything Cadence hates my guts and only tolerates me because I annoy her when we're in class, but Amy won't wanna hear that. She'll just find a way to turn it around again.

Right when I go to respond, she starts up again and I feel whatever patience I had slipping away.

"Maybe you can't see it because you've got a thing for the little retard too. Is that it, Dill? Maybe you don't wanna play a game with her after all. Maybe you wanna get into the mute girls pants?"

Yeah, that's it. I'm done with this bullshit. I knew I should have gotten up and walked away from her when she said that shit with Cadence sitting right here and I know it even more now. She's full of nothing but venom and I want no part of it. Let her think whatever the fuck she wants. I'm done.

"You know what Ames? Come find me when you pull the stick out of your ass. You're delusional and I'm over it."

I meant what I said. I think she's being irrational, but there's a part of me, despite what I believe that knows there's a least a little truth in what she said even though it's the last thing I'm going to admit to. Despite all of this starting out as a game, I do like her and I'm pretty damn pissed with the way everything just went down.

Shit. I'm obviously losing my mind too. I need to get my head on straight. Cadence is just another retard and I gotta remember that.

Getting up from the floor, flinching in pain as I stretch muscles that want no part of moving, I turn and start heading down the hall, picking up speed the further I go, determined to get as far away as I can from Amy and her bullshit. As I round the corner that will take me to the stairs, determined to just head up and wait until class starts, I run into the last person I want to see with everything I just dealt with.

Kayden's blocking my way and he looks pissed.

Chapter Seven

Cadence

Why didn't I fight my mom on this? Why did I have to come here knowing that this is the kind of crap I was going to deal with?

All of these kids are what the world deems normal. There is no room for people with disabilities and definitely not any room for people like Eric, Isabelle and the others. We're all just a bunch of deaf mute freaks that give these so called normal people hours of entertainment to get them through the day.

It doesn't matter to them that we didn't ask to be the way we are; that some of us were born this way and we're only trying to get along and survive like everyone else. No, instead they've got to go out of their way to call attention to the things that set us apart from them instead of embracing the ways we're the same. Not every person here is like that, I mean I've seen people that aren't, but finding someone like that is rare.

Taking off from the group and stuck with only two options, both of which I'm not really in the mood for, I veer off in the direction of a third option. A place where no one will come looking for me. Not Dillon and his stupid friends and definitely not Eric and the others. The place I should have gone the first day.

Pushing my way through the turnstiles and smiling weakly at Ms. Reid as I pass by her, I head into the stacks of books that no student would ever be caught dead in. History texts might be needed sometimes, but it's the one place no matter what library you find yourself in that's almost always barren. No one goes out of their way to go there unless they're doing what I am now and trying to find a place to hide out and escape.

I've been different my entire life. I've had people treat me like a leper for as long as I can remember and despite all of it, I managed to develop a pretty thick skin. It's the reason I could do what Eric couldn't that day in the hall. I could stand up to Dillon, his girlfriend and that other guy easily because there's nothing they can say or do that I haven't already experienced. I'm used to all of it and in coming to terms with the knowledge that the majority of the world are jerks and there's not a whole lot you can do to change it, I've been able to push ahead and rise above it, doing whatever I have to in order to prevent it from happening to other people.

The deaf girl sticking up for the special needs kids. It's a running joke for the idiots I just wasted twenty minutes of my life on for sure.

Despite my thick skin, I'm not immune to it. It wears on me the same way it would anyone that goes through it. It's why I'm hiding out in the library right now, wanting nothing more than a few minutes of peace in order to calm myself. As hard as I try to not let their words, insults and even assumptions get to me, I'm only human and what just happened, it's definitely eating at me.

It's been a really long time since I wished I was normal. Wished that I wasn't deaf. I came to terms with my disability years ago, but right now, I would give anything to go back out there, sit with those people that I can't even stand and interact with them the way a normal person would. It's half the reason my mom tried every single hearing aid on the market when I was little. She knew I would struggle with this and wanted to make it as easy on me as possible. Problem is, there isn't a hearing aid strong enough. I'm doomed to spend my life, at least here, on the outside looking in.

I want to go back to my school now. I don't even care that the place is flooded. I would gladly sit in a desk full of water, rain boots on my feet and a slicker over me while it poured from the ceiling if it meant that the way I feel right now could end. Maybe it's time I talk to my mom and beg her to let me stay home for the next week and a half. It would be preferable to this. She would never agree, but at this point I'm willing to try anything.

This, the pity party I'm giving myself because I'm not like everyone else, I need to stop it. It's not getting me anywhere. I haven't done anything like this since I was six. I'm better than this and I need to remember that and not let what just happened change me. Remembering Isabelle's words from the other day at lunch, I realize I do have an escape.

Reaching around to my backpack, sliding it down until I can unzip it far enough to grab the phone inside, I pull it out and scroll through the contacts looking for her name. Finding it, I bring up the message screen and begin typing. I'm not sure what I want to come from it but with the way things already are, I figure it can't get much worse.

Her response is instant and seeing the words on the screen, I brighten for the first time since Mom caught Dillon laughing in class.

I'm outside. Kayden took off somewhere and Eric never showed. Could use the company.

There's something about the happy emote on my screen that pushes me off the floor and out the door just as quickly as I came in. It's inviting and right now with as alone as I feel, I can use all of that particular feeling as I can get. Making my way toward the front door of the school, more than ready to meet her, I don't notice the shadows that come to a full stop until it's too late and I've run into one of them. Hard.

Getting my bearings I look up and where I expect to find some random guy with as hard as I knocked into him, I come face to face with the girl I just walked away from not fifteen minutes before and just like then, she's got a nasty looking snarl on her face and I know that whatever happens now is not going to be good.

"Just the mute bitch we were looking for. It's time we had a little chat."

Dillon

I knew it was only a matter of time before this happened, but I gotta say, I was hoping I had a bit more time. No doubt he knows about his car and is here to threaten me about it.

New Kayden won't come near me physically, but that doesn't mean he won't find some equally damning way to get back at me. He stayed true to his word a few months ago and hasn't laid a finger on me since the insanity at Homecoming. Now, anytime he's looking to deal with me, he goes through Daniels or one of the teachers.

Looks like that's about to change.

"Not in the mood for this."

"I don't really care what you're in the mood for."

"What the hell do you want? If this is about your car, go talk to Tim since he's the one that did it."

"No doubt because you told him to."

"I didn't tell him shit. I heard about it secondhand, not that I'm completely against it. You had it coming squealing like a pig the way you did."

"You mean stopping you from torturing someone, don't you?"

"Whatever. You got what you wanted. I'm being punished and I'm sure you're pleased as shit about it. If you got a problem with what happened to your car, talk to Tim. I've got nothing left to say to you."

"I can't believe it."

"What?"

I don't really care what he's getting at, wanting nothing more than for this conversation to end, but with the surprised expression on his face, I gotta ask. It's a look I haven't seen him wear in a long ass time.

"You're actually backing down."

"Guess I am. We done?"

"As much as I'd like to say yes because even the sight of you makes me sick, no; we're not done."

"Well can you get on with it? I've got like fifteen minutes before I gotta be upstairs and I'm not letting you screw it up."

"How's that working out for you?" He grins. "Gotta figure that's a fate worse than death for you, being surrounded by all those people you call retarded."

He doesn't know the half of it, but I'm not about to say it to him. I meant what I said, I don't want any part of this and I won't let him be the reason I end up late to class. I'm sure he'd like nothing more than for me to get nailed again, especially after what Tim and Amy did to his car, but he's not gonna get his way.

Attempting to make my way around him, his arm comes out and shoves me backward, letting me know that despite my desire to get away, I'm not going anywhere.

"That shit you pulled Monday with Eric and Cadence; it ends now."

Of course that's what this macho bullshit is about. Eric went running with his tail between his legs and tattled on me. Stupid baby. It makes me wanna pick on him again just for how weak and childish he's acting. Maybe I'd think about leaving him alone if he didn't feel the need to tell on me every five minutes.

"Message received. Can I go now?"

"No, because I don't believe you. Dillon; somewhere in there is the guy I met four years ago. The decent one that wasn't always so fucking mad at the world. I get why you do the shit you do, but take it from someone who knows, it's not worth it."

"Thanks Dad." I snap sarcastically.

"The girl that Amy took out, she's not like Isabelle and Eric. She's different and if you think I'm on you for the things you do to Eric, you haven't seen anything yet."

What does he mean by that? How is Cadence different from Eric and Isabelle? From what I've seen spending time with her, she's more like Isabelle than he seems to think. As much as I hate this guy and want nothing more than to kick his teeth in, he's obviously got information about the girl that I don't and I wanna know it.

"Is this where you tell me to watch my back? That you're not gonna fight me but find better ways to deal with me, because if it is, spare me. I've heard it and it's as old and tired as this conversation."

"I don't know what I thought would happen doing this. It's obvious you're never gonna change, but Dillon, wake the fuck up."

"That's actually a good question. Why are you doing this? What the hell do you want?"

"I've known you a long time. I've seen you before you made the team and gained the popularity, turning into the jerk that's standing here now. I've seen you care about people even though you didn't want anyone to know you did. I heard some stuff today and it's because I know the person you used to be that I'm here."

"Don't believe everything you hear." I laugh awkwardly. I can't let him know that the stuff he's saying is getting to me. I hate any reminder of the way things used to be and the more he goes on about it, the more I want to turn around and go back the way I came. I'm not that person anymore and it's doubtful I ever will be again. No matter how much he walks down memory lane.

"So you're not talking to Cadence, laughing in class because of the notes the two of you pass back and forth? You didn't just get up and walk away from your friends after they ran her off? All of that, it's all bullshit right?"

Shit. He knows.

"You don't know anything and tell your little spies to stay out of my business."

I slam my way past him, not wanting to hear anymore. I was sure no one knew what was going on in class with Cadence and now I know differently. It means that from now on, I need to stay as far away from her as I can get. I don't need any more of this getting back to Kayden or even Amy and the others. I'll never hear the end of it if it does.

"Dillon, you can run from what I'm saying all you want, but you're never gonna run far enough, trust me!" He calls out and there's something about what he's saying that stops me in my tracks.

"What's that supposed to mean?"

As people start coming in from outside, he stalks over to where I'm standing and leans in as close as possible. His final words to me sending a chill down my spine.

"That girl you can't stop thinking about; the one that makes you feel shit you don't think you're allowed to feel; Dillon, she can't hear a word you say. Cadence—she's deaf."

Chapter Eight

Cadence

When my mom came home one night last fall, after chaperoning a dance, she had tears in her eyes and I remember wondering who put them there and how hard it would be for me to find them and deal with them.

It's the way things have always been with us. Even though she's got my dad and he's as supportive as they come considering everything he's got to deal with, I'm super protective of her. She must have seen something in my eyes that night because she quickly went on to tell me exactly why it was she was coming home in tears.

One of her students, Isabelle had gone to the dance and been named Homecoming Queen. I remember thinking that it was pretty cool that someone who had special needs was actually included until she told me what happened next.

This opened her up to telling me about Isabelle's struggles at school. The way she was picked on, called names and thrown into the girls' washroom, beaten and burned. Back then, all I could do was watch my mom fall apart over the whole thing, unable to do anything to take her pain away, but also thankful that kind of hatred didn't take place at my school.

The girls stopping me in the hall, I should have remembered that conversation sooner because if I did, I would have known what was coming for me. Now I'm seeing firsthand what Isabelle had to deal with because it's happening again.

They don't say a word as they're pulling me along, but even if they did, with my eyes focused forward, I wouldn't have caught their lips moving and been able to tell what was coming for me. Slamming their way into the washroom, everything my mom told me comes back and I understand with crystal clear clarity what is about to happen now.

What they don't realize about me is I'm stronger than I look. I've never been in a situation like this one before, but I have been in enough altercations, stopping other people from getting bullied that I know how to get myself out of it. As much as I hate violence of any kind, if they're planning on trapping me in here like a caged animal, I'm going to do whatever I have to in order to get away.

The minute my back connects with the wall, I feel the sharp sting up my spine but I don't allow it to stop me. The minute the blonde grabs for my arm, I pull it up and hit her right in the nose. Bending over, tending to my move, the other two come at me, and soon as the other girls hand comes out close enough, I grab it and not thinking, bend and bite it.

It has the desired effect as she shrieks and backs up and away, leaving me alone with the person that put all of this in motion. It's just me and Amy now and until the two girls collect themselves enough to come back and help, I plan on doing whatever I can to get out of here.

At least I am until Amy grabs my hair and yanks it. Hard. Twisting me around by the hair so she ends up behind me, all the reaching around I try to do falls short as I can't get a grip on her. Whether I like it or not, until she lets go of my hair or changes her position, she's in control and there's nothing I can do.

Feeling her hands on my shoulders, I try to anticipate what's coming next, but with too many different things she could do with the way she's got me, I'm not ready for her as she uses all her strength to push me up against the wall, releasing my hair, spinning me around and laying her hand flat across my chest.

Even with my arms blocked, she hasn't done anything to block my legs so I start kicking them out but before they can connect she dodges them.

Damnit. I can see the other two starting to move toward me and I know that whatever they're about to do now is going to be ten times worse because of what I did before they had a chance to start. They're pissed. I have a minute tops to get myself out of this situation, or things are going to get a whole lot worse.

Amy's lips start moving and despite not wanting to hear anything she's got to say, I can't ignore her as she's speaking so hard that actual spit is flying from her mouth and hitting me in the face.

"I don't know what it is about you stupid mute bitches, but I swear if I have to bring another one of you in here and burn the hell out of you so that you learn to leave Dillon alone, I will. If you haven't already figured it out, he's mine. Not yours. He will never be yours."

She turns from me, toward the friend I bit and I'm thankful for the reprieve. With her looking away, it means her focus isn't on me anymore which is gonna give me the chance to get out of this before the next part of their sick plan.

Bringing my arms up around, I dig my nails into her skin until the pressure against my chest starts to lift. Pulling myself off the wall the minute I'm able to move, I push her and as her body lands against the edge of the first bathroom stall, I watch as she flinches from the impact. Seeing my chance, I run for the door, grabbing onto the handle before I feel my hair again being pulled backwards, this time not as strong as before.

Doing the only thing I can, I twist myself around, tangling my hair even around the girl's hand, but the minute I lock eyes with the blonde girl behind it, the one I don't know the name of, I react purely on instinct. Even though I'm tangled up in her fingers, I reach my head forward and with as much force as I can, I slam my head into hers, not caring where it lands, as long as I can break her hold on me.

She stumbles backward and I see as she does, that she's got a clump of my hair still tangled around her hand, the one she's now using to cover her nose. Not waiting around to see just how badly I hurt her, I turn to the door, this time throwing it open as wide as possible and running out into the hall.

There's no telling how long I've got before they come looking for me, so moving as fast as possible, finally feeling the sting at the back of my head, I race for the stairs. There's only one place I need to be now and it's not down here.

For the first time since I came here four days ago, I need my mom.

Dillon

Kayden is bullshitting me.

There's no way Cadence is deaf. She told me as much earlier when I asked her if she was gonna talk to me. She just doesn't like the sound of her own voice so she prefers writing. I don't know what Kayden's game is, if he's trying to get back at me for all the shit I pulled with him last fall or what, but there's no way he's gonna get me to fall for this.

"You're full of shit."

"Unlike you, I don't go around spreading shit about people, hacking into their phones and exploiting their most private moments for personal amusement. I don't want to tell you this, but with everything I've seen and heard, I think you deserve to know."

"You think you're so much better than me, but you're half the reason things are this way now. You're the one that put all this shit in motion. You can think you're better all you want, but you're still the same douchebag you were when I met you."

Where I expect my words to get to him, he stares blankly at me, like everything I just said means nothing. Considering who he's dating, I figure he would feel at least a little bit of remorse over the things he did when we first started hanging out, but he's standing here looking at me the exact same way he was when I bumped into him to begin with.

"You're not saying anything I don't already know. I've got no problem admitting what a complete asshole I am. That's where you and I are different. You can't admit the truth."

"I can admit I'm an asshole."

"That's not what I mean. Dude; put your shit with me aside and really listen to what I'm telling you. I'm willing to bet she hasn't said a word to you even though she can speak. I'm also pretty sure you've had moments where you said something to her and she didn't even acknowledge your existence."

There's nothing I would like more than to tell him that he's full of shit and wrong about all of it, but I can't. He's not wrong. She hasn't said a word to me and her reasons for that are because she hates the sound of her own voice. I've heard deaf people talk before, at least the ones on television and it adds up. I remember laughing at the way those people sounded. If she expected me to do the same to her than not talking makes perfect sense. Not acknowledging when I've said something to her though, that one hits even harder because she did that exact thing earlier, both in class and with my friends. I said something and she didn't hear me.

She has answered me before though, so if she couldn't hear me how did she do that?

"I've said stuff to her, K."

"Don't call me that."

"You tell me the girl I'm chatting up in class is deaf and you're concerned about what I'm calling you? Man; really?"

"I could be telling you that you have terminal cancer and I would still hate you calling me that. To answer your question, she can read lips. So if you've been looking at her when you're talking to her, that's how she can answer you."

"Okay, so she's deaf. What do you get out of telling me this?"

"This has nothing to do with you. I'm telling you for her. It's only a matter of time before Amy gets wind of you and Cadence and you know what's gonna happen. I won't let another person get dragged in the bathroom and burned. I mean it Dillon, it stopped after Isabelle."

Before I can respond, let him know that as far as the burning goes, we're in agreement despite how we feel about each other, the very girl he mentioned comes running up beside him and her face is frantic. It's a look I haven't seen on her since the night of the dance.

If Isabelle looks like this then it can't mean anything good.

"Kay, something's wrong." she whispers bending closer to him, obviously trying to keep it private.

I don't know why I care if something's wrong with her, but there's something about the look on her face that I can't seem to look away from. It's a look that shouldn't be there with as happy as she's been since her and Kayden worked their shit out.

'What is it?" I hear him ask her and I strain in order to hear whatever her next words are gonna be.

"I got a text from Caddy. She was supposed to meet me out by the tree. She said she wanted to talk about something, but she never showed up and the bell's about to go off."

"How long has it been since she sent you the text?" I ask, completely ignoring the fact that she was speaking to Kayden. When she turns, leveling me with a look of disgust, I know what's coming.

"What do you care?"

"Are you gonna tell me when she texted you or not?" I snap, ignoring the question all together. It's none of her business why I care. I just want information.

"It's true."

"What's true?"

God, I know that I felt something different towards this girl near the end of the stupid shit I pulled, but right now she's reminding me why I picked on her in the first place. I don't have time for this, I need to know what happened to Cadence.

"What Eric told us earlier; it's true." She repeats again and I'm still completely fucking lost.

"Yeah its true baby, but I don't think he's ready to admit it yet." Kayden says, which only makes me wanna hit him.

"Can someone please just tell me when she texted?"

"I waited for her for about twenty minutes and it was about five minutes before that. So twenty-five minutes. Do you think she could have just gone to her mom?"

Wait, what? Her mom?

"You never got her last name, did you?" Kayden asks, covering his mouth with his hand to try and hide a laugh. The one that still breaks through and makes the urge to hit him even worse.

"It didn't seem important. You wanna clue me in?"

"Taylor. Cadence Taylor. Dumbass."

She's Ms. Taylor's daughter. Shit. This situation was already a shit ton to handle with finding out she can't hear, but knowing she's the daughter of the Special Ed teacher whose class I'm stuck in, well shit. This is bad.

"Damnit."

"That's not the word I'd use, but yep. Damnit."

Focusing back on the reason Isabelle's standing with us and less on who Cadence really is, I start to think about the way everything went down before I walked away. Amy had been pissed at me and Cadence for what she thought was something going on between us, or at the very least Cadence having a thing for me. What are the odds she took it a step further when I left and went looking for her?

Very fucking likely.

"Uh, I don't think she's with her mom." I say, hoping that I'm wrong with what I'm thinking even though my gut is telling me a different story.

"What do you mean? What do you know?" Isabelle turns so fast, moving her body until she's standing directly in front of me, her eyes locked on mine and looking less than thrilled. "What did you do, Dillon?"

"I didn't do shit, alright! Stop looking at me like that. I invited her to lunch earlier. I thought if the others got to know her, that what happened Monday would be the end of it."

"Shit." I hear Kayden whisper and it just makes the horrible feeling in my stomach that much worse. He spent the last four years hanging with all of us. He knows Amy better than anyone. Hell, he dated her before I did. No doubt he's thinking the same thing I am.

"Isabelle, go up and check with Ms. T; see if she's there. We're gonna go find Amy and the others."

"You think Amy got her, don't you?" she asks, the cracking of her voice not lost on me. Isabelle has been on the receiving end of Amy and her anger before and I'm pretty damn sure she's not itching to repeat it.

"Looks that way, but don't worry. Dillon got her into this mess, he's gonna get her out of it or I'm gonna be the least of his worries."

As he kisses her on the forehead, I turn away, not wanting to witness any form of display between the two of them, but not because there's something wrong with it. It's because of the closeness. Amy and I have a good time together, but it's never anything like what these two have.

Isabelle takes off the down the hall and Kayden turns to me, his face displaying clearly what he thinks about the whole situation and for once, if he wanted to pound the shit out of me, I'd let him. He's right. I did bring this on. I only hope that when we do find her, we aren't too late.

If we are, Amy is gonna pay.

Chapter Nine

Cadence

I don't think I've stopped shaking since I got here.

The minute my mom caught sight of me, my clothes crumpled and my hair matted not only with sweat but with tinges of blood where the one girl had ripped parts out, she didn't even ask what happened. She ushered me into the class, shutting the door behind her and locking it.

There's gotta be five minutes tops before her students come streaming in for the afternoon lesson and she couldn't care less. She's that caught up getting me to tell her what happened.

"Do you want to tell me how this happened?"

"You know."

I watch as her eyes shine in recognition but am not at all ready for what she says next.

"Was it the girls that did this to you or the entire group?"

I know what she's asking. She wants to know if Dillon had anything to do with this. She doesn't come right out and say his name, but asking about the whole group might as well be the same thing. Just like it did this morning, it always came back to Dillon. For whatever reason, she seems to think he's the root of all evil and until a few minutes ago, I might have agreed with her.

"Girls."

"Well, no doubt that boy is the reason behind it."

Something comes over me seeing how easily she jumps to conclusions and I start signing fast, not stopping until it's all out.

You didn't listen to what I said, Mom. Dillon had nothing to do with this and blaming him for something he

wasn't even there for is wrong. I understand why you don't trust him but I don't get why you hate him so much. You always taught me not to judge people, but you seem to have no problem with it.

I've never talked back to her like this. There's just never been a reason to because normally she's so understanding, with her job and also in dealing with me that I've never had to go that far. I can't let her do this though. As much as Dillon is a part of it because of who took me into the bathroom, he isn't the one that did it.

"I'm sorry, Caddy."

I can't say I expected that to be her response. She's never been an angry person, but when you're sitting there and your kid is going off on you, even if she's signing it and not saying it out loud, I can't see it making any parent very happy.

"What did they do to you? Did they burn you?"

I shake my head, answering the burning question easily. I wouldn't have let it get that far. Even if they ripped all my hair out, I would have fought them. As for telling her what they did do to me, well that wasn't as easy. It's not that I can't find the words, it's just the minute she hears this, she's gonna go into full mom mode. She will do whatever's needed to protect me and in the end, despite me going off at her about it, Dillon will be the one paying for it.

Amy is his girlfriend. I know that. I know the reason this happened at all is because she thinks there's something going on that isn't. Despite my argument, he is the cause of this and there's a part of me that thinks he should pay, but it's only a small part.

He probably has no idea this even happened.

Beginning to sign out my answer, I slowly let it all come out and watch as her eyes go from locked on me and my hands to down into her lap. This is another reason I didn't want to tell her. The way she's reacting, I know she's hurting for me, for the daughter that is getting bullied because of her decision to bring me here. The daughter that's going through this because she's different.

I hate doing this to her.

"I'm going to take this to Principal Daniels. He needs to be made aware that these girls are up to their old tricks. It should have been dealt with when it happened to Isabelle, but since it obviously wasn't, I'm going to make sure it is now."

"Mom," I say and as she looks back up at me, ready to hear what I've got to say, I take my chance. "Don't blame Dillon."

"Is there something going on between you and this boy, Caddy? I'm aware that the two of you have been speaking, it's hard not to notice the way the notes keep passing back and forth when I'm trying to teach, but how far has it gone?"

She's definitely not in teacher mode now. As different as I'm treated because of my disability, in this way, I'm just like every other girl on the planet. The only difference between my mom and other moms is she's doubly invested in my answer. Not only does she want to know because she doesn't like Dillon, she also wants to know because she doesn't trust anyone with her baby.

I just hope that when I tell her that nothing is going on, more than what she's already seen, that she believes me and doesn't just assume I'm like every other teenager and lying to her. Hopefully she knows by now that I wouldn't do that, disability or not.

Again I sign out my response, not trusting my voice to say the words out loud even though they should come easily.

There is nothing going on, Mom. We just talk because we're bored when we're here.

"Are you sure that's all it is?"

I nod and she leans back in her seat, accepting my answer which whether she's aware of it or not, takes another load of my shoulders.

"How were they able to get to you? I thought you've been with Eric and the others at lunch?"

Dillon asked me to meet his friends.

"Oh Cadence," she says and with the way her chest moves I can see that she's sighing. "What did I tell you about that boy?"

Her eyes move to the door and as I turn to see what it is she's looking at, she stands and makes her way over to it. Looking down at the watch on my wrist, I notice the time and I'm pretty sure what she's going to find on the other side. Her students are going to be there, wanting to get in and whatever conversation we're having is going to have to wait until we get home.

As hard as it's been telling her this, it's only going to be worse doing it again when we're at home. I just want to get out of here and forget any of it ever happened. There's no way I can stay here while she teaches for the next three hours. Sitting in my virtual world of silence while surrounded by a bunch of teenagers, special needs or not isn't going to do anything to help what I've been through. Seeing their looks of sadness, understanding and pity just might make it worse.

That's what I'm telling myself instead of just admitting to the real reason I want to get out of here so bad. I'm not worried about the other kids at all. I'm worried about one guy in particular and spending an afternoon being ignored or ignoring him is definitely not something I'm in the mood for. The last person I want to see right now is Dillon Murphy.

As I watch my mom move away from the door, expecting to see her students come flooding in, my eyes sensitive to one body in particular, I see that it's not the entire class after all, but one. The very person I'd been attempting to go see when Amy and her friends cut me off in the hall.

Isabelle is here and as her eyes look over to me, there's recognition in them.

She knows everything.

Dillon

We've been to every bathroom on the first and second floor and there's no sign of Cadence anywhere. It's even worse because where I expect to see Amy or at least have a text or something from her, everything is silent and she's nowhere to be found.

There was a split second when Isabelle left that I thought I was blowing things out of proportion and Cadence would be fine. Her absence would have nothing to do with Ames and the shit she pulls with the girls. I wanted to believe that because I didn't tell her to do it, she would leave well enough alone and I'd find her hanging with Tim and the others just like every other time.

The longer we go without finding them though, it gets harder to believe in. It means when we do find them, not only is Amy gonna pay for what she did, just the way Kayden said, but I am too. This is all going to fall back in my lap and there's not a damn thing I can do to stop it because it's true.

I knew talking to Cadence that first day was going to come back to haunt me. Not because of who she is or even that she has issues. I knew that Amy would see her as a threat and I still kept going with it. I know exactly what my girlfriend is like and just like every other time I've picked on one of the people I consider weak and retarded, I threw another one under the bus. This time I didn't want to do it. It doesn't make me a good person but I wanted things to be different.

Cadence was never supposed to go through this, because she's better than this.

"If something happened to that girl, Dillon, I swear to god."

We've been so focused on finding the girls that we haven't said a word to each other the entire time we've been looking. I'm not surprised these are his first words to me. Ever since he started spending time with Isabelle, he's been an advocate for the kids like her. Kayden's become predictable.

"You really think I wanted shit to go down this way?"

He knows me better than anyone, he was right about that earlier. No one knows the way my mind works like him so he should know that I wouldn't do things this way. If Cadence had been a target the way the others were, I would have planned it way better. It's like the shit with his car. I wouldn't do that right after being nailed by the guy. It's too flashy and calls attention to me automatically. As much as I want them to think more like me, Amy and Tim just don't operate the same way.

"This has your stench all over it."

"Not this time it doesn't."

"Because this time, you like the girl."

Nope. Not going there. It wasn't all that long ago I did this very thing with Kayden in order to garner information from him. I don't think he's doing it for the same reasons I did, but there is no way in hell he's getting me to admit to anything.

"You don't know what you're talking about."

"Yeah, I said the same exact thing. Turns out I was just fooling myself. We might not see eye to eye, but you're doing exactly what I did."

"Can we just get back to what's important here? We need to find Ames and Cadence. The longer they're missing, the worse this feels."

Music starts playing and looking over, I see he's stopped and is pulling his phone out of his back pocket. Looking down, reading whatever's been sent, he wastes no time letting me know what it's about.

"Isabelle found Cadence. She's with her mom."

There's this second after he says it where I feel the tension in my body release and I'm able to breathe easily again. I know that we were on the lookout for both girls, but knowing that Cadence is fine, it's what matters most. If she's with her mom then that means Amy didn't get her.

"Look, Belle wants me to meet her upstairs. You gonna keep looking for Ames or you wanna come with?"

There's one thing I've been sure about since Homecoming. Kayden's hatred for me. After what I put him and Isabelle through, it's understandable and I just moved on from it, putting it in the back of my mind, even though I knew that he wouldn't ever let it go that easily. He's haunted my every movement since that day in the hall where he told me that everything was over, but I didn't even care. We weren't friends anymore so I had nothing else to say to him. Hearing him invite me along now, it's surprising. Considering everything going on, him wanting to be around me at all is a miracle.

"Pretty sure I'm the last person they want to see."

"You do need to be up there for class."

I can't argue with that. I did need to be upstairs, but for the first time in a long time, I'm afraid to go up there. Kayden needs to go on his own. I'm not ready to come face to face with her just yet, especially now.

"You go ahead. I'll head up in a couple minutes."

He nods his head and just as he's about to turn and walk away, he stops. Bringing himself back to where I'm standing, he leans in and as he does I catch the smile on his face.

"Do the world a favor would you?" he asks and going along with him, I nod. "Get rid of Amy before she drags you down with her."

Not waiting around for a response, he heads for the stairs and as I watch him disappear through the doors, I think about what he said. As perfect as I thought she was for me, how similar we are and the way she seems to get me, can I really get rid of her for doing something I've had her do a million times before?

The short answer is yes. If it comes down to a choice between Cadence and Amy, the choice is so damn clear that even I can't deny it.

I need to deal with Amy once and for all.

Chapter Ten

Cadence

I've never been so happy to be outside in my life.

Not a lot of people know, but this isn't my first experience with bullying. It's the first time it's happened here, but before Mom got me into my school, I was in regular elementary. I experienced kids and their hate firsthand and while it wasn't anywhere near what I just went through, it wasn't pretty either. People, kids especially seem to think that just because we can't hear the things they say about us that we have no idea it's happening.

There was this one time, when I was like ten, where I read a girl's lips at school and she had some pretty mean things to say about me and my friend Harrison. There was nothing different about Harrison, he was just like her, but because he made a choice to be my friend, it opened him up for the horrible words and taunts that were thrown around about me all the time.

It didn't sit right with me. I couldn't ignore it anymore. It bothered me that she said stuff about me, it hurt if I'm honest about it, but it was the things she said about Harrison that pushed me forward. I walked up and when she finally turned and acknowledged me, I slapped her across the face. A move she definitely hadn't been expecting.

I don't like fighting but that's not to say I've never been pushed to it. The girl, whose name I can't even remember, backed down after that. It's like slapping her, I woke her up and she started thinking I could hear her after all. The taunts stopped and though I still had people do them, they weren't coming from her and Harrison was able to go on being my friend and not worry about being attacked for it. I'd done what I set out to do.

Being deaf is not a weakness or it shouldn't be seen as one and that's what I wanted to get across that day. It's still what I want people to see. It's the same thing with the special needs kids. They are no different than I am, than anyone is really. Just because they might act in ways that *'normal'* people don't or experience life in a different way, it doesn't make them wrong or less than anyone else. We're not weak or what's wrong with the world. If anything, from the people that I've met and spent time with, we might just be what's right about it.

It didn't take long after Belle showed up for her to talk my mom into letting me leave. Having lived through this herself, she knows better than anyone that staying in the classroom, even if I am protected by a parent wasn't the right thing for me. My mom cracked under the pressure and with the promise of having Kayden drive me home, she let me go.

I'm outside sitting on the curb, not trusting my wobbly legs to walk the parking lot, waiting for Kayden to pull up in order to get me out of here. I'm enjoying the way the breeze feels on my face and how just a few minutes of sitting out here like this seems to make the events of earlier fade away, leaving me the most relaxed I've felt since my mom told me my school would be closing.

Seeing the car pull out of the spot a few feet away I stand up and prepare myself for when he pulls up, but the minute I go to take a step away from my place, I feel the brush of a hand on my arm. Thinking its Isabelle, I turn but it's not her at all.

It's Dillon.

"Why are you leaving?"

When I don't answer him, he tries again and despite every attempt not to, I'm drawn to his lips the minute they start moving.

"Did something happen?"

There's no doubt about it. I lied to my mom when I said there was nothing going on here. There is definitely something going on, at least for me and the proof is in the way I'm acting right now. The way I've been acting since the first day he walked into the class and spoke to me for the first time. I'm drawn to him and denying it isn't worth the effort it would take.

I just don't want to be drawn to him.

I nod my head, thankful that he's asked something I can answer.

He looks me over at my response and it's when his eyes come to rest on my head that he moves and before I know it he's behind me, his fingers on the top of my head. If he didn't know what happened to me before, he's fully aware of it now.

This is something I don't want him to see. I'm still not sure he wasn't behind the entire thing, so him picking through my hair and seeing what his friends did to me, it's not right.

After a few seconds of him standing behind me, his shadow hovering over mine, he breaks away from his inspection and comes around to face me again. I see the look on his face, reminding me again of the way I'd seen him in the hallway with his friends that first day. It's a look I don't think he wears often but one I knew was there just waiting to escape.

Seeing what he did, what they did to me, it's hurting him.

"I'm sorry."

Reaching out, I do the only thing I can in order to make him see I'm alright and that I know it's not his fault. As my fingers connect to his hand though, his eyes seem to become even more pained and I immediately take a step back. The pain reflected in his eyes makes me feel like I've been burned.

"This should have never happened. Kayden's right. This is my fault. I need to fix this shit. I know it means nothing to you, but Cadence; what happened, it won't happen again."

The speed at which his lips move reminds me of the way he'd been in class with me before and completely different from the way he'd been a few seconds ago. It's almost as though this time, he wants to get the words out so badly that he's not paying attention to how fast he's saying them and they're actually running together a lot more than they should.

I'm about to open my mouth and tell him that everything's okay, but just as my lips part he turns his back to me and walks toward the school again, faster than I expect, like he can't get away from me fast enough. Despite my desire to go after him in order to make him feel better, I don't do it.

Whatever this is that I'm feeling, I need to get it under control. Just because he didn't have anything to do with what happened, it doesn't suddenly make him a better guy. It just means that his friends had gotten the jump on him. There's no telling what would be waiting for me in the morning once he's had time away from me. He could easily turn around and join in with his girlfriend tomorrow and I need to remember that. What my mom said before is true. He's bad news and I need to stay away from him now more than ever.

Even if it's the last thing I want to do.

Dillon

Someone is going to pay for this.

I'm already going to get shit for not heading to class the way I should have. Well, that's not exactly true. I did go to the class, but the minute I saw Isabelle and Kayden walking Cadence out of the class, I ducked around the corner and waited for them to pass.

Instead of heading in, I followed them out and I'm glad I did. If I didn't go out there to meet her, I never would have known what really happened when she left me earlier. I know it all now and I swear to god, if I don't find Amy soon, I'm going to beat on the first person that steps in my path.

What happened to her, what Amy did, it's all my fault. That's why I walked away from her when she reached out. I couldn't take looking up into those eyes and seeing what I knew I would find there. She knows I had nothing to do with this, which means when she touched me, she was doing it to let me know she didn't blame me. I couldn't let her because honestly, I am to blame for this. I'm the one that created Amy and now I need to be the one to put an end to her.

There was blood matted to the top of her head for fuck sakes. We've been doing this shit with people for three years now and never once has someone come out with blood on them. Yes, they ended up burned, but they were never bleeding. Whatever happened in that bathroom, it ended with Cadence bleeding. I can't handle that.

This isn't about weakness and strength anymore. I know I've made it about that because of what Bruce drilled into my head, but what this girl went through, it has nothing to do with her being weak. I've only talked to her for two days out of the last four and even I know she's stronger than all of the people I call friends.

I know because she's stronger than me.

I was so preoccupied with the damage done to her hair that I didn't even think to ask if she'd been burned. I remember Isabelle after Amy got through with her and none of that was obvious with Cadence, which makes me think that they didn't get as far with her as they have with everyone else they've done it too. It also makes something else pretty damn obvious.

Cadence fought back.

Amy is a strong chick. There's not many girls that can take her down and it's even worse when she's got Charlotte and Eve with her. Those girls are unstoppable. If Cadence was burned, I would have seen it somehow. She might not react the same as Isabelle, or even the other girls that we've sent home in tears, completely broken down from the sick shit we do, but it still would have been obvious.

It doesn't even matter to me if she was burned or not. All I care about is finding Amy and dealing with this jealousy shit once and for all. She'd taken it too far this time and Kayden, as much as I hate the guy, is right. I need to get rid of her before she brings me down.

Drags me down more than I've already done on my own anyway.

Knowing that looking for Amy specifically isn't going to work since we couldn't find her earlier, I veer towards where I know I'll find Charlotte and Eve.

They were involved in what happened, which means they're just as guilty, if not more so than Amy is. They know how she is and they also saw the way Cadence was with them for the little she hung out with us. If they're really Amy's friends, they would have talked her out of this shit instead of going along with it.

My stomach is in knots just thinking about it and it's not because of the stuff I'm thinking. It's because I'm just as guilty as they are. I could have stopped Amy from doing this. I should have done it, but of course I'd stormed off, leaving my girlfriend with her festering thoughts and now Cadence paid the price.

I might to be blame, but it doesn't stop what's gotta happen now. I've got to end things with Amy and no matter what she says or does, I have to make sure that this time it's for good. I've been sick of the constant back and forth with us for a while, but too damn lazy to do anything about it. I don't know what the hell is going on with me and Cadence, but if anything she'd given me enough of a wakeup call to do what I should have a long time ago.

When I get to Charlotte's class, keeping myself hidden from the teacher's line of vision, I scan the room for the two girls I hope to find. When a complete glance over the entire class produces nothing, both girls as missing as Amy is, I finally do the one thing I've been avoiding the entire time. I pull my phone from my pocket and I text her. It's a long shot, but maybe if I say the right thing, she'll answer me despite being pissed with the way we left things at lunch.

Baby, where are you? Look, I'm sorry about what happened. I bailed out on class, so if you just tell me where you're at, I'll meet you.

I am not that guy. I think that's the first time I've sent a text calling her baby since we got together. I'm pretty sure she'll see through my bullshit attempt at getting her to answer me, but with nothing left to lose and needing to get this over with, I press send.

Library. Did something that if Daniels finds me I'm gonna get in shit for. Meet us there.

I wasn't looking to do this with an audience, but with the only other option being not doing it all, it doesn't look like I've got much choice. I'm not backing down this time. Turning back the way I came, this time heading in the direction of the library, I speed up until I'm standing right outside the doors.

I've been in here exactly three times since I started here freshman year. I didn't like it much then and I don't like it now.

When I first moved here I wasn't the way I am now. I was quiet and not knowing anyone, I wanted a place to escape for the first few days while I acclimated to the way this school was from my old one. I hid out here and ate my lunch, read books and other things that looking back, made me look pretty nerdy. After that I ended up going to the locker room but before it was my safe haven.

Being here reminds me of the way things were then and I'm sickened by it. The same way I felt with Kayden bringing up the past is happening again and it makes me want to leave. I want to go to my car, get in and drive away from here, not looking back until I'm out of this town altogether. I'll never do it and no matter how much I wanna flee from the memories, I can't.

I need to get this over with.

I see them the minute I slide through the turnstiles and catching the eye of the librarian, I motion to where they're huddled and then point to the hall. I'm going to get these girls out of here because judging by the look on Ms. Reid's face, she wants them anywhere but here.

As I reach them, Amy jumps into my arms and I squash the urge to pull her off me, instead going with the attentive boyfriend act I attempted when I texted her.

"We need to get out of here. She's on to you guys and all it's going to take is for her to call Daniels and we're all screwed."

Amy nods, Charlotte and Eve following suit and I'm struck again by how true Isabelle's words were. They really will follow along with just about anything that Amy does, right down to a random movement of her head.

"I screwed up real bad, Dill." She says and I just nod. I don't know what she's expecting me to say, but if she's looking for me to baby her about this, she's got another thing coming.

There really is a first time for everything. Who knew?

"Yeah, I know what you did. We need to get out of here before she calls Daniels." I repeat before turning to Charlotte and Eve and leveling them with the reality of what needs to happen now, or at least what I want to happen. "You two need to go to class and pretend like nothing is going on. Fake cramps or something so he doesn't suspect you."

They nod and before I can say anything more, they're moving toward the door, doing exactly what I told them.

If this were any other time, I might actually sit back and enjoy how easily these girls listen to me. I used to love it before. It's like they worship the ground I walk on with how easily they did what I wanted them to and there's a definite rush to be had from it. I don't feel that way now though. It's the complete opposite.

I just want them gone.

"I was so mad at lunch. I'm sorry."

Her words, they do nothing for me. She's not sorry, at least not for what she's apologizing for. She's sorry that she pissed me off to the point where I walked away from her maybe, but that's about it. I've been down this road before, over stupid crap like this and there's no way I'm doing what I did then with her now. The time for accepting it and moving on is over.

"We need to talk about that but not here."

I motion toward the hall and she starts moving. I follow behind until we're both safely out and away from the prying eyes of the librarian. Not that I'm all that concerned with her hearing what I'm about to do. She remembers the way I was on my first day, having been there when it happened, so I like to think she's the only person in the school that doesn't totally hate me.

"So what did you wanna talk about?" Amy asks as I scan the hallway for anyone who might be able to listen in. I know what's going to happen the minute I do this and I definitely don't want an audience.

"What did you do that made you hide out? You've never run off before."

"That bitch you brought to lunch. When you took off, I went looking for you, but ran into her instead. The way she looked at me Dill, I lost it. We dragged her into the bathroom and well, all hell broke loose."

She's got my full attention now. I want to know what she means by hell breaking loose and more than that, I'm more than a little interested in how Cadence supposedly looked at her for all of this to start, even though I'm pretty sure I know.

I've seen the way Cadence is. She's tough. The way she looked at me in class, especially when she flicked the shit out of me for rolling my eyes gives me all the information I need in terms of her looking at Amy. She stood her ground no doubt and ended up paying for it.

"What do you mean all hell broke loose?"

"She wasn't like the others. I expected her to act like Isabelle; maybe not pissing herself, but scared. She didn't do any of that. She bit Eve and she knocked Charlotte in the face. It was brutal."

I don't want to, but the overwhelming sense of satisfaction I get from hearing what Cadence did to the other two, makes me smile. Looking Amy over, I can see that there's not a scratch on her, which means nothing happened to her.

"Anything else happen?"

"I got up her against the wall, told her off about what she was doing trying to get with you and the minute I turned to check on Eve, she tried getting away. That's when we got hold of her hair again and yanked a bunch of it out."

There is it. I've heard enough. Cadence got away, since I saw her a couple minutes ago and she's safely out of the school.

I don't need to know anything else. Amy admitted to everything I needed her to.

"Ames..."

"I know okay. I know you're pissed and I said things that weren't true, but baby, I know girls. I saw the way she looked at you. She wants you and there's no way in hell I'm letting her get you."

"You're crazy. You get that right?"

"Screw you! You're blind to what goes on around here. What people say about you; what the girls talk about. Things they want to do to you if they could just get five minutes alone with you! I've been listening to it for a year now. Seeing the look in their eyes when they pass you in the hall and I never say shit."

"You're saying a whole lot of shit right now."

"Why are you acting like this?" she screams and I know that I've reached the point of no return. It's time to get this over with and get the hell out of here before she completely breaks down, though with the way her voice is already raising, she's pretty damn close to that point already.

"You don't see it do you?" I yell back at her, making sure there can be no doubt of what she's about to hear. "I don't give a fuck who looks at me. I don't give a shit about any of it and I don't give a shit about you!"

Her eyes go wide and where she'd been close to me before, she starts backing up now. This reaction should bother me, with what we are to each other, but I'm so far beyond done with her and the way she's been since we got together that I feel absolutely nothing. I'm not happy, bothered, nothing. I'm completely numb.

"You don't mean that."

"I mean every word. I've been putting up with you and this jealousy shit for a year. Half the reason Isabelle got picked on is because you saw the way I looked at her one day and lost it. Every single girl we've ever chosen is because of you even though I went along with it. It always comes back to you thinking they want me when they actually want nothing to do with me!"

"That's not true."

"Yes, it is true! You seem to think I'm God's gift and maybe for a little while, I bought into it too, but come on!"

"You don't get girls the way I do."

"Are you even hearing me right now? This has nothing to do with other girls. It has to do with you! I told you six months ago to knock off the stupid shit you were doing or I was gonna walk. Well it took me way too damn long, but I'm walking now."

"No, you don't mean this. You're just pissed about lunch."

She reaches out to grab on to me and the minute her wrist comes into my view, I grab onto it. All it would take is one small twist and I could break it and her in the process. I gotta get out of here before I end up doing something I can never take back. With as angry as she's making me with her stupidity, this is not going to end well if I don't.

Pulling her to me, not letting go of the hold I've got on her, I speak again and this time I say everything that needs to be said because once I walk, I won't be coming back. This is it. I'm beyond done. The way she's acting is just further proof that I'm doing the right thing. It might have started with me wanting to do it because of what she did to Cadence, but it's so much more than that now.

This isn't about Cadence, it's about me.

"We're done. This sick thing we call a relationship, it's over. I might not have been the best boyfriend in the world, but I never gave you a reason to act like this. I was loyal as shit to you. You wanna be pissed at someone for what's happening now, go find a fucking mirror, because you've got no one to blame but yourself."

Releasing the hold and turning my back on her, taking a few steps away, I hear her speak and it only proves that what I've done is the right thing. Even with me walking away from her, she's still so out of her mind that she's turning it around on everyone else.

"Thanks for proving that I was right earlier. You really do have a thing for the stupid mute bitch!"

I'm starting to wonder what it was I saw in her in the first place because what I see right now, is enough to keep me off girls forever.

"You go ahead and believe that, Ames. It's not my problem anymore."

The farther away I walk, the more the knot in my chest alleviates. It's like in some way my body is letting me know that walking away from her, dumping her the way I did is healthy—right even. By the time I turn the corner and she's completely out of my view, I feel lighter than I've ever felt.

There's only one more thing I need to do, but with the way everything happened today, it's going to have to wait. I just hope I don't have to wait too long.

I need to make things right with Cadence.

Chapter Eleven

Cadence

There was this moment last night where I wasn't sure I wanted to come back here. I knew what would be waiting for me after the failed attempt in the bathroom and I wasn't looking for a repeat performance.

My mind was so made up that I told my mom I'd much rather spend the next week in the room doing absolutely nothing than go back there.

It worked. She agreed with me. After speaking with Principal Daniels, letting him know what happened to me, she explained that if I didn't want to go back, she wasn't going to force me. Even though the girls would be handled, she knew that what they started would only be continued in their absence and she didn't want me having to deal with it.

Honestly, it was a relief. If I never saw Wexfield High again, it would be too soon. I wanted nothing to do with the way things worked there and even though there were people there I liked and would miss, it wasn't enough to change my mind. It's only when I woke up in the middle of the night, the tossing and turning becoming too much to handle and sat down at the computer, logging into my Facebook account that things began to change.

At the top of the screen where friends could be added, there was a bright red one wrapped in a bubble and right beside it, the little message icon was also glowing red. I didn't think anything about it considering Eric asked me for my info and I assumed now Isabelle or Kayden were too. It's only when I clicked on the message icon that I found out it wasn't any of them.

Dylan Murphy
It took me three hours to find you since we don't have anyone in common, but I need to talk to you about what happened today. Explain or whatever. Please come to school tomorrow so we can talk?

It wasn't anything major, he didn't bear his soul or anything, but what he did say was enough. As sure as I was that going back was definitely not the right move to make, there's something about what he wrote that made it exactly what I had to do.

With that message in mind, I walk the hall now, on the way to the stairs that will take me to the class where I'm going to see him again. As nervous as I am, checking around every corner for any sign of the three girls that turned my world upside down less than twenty-four hours ago, I'm comforted in knowing that once I did reach the class, I wouldn't be alone. Sure, Dillon might be there and he might want to talk, but Eric and Isabelle are there too and neither one of them will let anything happen to me.

The minute I enter the class I see my mom and she throws me a weak smile, the concern she has over me being here evident in her eyes. When I got up with her in the morning, grabbing my backpack before making my way out to the car, I'd taken her off guard, but after having the drive to school to get used to it, she'd gone along with my decision and hadn't voiced her fears even though I knew she had them.

Those same fears she's displaying now without saying a word.

Walking to the back of the room, fully prepared to take my seat, pull out my book and dive into it again, I come to a complete stop the minute I see the folded lined paper in the middle of it. Darting my eyes over to the seat next to me and seeing it empty, I breathe a sigh of relief. I'm overthinking things. With me not being here yesterday, someone else probably sat here and left the paper behind.

Tossing my bag on the floor beside me and sliding into the seat, I pick the paper up and open it, determined to see who it belongs to so I can give it back. It's only when I see the familiar scrawl on the page and my name at the top that I realize that I hadn't been overthinking it at all. Dillon strikes again.

Cadence

I really hope you got my message last night and you showed up otherwise this is gonna be a wasted piece of paper.

~~Shit~~

Let me start this again.

I don't have a clue what I'm doing. I've never done anything like this before and it's a little messed up. I'm leaving this here super early, before anyone can see because I don't want to see your face while you're reading it.

If you hate what I'm saying to you, I don't want to see your eyes go all dark and hard the way they did after what happened with Eric. I know that look really well because I'm always wearing it.

What happened to you yesterday, it shouldn't have happened. When you got up and walked away from us, Amy kept saying shit and I got up and left too. I was actually coming to find you. I wanted you to know that the ~~shit~~ stuff she was saying, I didn't agree with it. It wasn't what I thought about you or anything.

I know what they did to you after I left. Amy admitted it to me and I hate it. I hate that because I tried to do something, it got twisted and you got hurt.

You're the best damn thing about being stuck in that class. I did a lot of horrible ~~shit~~ stuff that got me put there and I swear, I thought it was gonna be hell until you started busting my balls. Lol

This is supposed to be all serious and I'm doing my best not to be a jerk and curse, but I keep screwing that up too. If you're still reading this, I'm sorry.

I'm sorry for the letter and all the lines and scribbles and being all over the place with what I'm saying and I'm sorry for what Amy did to you. I brought you to lunch that day because I wanted my friends to meet this cool person I got to spend the class with and I just screwed the entire thing up.

I want to come to class today, see you sitting there, smile at you and have you smile back. I want to be your friend. I hope that when I do show up, you'll talk to me again. I don't think I can get through the class without it.

God that sounds so gay. Ugh. I'm just gonna stop writing this now.

I'm sorry. Please forgive me.

Dillon

Folding the paper back over and placing it back on the desk, I stare at it, as if doing that will somehow make everything I just read easier to take. It's easy to see that he's never done anything like it before because there were a lot of scribbles and curse words crossed out. Why he thought he had to speak any different than he always does is beyond me, but there's no doubt it was awkward.

He wasn't attempting to be funny, but he was, a lot more than he should have been. It's half the reason I kept reading even though the stuff he was talking about I didn't want to think about. What happened to me yesterday is still fresh, so the last thing I need is a reminder, friendly or not.

It's not the stuff with Amy that gets to me most. It's the way every time he said something even remotely nice, he had to backtrack and call himself gay or say it sounded stupid. Whatever he's been through; the person he's changed into, it's made him think that even saying something nice is bad and there is something so wrong about that.

It shouldn't be a bad thing to be nice and whoever told him otherwise needs a smack upside their head because they lied.

It's been a couple of minutes since I read the words and even now I'm so sensitive to every shadow that passes by me that I keep looking up, hoping that the next person I see will be him. He said he was going to show up, but do it after I was finished reading. Well, I've been done for a while now and there's still no sign of him.

Even when he does show up I'm not sure how I'm going to handle it. His words got to me because even though he was all over the place, you could easily see how hard he tried with it. He wants to make things right, blaming himself for what happened yesterday and I owe him the chance to try.

This whole thing is awkward. I was supposed to come here, sit silently in the back and mind my business while my mom taught the class, going home with her at the end of the day and repeating the same cycle over again for the next two weeks. I was never supposed to get involved with the people here or even form attachments, but that's exactly what I did.

I got attached to Dillon Murphy and now that it's done, the only thing left to do is ride it out until my school is fixed and I can go back to the way my life is supposed to be.

It's just not something I'm sure I'm gonna be able to do.

Dillon

Something's going on with me and I'm not sure how I feel about it.

It started last night when I got home and it hasn't let up since. After spending hours going through every profile I could possibly find until I found the one that would connect me to hers, I sent her a friend request first and then messaged her. I'm not much of a writer, this being the first time I've ever written anything on Facebook that wasn't related to football or perverted somehow and by the time I finished, it was a really long message. After sitting there staring it for an hour, I finally deleted it and went with something shorter.

I spent the entire night stressing over it to the point where I didn't sleep for shit and finally getting up and making my way down to the kitchen, I put the plan together that I'm now hiding out in the hallway waiting to happen.

Everything I said to her in the original message I was gonna send, I wrote out by hand. Even though I think it looked like shit and if I were her, I wouldn't want anything to do with it, I left it on her desk, sneaking in before Ms. Taylor got there, hoping that she showed up so it wouldn't fall into the wrong hands.

The last thing I want is someone getting their hands on what I wrote her. Not because I'm embarrassed by any of it, but because it's just not something I do. I don't go out of my way to make a girl forgive me. I don't go out of my way for anyone period. This is my first attempt at even being civil with someone like her and that getting out would throw my reputation in the toilet pretty quick.

Maybe I am embarrassed after all, if I'm that concerned about the way people will look at me if they saw it.

The way I'm acting, it's throwing me off. I know that I want to do the right thing by this girl but I honestly have no clue what the right thing is and there's this conflict inside me over it. On one hand, I'm beating on myself pretty hard because the way I'm coming off looks stupid and on the other hand, I'm hoping that it has the desired effect. I can act sweet when I need to get what I want, but I don't have a clue how to actually be sweet.

I watched her enter the room, watched the look between her and her mom before she went to her seat and sat down. I saw her pick up the paper and I'm assuming that her eyes scanning over the page means that she's read what I wrote. It's time for me to get over the fear and awkwardness I have and enter the class, but I still can't will myself forward.

It's the fight going on inside me. I have no clue what sides gonna win and I'm afraid that the minute I sit down, that part of me that wants to do the right thing is going to get squashed and I'm going to turn into the ultimate asshole again. It's the way I've always been and I've been doing it so long now that I swear it's the only thing I know how to do. Being different isn't even on my radar.

At least it wasn't until Cadence.

"Dillon, are you going to join us this morning or are you planning to skip again?"

Damnit. Standing here not focusing got me nailed. Now I'm gonna have to explain what happened yesterday and hope I don't get in shit for it and pay the price for lingering outside now.

"I'm coming in. Sorry about yesterday Ms. T. Something came up that I needed to handle."

"There always seems to be something with you, Dillon. We can discuss yesterday and where you were later. For now, please come in so we can start the class."

Doing as she says, I walk in and immediately turn to head to my seat. It's when I'm about a foot or so away that the girl I've been watching for the last fifteen minutes looks up and our eyes meet.

Sticking to what I said I wanted in the note, I smile, even though it's a pretty weak attempt and my brain goes haywire waiting for her to return it. When she does, my heart and my head settle and I slump my body down into the seat, feeling the ache in my muscles the minute my ass hits the chair. It may have been a couple of days since the fight, but I'm still feeling the pain from it.

I flinch from the impact and a few seconds later, I see a blue paper make its way up into the air.

Are you okay?

With everything that happened to her yesterday, I put a lot of what Kayden told me out of my head, but now, seeing the note and the words on it, I'm reminded again. Where I believed she was just a random girl that didn't like the sound of her voice, there's more to it and even more to the notes she's been writing me. Cadence isn't like any other girl because she's deaf.

This would have been material for me to use picking on her before, but knowing it now, with all the stupid changes going on with me, picking on her, it's the last thing that comes to mind. Her being deaf should prove to me that she's even weaker than the others, but it doesn't do that. I'm completely going against everything I know because her being deaf doesn't mean anything to me.

She's still the same Cadence she was the first day and I refuse to look at her differently. In fact, I'm not even going to bring up that I know because I don't want it to change anything that's already going on between us.

I meant what I said in the letter, I want to be her friend.

"Yeah, I'm fine." I say, making light of the fact that she caught me flinching in pain. Always the tough guy, even when tough is the last thing I'm feeling.

Liar.

There she is. Calling me on my shit again. Exactly what I want her to do.

"Yeah, you caught me. I'm not okay."

That's better.

Not knowing what to say back to that, I just smile awkwardly and hope that she'll say something else that can kick start this conversation. Now that she's here, getting both of my messages, the last thing I want to happen is for it all to end before we've had a real chance to talk. This is the point where I should bring up the letter that's still sitting in the middle of her desk, sticking out just under her elbow, but I don't because for some reason, I'm a total pussy and don't wanna bring it up first.

Run into any more trucks lately?

She smiles as she holds up the paper and I laugh, this time doing it just loud enough so only the two of us are able to hear. The last thing I need is for her mom to catch on. I've got a feeling that there'd be another warning coming and this time, not because of skipping class. I don't need to call even more attention to the way I'm acting with her daughter lately. I'm doing it enough on my own as it is.

"Not lately, no. Still healing from the last one."

She smiles again and that's when she lowers her head to the paper in front of her, looking back at me and then pointing down to it, her eyes zeroing in on it intently. Scribbling something on another post it note, she holds it up and this time, there's a crinkle in her eyes, a brightness that I haven't seen since she came here. It's only when I see the words on the paper that I realize why.

You're forgiven, Dillon.

Seeing those words on the paper, knowing what it means, for both of us, it hits me. The one thing I haven't wanted to admit to, but that I've felt for the past four days despite my best attempt not to.

Amy was right yesterday.

I like this girl.

For the first time since I moved here, maybe even before that, admitting something like this, it doesn't get to me the way it normally would. I'm completely okay with the admission despite knowing that liking her means shit in the long run because when her school is up and running she'll be gone and I'd still be here going it alone.

It also doesn't mean anything with the way her mom feels about me. I've made quite the name for myself and there's no way that the woman standing at the front of the room now doesn't hate me. I've more than earned everyone's hate and I'm sure the teacher is no different.

Knowing all of this, it doesn't stop me from what I've got to do next. It's because of the way I feel, what I'm realizing that I'm not going to be able to move ahead until I do it. So instead of sitting here and going over it a hundred times and talking myself out of it, I turn to her and do the one thing I've wanted to do since I sat down.

"I know it's a long shot, but um—will you let me take you out for lunch?"

Her head lowers to the desk and I instantly think the worst. The light I saw in her eyes a second ago is gone and there's something there in its place. Indecision. She's not sure what the right step to take is even though she's read my words and interacted with me the way we did from the beginning.

Where I would have been pissed at that before, not getting what I wanted from a girl, this time, it makes sense.

If I were her, I wouldn't know what to do either. I wouldn't trust a word that's coming out of my mouth. I want her to trust me though and if she would just say yes, I'll do whatever I have to in order to earn it, because Cadence, she's different.

She's worth it.

Chapter Twelve

Cadence

If my mom gets wind of what I'm about to do and with who, I'm pretty sure she's gonna lock me in the classroom and not let me leave until she's ready to go home. Despite knowing that, I know what my answer is going to be to his question. I just hope that in the end, it doesn't turn out to be the wrong one.

The last time he asked me to spend lunch with him, I ended up in the girl's bathroom with three crazy girls attempting to attack me. That's the last thing I want this time. I've already written out my answer, which is why I turned to the paper in front of me and away from him, but looking back now, ready to answer and seeing him staring a hole into the desk, I'm not sure what to do.

Do I reach out to him and show him my answer or do I just leave it alone? Knowing the way that Dillon acts and the way he's been with me is what makes all of this confusing. It's like I'm dealing with two different people, so at any given time, I have no idea how to respond to him because I can never tell which one is asking or will answer.

Against my better judgment, I reach across and brush his arm with my fingers, causing him to look up. Holding up the paper, high enough so he can read my words, I watch as I'm rewarded for my move with a smile and this time, it's one that rises all the way from his lips, past his cheeks and straight up into his eyes.

Where'd you have in mind?

Wanting nothing more than for this moment to freeze right now, so that I never have to see the smile he's wearing disappear, I prepare myself for the disappointment that's sure to follow the minute he responds to me. Where I'm hoping the look won't entirely go away, I know that it can't stay forever. The way he is; the way we are, it can't last. It never does even though it feels pretty awesome while it's there.

"The ravine."

I try really hard not to do it, but I can't help it. The minute I hear that he wants to take me to the ravine, I laugh. It's the first move vocally I've made around him since I met him and just as I realize it and go to cover my mouth, his hand flies out across the space between us and holds mine in place.

"Why are you laughing?" he asks, though I'm pretty sure with the look in his eye now, he wants to call me on what I was about to do in order to silence the obvious slip up I'd done laughing at all.

I motion with my free hand down to the paper and he releases the hold, letting me write him, though I get the feeling he wants to hear me actually say the words this time instead, something that while I can do, I'm still not ready for.

The ravine has the grossest water in Wexfield. It's brown and murky.

"Sounds like the perfect place to me."

His words, while confusing, intrigue me.

Why's that?

"Never mind, it's stupid."

He's not getting off that easy. Now that he's got my mind working, trying to sort out exactly what it might mean, there is no way I'm going to let him back track and act as though he never said it at all. He should know this by now with the amount of times I've gotten on him during our time here.

Just tell me. I'll get it out of you some other way if you don't.

This is dangerous territory for me. I'm basically flirting with the enemy and I don't have the first clue how he's gonna respond to it, much less what to follow it up with if he does.

"I wanna know what those other ways are later, but when you said brown and murky I thought about us."

What about us?

"We both have brown eyes and well, at least for me, all of this, it's awkward and murky seems like another word for awkward. See? I told you it was stupid."

It's not stupid. It's perfect.

There it is again. The smile from before, the one that I didn't want to go away. What I've said, it's made him happy and I'm being rewarded. He has no idea, but the way he looks right now, it's a look that he needs to keep. It suits him.

"So you'll go with me?"

I nod my head and hold up the paper with the word yes on it at the same time and if it's possible, the smile gets even brighter. This might not be a smart move and if my mom found out, she might decide to keep me home for the duration after all, but with the way he's smiling at me right now, I'm willing to take the risk.

There's more to Dillon than everyone sees and despite knowing it could end badly for me in the end, I'm determined to see it through. I want to get to know the real Dillon and nothing is going to stand in my way.

Not even my mom.

Dillon

Brown and murky.

I haven't been able to get those words out of my head since she wrote them to me and standing here now, looking at the water and seeing the familiar shade of brown, the water so clogged with dirt and garbage from years of mistreatment, they're even more important. She was right about the water and I was right about it reminding me of us or at least me.

There is nothing murky about her. Cadence has been the same person the entire time I've known her. She puts me in my place, she answers my smart ass remarks with ones of her own and is genuinely nice while she's doing it. Where I'm conflicted, confused and a general mess, she's as put together as a person can be. I'm definitely the murky one here.

The first day I met her, I couldn't get over the way she looked, but I swear I haven't thought about her or that body once in the last two days. It's like whatever hooked me to her in the beginning is gone and it's the parts of her that I'm left with that keep me here. The way she is makes me like the person I am when I'm with her, something I haven't felt in forever.

It also makes me want to get to know her better, so motioning to the first bench I see after we've been walking for a while, I decide that's exactly what I'm going to do. Starting with getting her to tell me she's deaf. If I'm lucky, once I get past that barrier, the one thing she still hasn't admitted to, I can get to the other thing I want from her.

Hearing her speak.

Armed with the little notebook I used with Isabelle, I pass it to her the second we're both seated and wait while she opens it and starts writing along the pages.

Why did you wanna stop walking?

Not willing to speak until her eyes are on me, knowing that anything I say will go unnoticed unless she's watching my lips move, I think over my answer to her question. It's a pretty simple answer, but I hope it's not one she's gonna hate because I really do want to get her to open up to me.

"I wanted to talk. I need to tell you something."

Tell me what?

"I know why you don't talk. Well, I know why you hate talking."

Two things happen the minute I speak. At first she looks confused, like what I said doesn't make any sense and when I see it, I want to try and word it the right way again, but before I can think of a better way, I see recognition in her eyes. She knows that I know.

You know.

I nod, but instead of speaking, I look down at her hands and before I can question it, I slide my hand across until it's resting on top of hers, barely touching but a connection all the same. I don't have the first clue what I'm doing, never having been this close to a girl without having her doing something for me before, but I do know that I like the way it feels and I'm definitely not pulling away unless she does it first.

"I know, but I want you to tell me."

Why? If you already know, what's the point?

Another question with an easy answer.

"Because until you tell me, I won't believe it."

It's pretty obvious it's true.

That's where she's wrong. Not wanting to talk, hating the sound of her own voice the way she said, even though I know she can't even hear it, it's something I would expect a girl to say. Girls, even though they don't need to be, are insecure about things like that, especially when it comes to the way a guy looks at them. It's a pretty normal thing. At least it's normal to me.

Every move she's made before I found out the truth could easily be explained away as anything other than her being deaf and I'm pretty sure if she thinks about it, she'll see that I'm right.

"That's not true. I didn't have a clue before Kayden told me. So, until you tell me, I'm going to pretend I don't know."

She frowns and despite hating the way it looks, I laugh. I'm not trying to laugh at her, or make fun, but the way she hates what I said enough to frown is what makes me find it funny. Even now, alone with me like this she isn't letting up. It's actually kinda cute.

I'm deaf. Happy now?

"Yes. Well, happier anyway."

I don't understand.

I've been happy as hell since she returned my smile this morning, but I'm not sure I'm ready to let her know that yet. I'm still having a hard time dealing with the way I feel when I'm around her, so until I can come to terms with it, I'm gonna keep my mouth shut. The last thing I want to do is say anything that will end up ruining whatever's going on here.

"I'm just happy today. There is something that would make me happier though."

Her eyes raise and the minute she slides the notebook over to me, I see the question marks on the page and prepare myself for what I'm about to do. I want to hear her speak and if the way she still hasn't pulled her hand out from under mine is any indication, I think she's comfortable enough with me to do it. At least I hope she is, otherwise this is going to blow up in my face pretty damn quick.

"What's the real reason you don't talk?"

I told you the real reason.

"Maybe you told me part of it, but you didn't tell me all of it."

The way people look at me when I speak; it's why I don't like to talk out loud. I can do it, I guess you know that too, but I hate it.

"Are you afraid I'm going to do the same thing?"

She nods this time instead of using the pad to write and my chest starts aching the second she does. She has every right to worry about that because I know I would have done it before. If I can call out and exploit weaknesses I see in people that aren't deaf, then it's not a stretch that she thinks I would do it to her. I want to say that I wouldn't judge her like that and she can say anything she wants to me, because I really do want to hear her speak, but the more time I spend thinking about it, the more I realize I can't do that.

She wouldn't believe me and I'm not sure I believe me either.

Words mean shit to this girl, I can tell. She knows the way I am, experiencing it herself so anything I could say right now would just go straight through her, not affecting her at all. I don't want that. When I say or do something with Cadence, I want her to know it's for real and it's the truth and not just me playing a part.

I don't want her to think I'm playing her even though that's how this entire thing started.

"Can I tell you a secret?"

Sure.

"I wanted to stop and talk because I wanted to hear you speak. I was going to ask you to talk to me even though I know how you feel about it. I don't think I want that anymore."

What do you want?

This, is an easy answer, but it's not easy the way everything else has been. It's harder than all of that because what I'm about to say, it's not something anyone would expect to ever hear from me. It's going to sound unbelievable, but I want her to believe in it despite that.

"I want you to talk to me when you're ready. I don't want to push you into it or make you think that you have to do it in order for me to stick around. I meant what I wrote you this morning. I want to be your friend even though I'm starting to think I don't have the first clue what a real friend is or how to be one."

Can I ask you something?

"You can ask me anything."

What if I said I didn't want to be your friend?

I'm not sure what to do with this. I know where my mind goes the second she says it, but with this girl, I don't think that anything I come up with is going to be exactly what she means. It hurts though. Her not wanting to be my friend, it hurts on a level I haven't felt in a very long time and I don't want to feel ever again.

"Um—that would suck, I guess. Is that what you're saying?"

Yes Dillon, that's exactly what I'm saying,

Right now, seeing those words on the paper, I want to get up and walk away. I don't know what the hell I was thinking wasting my time the way I did. Sure, she's beautiful and her attitude, the way she is makes me want to be around her and I feel things I haven't allowed myself to feel in a long time when I'm with her, but that means shit really.

I don't need to be feeling this stuff. I don't need to feel at all. It's exactly like my dad says. Emotions and feelings only turn you weak and right now, I'm the weakest I've ever been because her not wanting to be friends with me is killing me inside. This girl, with all her fucking issues has made me weak and it makes me sick.

Sliding my hand off of hers and bringing it back into my lap, I lift myself off the bench and back away, more than ready to get back to school, leaving her here alone to find her own way. It's a dickhead move, but right now, if she doesn't wanna be my friend, there's no point in me giving a shit.

As I turn, I see her stand and before I can get more than a foot away from her, I feel her hand brush mine and I'm frozen in place. Even if I wanted to move right now, the softness of her hand touching mine completely stops me from doing it.

"Dillon, don't go."

Cadence

I knew he was going to take that wrong.

Dillon isn't used to being with people the way he is with me. Being here, sitting just off from the bike path, the water only a few feet in front of us, he's completely out of his comfort zone. I'm the one that he would normally be making fun of, not the one that he feels things with.

Admitting the things he did, what he wanted from me when he asked me to come here today was a big step for him, I could tell by the way his body tensed. He's acting out of character. He's always been a certain way and now, being shown a different way, being guided by whatever it is that's pushing him forward, it's a struggle. It's made even worse when he puts it all on the line and admits that he wants to be my friend even though he doesn't have the first clue how to do it. He's open and vulnerable for the first time in his entire life and it's because of him being that way I ask what I do.

I don't just want to be his friend. I've been thinking about it since we came here. I don't have any experience being with someone; especially someone like him, but I do know what it is I'm feeling when I'm with him. I know what the weird flip in my stomach is about, the fascination I have with watching his lips move when he talks to me. It's all because I like him a little more than I should.

The thing is, the question I asked, I knew he was going to take it that way and now I've got to fix it before he walks away and never looks back. So in an effort to stop him, I do the only thing I can and I reach out of my comfort zone, doing the one thing I've been keeping from him for the past week.

I speak.

He's not walking away anymore, but it's not much better since he hasn't turned around since I said it. I've given him what he wanted and I'm starting to think that maybe I did it a little too late. That what I asked him, what he's taking the wrong way is too much for even the sound of my voice to stop.

Taking a chance and moving closer to him, this time gripping his hand tightly in mine, I come around to face him, reaching out with my free hand and touching his chin, wanting him to look up and see me, say something so I can see it and we can get past whatever it is that's going on inside his head.

Responding to my touch he lifts his head and the minute his eyes lift and reach mine, the brown of his softer than I think I've ever seen them, his lips start moving and I focus on exactly what it is he's about to say.

"Did you just—"

"Yes." I say again so that this time he doesn't even have to question it. I have no idea what he's hearing now, but where I expect to see a look of disgust or even worse, pity, I see nothing. If he thinks the way I sound is funny or bad, he's not showing it. It's the first time other than with Eric, Isabelle and my parents that I don't feel like a freak.

"Caddy." He sighs. "What are you doing?"

"Don't go." I answer, aware that I'm not answering his question but still preoccupied with him walking away from me and needing to stop it.

"Why should I stay? You don't want to be my friend, so I'm just wasting my time and yours staying here."

I shake my head. I can't answer for him, because I don't know if he really sees all of this as a waste of time, but there's no way I can let him think this is a waste of mine. I wouldn't have come here at all if that was the case. This is the farthest thing from a waste of my time. I'm exactly where I want to be and now I need to make him see that.

"Is it because of the shit I did to Eric? Is that why you don't wanna be friends?"

I shake my head again and his chest catches and releases in another sigh.

"Then what the hell is this Caddy? What are you trying to do?"

"Let you hear me."

"Why?"

I can't take this anymore. I don't want to talk because I'm not sure I can find the right words to answer his question. There's only one thing I can do, one move I can make even though I have no clue what the heck I'm doing that will get the point I'm trying to make across. I just hope that when I do it, it doesn't backfire in my face and cause him to pull away even more.

Moving as close to him as I can, I bring my finger to his lips first, the feel of them under my fingertips enough to shake off the nervousness and bring me to the next step. As I feel his breath escape over my finger, I lift myself up until I'm standing on my toes and closing my eyes, not wanting to see his reaction, I press my lips to his.

Half expecting in the moment for him to pull away in disgust, I'm shocked when he presses back harder, his hand which had been holding mine a second before, coming up to rest around my back, pulling me even more into him, a rumbling vibrating from his chest, like a possessive growl escaping from somewhere inside him.

It's in the moment, feeling the way his lips are pressed to mine, the way they felt when I ran my finger across them seconds before that I'm reminded again of the question that had almost sent him running and the reality of what's happening hits and I give into it completely.

Looks like I'm not the only one that didn't want to be friends.

Chapter Thirteen

Dillon

What the hell am I doing?
So much has happened in the last few minutes and I'm having a hard time keeping up. Before I even get a chance to deal with the fact that she spoke to me, I actually heard her voice and what hearing her makes me feel, her hand is locked up in mine and she's standing in front of me.

My senses hit overload the minute our eyes meet and not only can I smell her, the scent of some kind of flowers rising between us, but the pink tinge to her ivory colored skin is impossible to look away from. With the way her voice sounded when she said my name, I don't think I can take much more. I've never been so aware of a person before.

The feel of her hand is more than enough but she doesn't let it end there. After going back and forth with me about what she's doing here, what she wants from me, she puts her lips on mine and the loose thread that was keeping what was left of my sanity together breaks and I'm completely lost.

Jesus. This, kissing her, I've never felt anything even remotely close to this with any girl, ever. I don't even know how to describe what's happening to me, that's how completely crazy and unknown this is. I need to pull away, break this spell I seem to be under, but I can't. I want more. So instead of pulling away the way I probably should, I press my lips harder back into hers and pull her tighter to me.

She feels so damn good in my arms like this. She fits so perfectly it's like she belongs there, but I know better. She doesn't belong with me because despite how right this feels and how badly I want to continue doing it for as long as she'll let me, I can't be the person she needs me to be.

Removing my arms, releasing the hold I have around her, a lot tighter than I realized when I'd done it, I put my hands on her shoulders and attempt to push her backwards in order to give us the space I think we need right now. I feel like shit the minute I do it, but I can't let the way it feels override what's right.

We can't do this. She's someone that I want as a friend; despite what just happened and there's no way in hell I'm going to let whatever this is get in between that. I just broke up with my girlfriend anyway, thinking about kissing another girl should be the last thing on my mind.

Who the hell am I kidding? This has nothing to do with Amy and our breakup. We weren't even really together anyway, we were just tolerating each other or at least that's how it was for me. I kept Amy as close as I did because it was comfortable and as long as I was with her, I didn't have to worry about getting sidetracked with anyone or anything else. I could treat Amy however I wanted and it didn't matter.

It does matter though because I never felt anything remotely close to this with her. I was with the girl for a year and not one second of that time did I feel the way I do with Cadence right now.

"Dillon..."

Shit. I need to say something. I've just pushed her away and I can see she's confused, so I need to say something, anything that will stop her from looking at me the way she is.

"We need to go back. I don't wanna end up getting both of us in shit."

"Wait!" she cries out even though she's closer than ever to me.

"What?"

"Talk to me please."

Instead of answering her, I focus on the way her voice sounds. Each word is long and drawn out, low pitched where with most girls it sounds higher. I can see now why she hates talking and why people look at her strange when she does. It's because it doesn't sound the way you expect someone to sound when they speak to you. The thing is, she sounds fucking beautiful and I want to tell her that so badly it's giving me a headache just thinking about it, but I don't because I can't lead her on.

I'm only going to hurt this girl. I hurt everyone I touch. It's the way I'm wired. I don't give a shit about anything or anyone and the only real pleasure I get comes when I'm hurting someone else, physically or emotionally. I can't do that with her. I need to do what I said from the start. I need to be her friend and that's it.

The only way that can happen is for me to do the one thing that right now I know is going to rip everything we just shared apart. I need to treat her like shit and push her away.

"Stop talking Caddy. I can't stand hearing you anymore."

My stomach turns over in protest at how sick I sound and the minute I catch the look on her face, I can see that they've done exactly what I needed them to do. The wounded look I saw on Isabelle's face that day in the parking lot haunts me as I look into Caddy's eyes now. It's the same look. I hurt her and any second now, she's going to break on me.

Her shoulders slump and she turns from me, heading in the very direction I'd been going when she stopped me. I want to call out as she's walking, tell her to stop and that I didn't mean what I said, but as much as I want to, I can't. It needs to happen this way and she wouldn't hear me anyway.

It's pretty evident the farther away she gets that my big idea of remaining friends with her after this is going to blow up in smoke. There's no way after telling her to shut up that she's going look at me the same again. The struggle inside me, it's even worse now. There's the part of me that knowing I hurt her, is happy because I've broken yet another weakling down and the other part that fights against it, wanting me to run to her, pull her to me and never let go.

As I finally start moving, her body so far away from me now that I can barely see her at all, I swallow both of them down, desperate to go back to the way things were before I met her when I didn't feel anything at all. It's turning myself completely numb that's going to get me through this.

I'm doing the right thing. Cadence is too good for someone like me and if it takes walking away completely, even giving up on the hope of a friendship with her, then so be it. There's no way I would let the way I am touch her.

She deserves better.

Cadence

The minute we get back to school, I escape from the prison that his car has been for the last few minutes and race inside, no real destination in mind, but knowing it has to be somewhere far away from him.

I thought kissing him would show what my question really meant and when he kissed me back, pulling me to him, I thought he understood and wanted the same thing. I can't believe I was so stupid. I misread the entire thing.

He didn't want me kissing him. The growl I felt had been a figment of my imagination obviously. When he finally backed away from me, it was like he couldn't get rid of me fast enough and just thinking about the look on his face when he told me to be quiet, I feel like ripping my eyes out. I never want to see a look like that again. I've never felt so disgusting in my life.

I want to cry so badly but the tears won't come. At first, when I wanted to cry most, I had been in front of him and didn't want him seeing me break. He's a bully, so seeing someone break is fun for him and there's no way I was giving him the satisfaction of seeing it happen with me. Now though, being away from him and able to let it out even though I'm in a hallway filled with people, it still won't come.

The stairs that will take me to class and my mom are right in front of me and even though I know I should go to them, head to class and pretend nothing happened during the time I was away, I can't do it. I can't face my mom; especially when she asked me what I was doing for lunch, I lied right to her face saying I was going to head to the library and read.

I can't take the way she'll look at me when she learns the truth and honestly, with the way I feel right now, there's no way in hell she won't be able to tell that I lied or at the very least that something a whole lot bigger than reading happened during the hour I've been away from her.

"Stop talking Caddy. I can't stand hearing you anymore."

Of course he's going to be like everyone else. He's worse than the others because with him, I believed in him. The way he responded when I spoke for the first time made me see him differently than every other person I've spoken in front of. There was a look in his eyes that had nothing to do with disgust and everything to do with caring. Obviously another way I misread everything.

I'd become so caught up in him, feeling things, I made myself blind to the reality. I imagined all of it. He was no different than anyone else and he never would be. I should be happy that he reacted this way because he just proved my mom, Eric and every other person that told me about him right, but the last thing I feel about any of this is happy.

I can't keep doing this to myself. I'm better than this. I'm better than him and the horrible thing he said to me. That's what I need to remember. He's the one that screwed up, not me. The only mistake I made was believing in him. He had done the rest. I can't let the way he is change me. I've spent so long handling my disability with dignity. Dillon Murphy is not going to the one that brings all of that hard work crumbling down.

That's going to happen over my dead body.

I've almost got myself believing in it, starting to feel the hurt drain away, but just as I'm about to make my way toward the stairs, prepared to go to class and face down my mom, I feel the first tear fall from my eye, followed quickly by another and another until they're coming so quickly I can barely even make out the staircase in front of me.

So much for all that so called strength. I'm exactly what he believed me to be from the start.

I'm weak.

Dillon

Doing the right thing isn't supposed to hurt this bad.

When you're faced with a choice and you choose the right one, there's supposed to be this big moment of clarity you experience. It's an overall kind of feeling; where you just know instinctively that the choice you've made is right and you move ahead feeling lighter and better than you've ever felt because of it.

There's no big moment of clarity for me because I didn't make the right choice. What I did do is choose the coward's way out.

Most people when they make the wrong choice or decide to do something that's not right, they feel sick to their stomach, twisted up in knots because deep down they just know that they've taken the wrong step. I've never felt good or bad about any decision I've made because I've spent so long trying not to feel anything at all. Right now though, I'm definitely twisted inside.

It's so strong I feel like I'm choking on it.

This girl, with the eyes that mirror mine in every way; the one that when she looks at me, it feels like she can see right through me, I pushed her away in the worst way possible and there's not a damn thing I can do to change it. In trying to protect her, keep her at arm's length so that in the end I wouldn't be the one to break her apart, I did exactly that.

What I did, wasn't just to protect her, but me too. The way I feel when I'm around her, it brings up memories of an easier time; a time that I haven't lived in so long I wouldn't have the first clue how if given the chance again. In an effort to protect myself from feeling all of that, I reverted back to the one defense I had. Being a complete dick.

Watching her as she stands at the door to the stairs, the ones that will take her to our class, the way her body goes from being completely rigid to shaking, the sound of her crying making its way down the hall so that not only can I hear it, but everyone around me can as well, something breaks inside of me. The same way it did when she pressed her lips to mine less than a half hour ago.

Pushing her away was supposed to be the right move, but it's not and just like yesterday when I found out what Amy did to her, the urge to make everything right with her takes over and before I know it, my feet are moving forward, no longer focused on the people around me, but on one person in particular.

Grabbing her by the arm and turning back the way I came, I pull her down the hall until I see the door to the bathroom. The one room in the entire school right now that will give me the privacy I need and get her away from all of the other eyes that are now watching us as I take off with her in tow.

The minute I push my way through the door, dragging her in and waiting as it slams shut from the impact behind me, I stop and lock it before putting my focus back on her. She might hate me and she has every reason to after what I said, but being in here, locked in with me, it's where she needs to be until the sobbing I heard in the hall can pass and she can get herself together.

For the first time since everything happened, I finally feel the peace that comes from making the right decision. I finally got something right even if it had taken a million wrong turns to get me here.

"Let me go."

"You're not going anywhere."

Her body tenses and I've never wanted to kick myself as hard as I do right now. The way I sound, how clipped my tone is, there's only one way that it could appear to her reading my lips the way she is. She thinks I brought in here to finish what the girls started yesterday.

The last thing I want to do.

"What I mean is, I need to say something to you. I need you to hear me."

If I hoped to stop the tears, I failed because it's obvious that my choice of words only makes everything that much worse even though I didn't mean it the way it sounds.

"I can't hear you remember? I'm deaf."

"I didn't mean it like that. Cadence…"

"Let me go, Dillon."

"I can't. Not until you hear me out."

"No."

There's something in the way she says no that drives me crazy and before I know it, my hands are around her and I'm swinging her around, pushing her backwards until she's completely blocked in against the wall, her face raised up and meeting my eyes, a look of complete fear reflected back at me.

Shit. This is not going at all the way I wanted it to when I made the decision to pull her in here. That moment of peace, the feeling of doing the right thing is gone and it's replaced with the gut wrenching agony that comes when you completely screw everything up.

"This isn't the way it's supposed to be."

She's staring right at me so I know she saw what I said, but where I expect her to answer, to question me in some way, she does the complete opposite and before I know it she's shoving her hands into me until there's a gap of space between us and she can move herself off the wall.

"You were supposed to hate me. Come back after what I said at the ravine, ignore me, not care that I even exist at all. Go back to your life. You weren't supposed to fucking cry Caddy!"

"What does that even mean?" she asks, not making any motion to come near me, but also not making any effort to leave either. She's standing completely in place, a few steps away from the wall, her arms now crossed across her chest, foot tapping as she waits for me to respond.

"It means that I screwed up!"

"Yes, you did."

Her feet start moving forward and I know what's coming. She's going to walk straight out the door if I don't do something right now; something big to stop her.

Reaching out and grabbing her hand, I lock my fingers in hers, not willing to let her leave, not until I've said what I need to say. If she wants to walk out after that, I can't stop her but I can't let her leave like this. Not yet.

"Cadence…"

"What Dillon?"

The right thing. It's there in the way she says my name. It's music. She has no idea how perfect it is because I made her believe that it wasn't. I did the one thing that makes me no better than any other person she's spoken to before. I made her feel like less when the truth is, she's more. So much more.

"Did you mean it?"

"Mean what?"

"What you said to me the first day. What you believe about me. Did you mean it? Is that how you see me?"

She nods and I resist the urge to pull her to me. There's still something I need to know and I can't take a step like that with her again until she gives me the answer. No matter how badly I want to. What she tells me when I ask her this question, it's going to determine where I go from here and exactly what I do next. It's going to be the answer that determines everything.

"After what you went through yesterday; everything you've seen me do and be a part of, do you still see me that way?"

"Yes."

For the first time in five days, I've got everything I need in order to do the right thing. Not the same tired stuff I've been doing for the past four years, but what I should have been doing from the start. In order to do the right thing, we've got to start over, from the very beginning.

It's time for Cadence to meet the real me.

Chapter Fourteen

Cadence

When Dillon told me on Friday he wanted to start over with me; that he wanted to do things differently this time around because the way we met and everything that happened after wasn't the way he wanted to remember our time together, I didn't believe it.

Not believing him, it has nothing to do with the things he's done before and what he would probably do again in the future. It was because words are too easy to come by.

It's easy to tell someone something you know they want to hear. What's not so easy is following up on those easy words and making what you said come to life. It's in taking the words and turning them into actions where most people give up and bail out. This is what I see happening with Dillon, which is why I don't give much thought to his words even though the minute we're back out of the bathroom he starts putting them in motion.

We've been holding hands since my attempt to leave when he yelled at me and it stayed that way the entire walk from the bathroom, up the stairs and straight to the door of my mom's class. It's only then when he changed things up and released my hand, walking straight through the door, knowing that because we were late, he was going to get in trouble.

My mom gave him a look when he walked in and it's one I've seen her do loads of times before. She's even done it with me, that's how often she uses it. She rolls her eyes at him, as if walking in late is something she'd been expecting and it just proved her point about what a flake he is. It's only when I walk in behind him that the entire dynamic of the room changes.

Her eyes raise in surprise and I know that she wants to ask me just what the hell I'm doing with Dillon. Being where she is right now, all the eyes trained on her, she can't. It means I'm definitely in for a long talking to when she gets me out in the car later, but for now, not having to answer her look brings me a whole lot of happiness.

It's none of this that surprises me though. Sure, I'd been surprised when he started walking with me to class because I thought it would be the last place he'd want to be after everything that happened, but past that, everything else was as normal as always. It's what happened when we were both seated that changed everything.

Waiting until my mom's back was turned back toward the board, he leaned over and tapped me on the shoulder, his hand laying out in front of him. One side of his mouth is raised in a smirk and as if knowing that what he's doing makes absolutely no sense to me, his lips start moving and just like always, I'm completely locked on them.

"Hi. I'm Dillon."

It takes a minute but putting together the way his hand is held out, now hanging across the space between our desks, and the way he just introduced himself, I see what he's doing and despite not totally believing his words, I can't help but smile at the attempt he's making.

Reaching into my backpack and grabbing the pad of post it notes, I scribble my response. I could have easily spoken to him, but with the way my mom looked at me when I walked in and how sensitive I am to how she really feels about him, the last thing I want to do is call even more attention to it by speaking out loud for everyone to hear.

Holding up the paper with one hand and reaching the other out to meet his, I shake his hand and as I watch his eyes read my words, I'm comforted by the way the other side of his mouth raises until he's full on smiling at me.

Nice to meet you Dillon. I'm Cadence.

~*~*~

It was that moment, where he started to make good on his words about starting over that the disbelief I had in him began to fade. It wasn't gone completely, but with the way he's trying, I'm as into the new start as he is.

If the way he was in class that afternoon wasn't enough, he took it a step further this weekend, showing up at my house the way he did. It wasn't only me that he wanted a fresh start with. It was my mom too and by the end of it, I'm pretty sure he even had her believing in him, which given everything she's witnessed him do, is a pretty big deal.

After hearing the speech from her again on the way home, yet another warning about Dillon and her belief that I needed to stay as far away from him as possible, even going so far as to warn me that she would keep me in class with her if I didn't go along with what she wanted, I didn't think anything would get past her protective defenses. As it turns out though, I didn't give Dillon nearly enough credit.

Spending the day together like we always do on the weekend while my dad works, we settle into our routine of lounging around on the sofa and flicking through the channels looking for something to watch together. It's only when the light she installed so I'd always be able to tell when someone rang our doorbell starting flicking off and on that I pulled myself away enough to go and find out just who would be waiting on the other side.

~*~*~

"Hey."

"Hi?"

"I know it's weird, me being here like this, especially when I tell you what I had to go through to find out your address, but um—do you think I can come in?"

The talk my mom had comes to mind and I shake my head, pointing inside where she's sitting, hoping that he'll get the hint. If she's home, it means he can't be anywhere near me or this house.

"I'm actually here because I want to talk to her. So can you ask her if it's alright for me to come in?" he asks again, the smile never once leaving his face, meaning that whatever he's here to do, he feels pretty secure with.

I do as he asks and disappear inside the house and the minute I get to the living room and catch her eye, I motion to the door and sign to her.

Dillon is here. He wants to talk to you.

If I thought I was surprised with opening the door and finding him standing there, the look on my mom's face is even more so. It's obvious that Dillon being here is the last thing she expected and I can't say that I'm not right there with her. I know he said he wanted to start over, but is this really one of the ways he has to do it?

It's not exactly a secret how my mom feels about him, so I just don't see this going the way he assumes it will. At this rate, she's gonna have me cuffed to her until my school is fixed.

"Well don't leave him standing out there, Caddy. Let the boy in."

Going back to the door, I smile and motion for him to come in. Closing the door once he's made his way inside, I point toward the living room and following behind me, he doesn't say another word until he's standing about three feet away from my mom.

Tapping me on the shoulder he hands me a paper when I turn to him and before I have a chance to question exactly what's going on, he focuses his attention back on my mom and his lips start moving.

"I know that showing up like this, it's not right, but I need to speak with you about something and I didn't want to wait until Monday. I hope that's alright."

Turning to my mom I see her nod her head, her face a completely blank slate of emotion which doesn't do anything for the nervous flipping going on in my stomach. If she's not showing *how she feels then I have no idea what she's thinking or what she's going to do next.*

"I can't say that I've ever had a student show up at my front door, on a weekend no less, but if this can't wait until Monday then it's fine. What is it that you want to talk about, Dillon?"

"Do you think we could do it privately?"

What he says, it makes me laugh and it's not really the question that does it, it's the way that even knowing what he does about me, he still treats me like I'm the same as everyone else. He doesn't want to talk around me even though he knows it doesn't get more private for him then the way it is now. It's not like I'm going to hear a word he says unless I spend the entire time focusing on his lips.

Wait; never mind. Maybe he gets it more than I thought.

"Of course. We can go into the kitchen. Cadence," she says, shifting her body in my direction and away from the boy standing behind me. "I know how tempted you're going to be to follow us, but I'm asking you to stay here."

With the paper still in my hands, no doubt something he wrote in order to explain what the hell he's doing here, I'm pretty sure this one time I can heed her warning. I don't plan on going anywhere until I start making sense of this whole thing. I might wanna know what it is that he wants to talk to her about, but not enough to risk him being unable to say it at all.

***Okay.** I sign and as they both turn and leave the room, I slide open the paper and see the familiar scrawl across the page, this time, far less spacey and easier to understand. In a few lines, he's given me all the answers I need. I just hope he gets what he wants.*

I know you're gonna be pretty freaked that I'm here. I swear, I'm doing this for you. I meant what I said yesterday. I want to start fresh and that means starting fresh with your mom too. I don't think I'll ever be able to make her see me differently, well, at least not without a lot of work, but if I don't try then we're never going to be able to move forward and I want to move forward. I'll explain what I mean by that later, promise.

Wish me luck, I'm gonna need it.

~*~*~

Whatever he said to her, it must have worked at least a little because for the rest of the weekend, even though she wouldn't tell me what they talked about, she also didn't warn me away from him. He's right; with her he's gonna have a lot of work to do with everything he's done to the students in her class and his part in what happened to me, but seeing her giving him a chance, it gives me hope.

She's not nearly as anti-Dillon as she used to be and this morning, passing notes back and forth with him in class, her even witnessing it a few times, it's the first time since my school shut down that I'm completely comfortable.

Lunch at the ravine?

Yes.

Good because I already asked your mom and she said it was okay as long as we didn't skip out on class.

It never ceases to amaze me, the lengths he's going to in order to make me believe in what he said Friday. Just when I think he can't do anything more than he's already done, he finds a way to do it and leave me even more speechless than I was when I first met him.

Dillon doesn't realize it, but what he's doing, the steps he's taking to prove to me that he can be a decent guy, he's restoring my faith in something that I gave up on a long time ago.

He's reminding me that people really can change; if they want it bad enough and are willing to do whatever it takes to make it happen and if I didn't already know it beyond a shadow of a doubt, knowing that he asked my mom before asking me would have sealed it.

I like him. I like him a lot.

Chapter Fifteen

Dillon

I've been searching for one thing since right before my twelfth birthday and it might have taken a really long time, but I think I found it.

I noticed it that day in Daniels office. The way my mom kept trying to make excuses for me despite knowing I did what I was being accused of. She might be completely out of it, but she knows the way I am and she knows a lot of the reason why I am this way. Sure, it's not all my old man's fault, but if he hadn't decided that my underlying anger could be used in an underground fight club that he could make a profit from, it might never have happened at all.

She sweeps what she knows under the rug and does everything in her power to defend me even though I'm not someone that can be defended. I might have been back when I was like ten or eleven, but now, definitely not. It's because of the way she was in the office and the way everything has played out since that I see exactly what it is that I've wanted for so long but have never been able to have.

I want to be put in my place. I want someone to see the stupid way I act, the shitty things I do and deal with me in a deserving way because I'm not strong enough to penetrate my thick head with the truth on my own. Someone needs to show me the way; push me to see the wrong in what I've been doing and not let up until I do whatever I need to in order to change it.

Cadence did that for me. She's the strong one. The one that can get through to me when I can't get through to myself. Flicking me for rolling my eyes at her mom, smacking me when I moan or bitch about things that aren't all that important, she's pushing me to see the person that's buried underneath all the bullshit. The kid I used to be.

It's because of her not letting me off the way my mom does, the way even my dad does when he does get wind of something I've done that I'm able to do what I am now. I thought about it Friday night after I went home and I didn't stop thinking about it until I'd written the letter to her and ended up on their doorstep. If I'm going to make her believe in me, in her own view of me then I have to do it all the way through. I have to make starting fresh a whole experience and not just one part that centers on her.

What Kayden tried to get me to see, the person that he said he remembered me being, I don't want to run from that kid anymore, even though he might not be the coolest and most exciting person on the planet. I want to go back to him and knock some sense into him now before he turns into something even darker in the future. I want to own the shit I did, the horror I created for four years and I want to do everything in my power to fix it.

Does that mean that I don't still feel the urge to push people that are weaker than me around? No. I mean I'm still the same guy, at least that way. There are some things about me that even though I don't entirely agree with anymore, I can't entirely get away from. I'm still a pretty angry guy and the urge to take that out on kids that are different than me, it's so damn strong, but I've got to push it down if I want this change to stick.

I wasn't always such a douche. I like to think I was a pretty decent kid before everything blew up in my face. I didn't have the social standing then that I do now, but I did have one or two people in my life, kids like me that made life pretty damn fun. I didn't hate people, hate wasn't even a word I understood back then. I would hang out with anyone as long as they smiled, liked the same things as I did and didn't mind that sometimes I seemed a little spacey.

My mom used to call me a dreamer. I was always caught up in my own thoughts, staring off into space and imagining what life would be like when I was older. All the awesome things I would do, people I would meet and things I would do to change the world. Yeah, I know, it seems like a bullshit story to me too, but it's the truth. I saw everything in color instead of the way I am now with everything being so damn black and white.

Something happened when I was eight or nine and the color got all distorted and not long after I changed. My mom and dad were always fighting, he started drinking and she started drowning herself in the pills in order to cope with the way everything changed with them. I pulled away from all of that, the friends I had and preferred being alone to being around people. A few months before my twelfth birthday, my dad was taking me out for dinner and instead of going to get food, he took me to get my ass beat instead.

Nothing was ever the same after that and for the last six years I've just gone along with it, riding the wave because it's easier than stopping, standing in place and going against the norm. I allowed myself to become more twisted with each passing day until the kid that hung out and played hockey and soccer with his friends was gone and a monster who beat the shit out of people was left in his place.

Kayden, he thinks that he made me the way I am. He actually told me that once, before he started hanging with Isabelle. It was such a random thing that at the time, I blew off but the more changes I'm trying to make, the more focus I put on it. He didn't turn me into what I became, I did that on my own and the truth is, I think I'm the one that made him the way he was.

Talking to Cadence's mom, I went in with no expectations. I had a lot of shit to make up for with her and the one thing I was sure of going into the talk was that she wasn't going to believe a word of what I had to say. I was going to have to show her, the same way I have to with her daughter and well, I've been spending every waking moment doing exactly that.

It's no secret that I don't care a whole lot for authority figures. The way I feel about Daniels is proof of that. I think the guy is a total joke and I enjoy doing things that I know will piss him off. I mean the way he dealt with everything at Homecoming shows what a joke he is. It's something that I'm pretty sure me and Kayden see eye to eye on. Instead of shutting the machine off the minute the shit storm I created started, he let it go right until the end. I mean if you want someone to take you seriously as an authority figure, shouldn't you do things that inspire it instead of making yourself look like a joke?

Ms. Taylor though, she's different than Daniels and I knew it before I took one step through her front door. She wasn't going to go easy on me. She was going to do exactly what her daughter did the first day and give me back everything I gave out. She just might be the first adult in a very long time that I can look to and actually respect and it has nothing to do with how I feel about her daughter.

"Alright Dillon, you have my attention. What brings you here?"

"If I told you that I'm here because I want to change; what would you say?"

"I would say I don't believe that. I think you're just looking for a way to get out of my class."

"That's fair."

"Are you telling me what I believe is wrong?"

"No—well, maybe a little. When I first got thrown into your class, I saw it as a death sentence. I even told Cadence that exact thing the first day. I knew I was going to hate every minute of it. I also knew that because I didn't give a shit what Daniels did to me, I would end up being in your class for the rest of the year because I wasn't planning on changing."

"And now?"

"Now, as much as I hate even admitting it because it makes me sound like such a chump, I think I'm starting to see what the point was."

"What does that mean?"

"When Amy threw Cadence on the floor Monday, it bothered me. That's when I started changing, but I wasn't ready to admit it. I blew it off the same way I always do and just went back to doing the same thing the next day. I asked her to lunch because I thought that if she got to know my friends, I could get her away from the freaks. Deep down I knew that Amy and her weren't going to get along, but because of the way she was in class with me, I wanted to give her another option. She was somehow better than Eric, ya know?"

"I'm not sure I do. She's my daughter and I can get behind you telling me that you saw something in her that was great, but as far as seeing her as better than Eric or any of the others in my class, I can't agree."

"I didn't think you would. I was just saying what I thought. What happened to her, what Amy did to her or tried to do in the bathroom, that's when I knew for sure that things had to change. I had to change, all of it just had to change. She never should have been in that bathroom or even in Amy's line of fire. I was the one that put her there and that day, I made a decision to fix it."

"Dillon, before you go on, can I ask you something?"

"You can ask me anything." I answer easily. I'm standing here in her kitchen, opening up in a way that I haven't done in years because I want to start fixing things that I've spent years breaking, the least I can do for being allowed this chance is to answer whatever questions she has.

"Did you tell Amy to do that to Cadence? The reason I ask is because you seem awfully guilty for someone that didn't have a hand in what took place."

"After Amy ran her off, I took off too. I didn't know Amy was going to do that though I should have seen it coming knowing her the way I do. You see guilt because I'm the one that threw her into it. Even if I didn't do it, I'm the reason it happened. I'm going to feel bad about that because it's not right."

"Well, I have to say, it all makes sense now."

Now she has me stumped. I'm not sure what makes sense to her, but I'm definitely curious.

"What does?"

"My daughter. She saw something that I just couldn't allow myself to see because of history."

"I still don't understand."

"Dillon; right from the first day, she has done nothing but defend you at every turn. Even when I told her last night to stay away from you or I would force her hand and keep her in the class with me during breaks, she didn't back down. It makes sense now. She was defending you because for the first time, you're worthy of it."

Cadence has been defending me the entire time? I know that I came here with no expectations, but I can't deny that I also came with a small hope I'd be able to get through to the woman and have this work in my favor. I just had no idea that I'd be getting this too.

"Is this change in you because of Cadence? Are you doing this so that you can get close to her the way you did with Isabelle and hurt her?"

"No. Not at all."

"I am aware of Eric and the way he feels for Cadence, so if this is your attempt at attacking that because you believe he is the reason you were punished to begin with, it needs to stop."

"Ms. T, what I'm doing here, what I'm trying to tell you; it has to do with Cadence, but it's not because I'm trying to use her. It's because being around her, it makes me want to be better."

"You mean that don't you?"

"Yes ma'am."

That may have been the first time I ever called an adult ma'am and I can tell by the look on her face that it was the last thing she was expecting to hear.

"Until Kayden told me, I didn't even know Cadence was deaf. I had no idea that she was your daughter. All I knew was that there was this gorgeous girl in your class that no matter what I did, wouldn't stop busting my balls. Um—I'm sorry about the language."

She laughs and I let myself relax. If she's not going to ride me about my language that I'm not gonna spend so much time stressing out about it. It's not really what's important anyway.

"Here's what you need to realize, Dillon. I am fiercely protective of my students, but even more so with Cadence. I'm sure you can understand why that is. I will not allow you to hurt her or get close enough to even try. I believe what you've told me. I think that for whatever reason, my daughter has somehow gotten to you, made you see something that until now you haven't been willing to, but that does not mean I trust you. Actions speak much louder than words and if you mean what you're saying to me now, then this is your one chance to prove it."

"Does that mean what I think it means?"

"Yes. Cadence sees something in you, something that honestly, I just can't see. I'm going to trust my daughter and take a step back. It doesn't mean I'm not watching you because son, I won't ever stop watching you, but I am willing to give you a chance."

I'm pretty sure in giving me a chance, she wasn't giving me her blessing to do what I'm about to do when class lets out, but that's something I'm just going to have to deal with when the times comes and not focus so much on right now.

I want Cadence to be mine.

Hearing her mom talk about Eric and the way he feels about her, it got me thinking about what I would do if he somehow got close enough during this fresh start to ask her out and she accepted. I'm pretty sure I'd lose it and not in a good way. I would end up doing something stupid since it's what I'm good at and wanting to make things right with her would be completely blown to shit.

I can't risk that happening, which means I've got to jump a few steps ahead in this new beginning and do the one thing that I've secretly wanted to do since she put her lips on mine at the ravine a few days before.

I've got to make Cadence Taylor my girlfriend.

Chapter Sixteen

Cadence

Something's going on.

About ten minutes before class ends, Dillon jumps up out of his seat and heads to the front of the room. I can see that he's talking to my mom about something and she's answering him back, but it's only toward the end of the conversation that I see it. I don't believe it, so of course I start rubbing at my eyes in an attempt to make sure I'm actually witnessing what I think I am.

My mom is smiling at him.

I'm determined to ask him about it the minute he comes back and sits down, but the more time that passes without him heading back, I start to realize that I'm not going to get to ask until I meet him for lunch.

When everyone starts moving out of their seats, I throw my book, all the paper I've been using to answer Dillon and my pen into my bag and make a mad dash for the door. Before I can head out though, my mom stops me and when I turn around to face her, she's wearing the same smile from earlier and she hands me a paper.

If it wasn't weird enough seeing her smile at Dillon earlier, it's even weirder now.

Thinking that something was going on is confirmed the minute I open the paper and see Dillon's handwriting on the page. It also gives me answers that I didn't even know I needed. Where I thought he'd be out in the hall waiting for me when I was done with my mom, I now know different.

Caddy, there's something I gotta do for my coach. It's gonna take a few minutes, can you meet me at the ravine?

Looking up at my mom, hoping in some way that she's got answers for me, she smiles at me again and motions her hand toward the door.

"He told me that he wanted to take you to lunch. I'm okay with it, but if you don't go now, you're not going to get back here in time for class and this time Caddy, you're going to be here when class starts."

Her wearing the smile the way she is totally destroys any hope she had of coming off halfway serious so I just ball the paper up and toss it in the bin before doing exactly what she said and heading out, my destination clear.

If he's gotta deal with something with the coach then I'll play along with him for now. I'll go to the ravine even though I can't help thinking that this is Dillon reverting back to the way he was when I first met him and doing it is gonna lead to me getting hurt. I trust him, despite his past giving me more than enough proof that I shouldn't and even thinking that he would hurt me is enough to turn my stomach, but I can't help it.

The last thing I want after the morning I've had is for him to turn it all around and hurt me. Not even my mom smiling before I walk out can erase the unease I feel as I make my way down the stairs and out the side door, each step bringing me closer to what's going to be waiting for me the minute he gets there.

Crossing the field in record time, I turn onto the main street until I see the entrance and veering off the actual pathway, I decide to walk through the trees this time, moving along with them as they blow around me. It's only when I come out through the final cluster of them that I see something I hadn't been expecting.

Dillon is standing about halfway down the bike path, beside a large rock and there's a can of something I can't quite make out in his hands. The closer I get to him, I see what he's holding and the confusion I felt at seeing him standing there alone is amplified even more.

What he's doing with a can of spray paint when he has to know it's against the law to tag here is beyond me, but it doesn't take me long to find out.

"So I lied." He says the minute I'm close enough to read his lips.

"I see that."

"Don't be mad okay? I swear there's a reason for it and for bringing your mom into it too, though she doesn't exactly know the real reason I needed her help."

"Okay."

He's not making any sense, but it's something I'm getting used to with him. The way he is now reminds me of the way he'd been when he wrote me that note a few days ago. He's all over the place, but he won't stay that way forever.

"Spray paint?" I ask, pointing to the can, and the minute I do his eyes light up and he looks down at it with a smile, something that again does nothing but confuse me. What exactly is so great about an aerosol can that can make him light up this way?

"Yeah, spray paint. I'll get to that, but first, there's something I gotta ask you."

He points to the rock he's standing beside and then looks back at me, the smile even brighter than it was a minute ago.

"Sit please."

Doing as he says and watching as he sits down beside me, the knees of our jeans touching the minute he does, he turns to me, reaching out and taking my hand and placing it in his own before looking up and locking his eyes on mine.

"I've got two questions for you."

"Okay."

"The last time we were here, I totally misunderstood what you were trying to say and you spoke to me. You also did something else and I haven't been able to get it out my head ever since even though I acted like a total ass. What I want to know is, if you had the chance to do it all over would you still do it the way you did?"

If he's asking if I would kiss him again, I think that should be pretty obvious, but since it seems like it's only obvious to me, I nod and hope that's a good enough answer for him.

"Okay good. That means what I'm about to ask you won't be a total fail."

I tip my head to the side in confusion and he laughs.

"Caddy, can you promise me something?" he asks, the laughter gone and his face growing more serious by the second.

"Okay."

"Promise me that when I ask you what I'm about to ask, that you don't give me the answer you think I wanna hear, but the real answer you want to give."

I don't want to admit it but with how serious he is about this, I'm starting to feel a little scared. Whatever it is that he's about to ask me, it's big enough that it's throwing his normal confidence off course and I'm not sure how good I feel about hearing anything that does that. He shouldn't have to feel awkward, least of all with me.

"Okay." I answer though I'm pretty sure by now he already knows what my answer is going to be. I've been saying nothing but okay since I got here.

"That day in the bathroom when I yelled at you, I caught you in the hall crying after I brought you back from here. You were breaking because of me in the middle of a hallway full of people and there was just something so wrong about it. Being with me, wanting what you did that day; that should have been what broke you, not me pushing you away. Ugh, this isn't coming out right. Let me start over."

He takes a breath and taking his other hand, the one that's not wrapped around mine he starts fidgeting with his hair, whatever it is he's trying to get out obviously harder for him then even he thought.

"What I'm trying to ask, it's—ugh. I'm just gonna spit it out. Even though I'm no good for you and I'll do something to completely blow this, will you go out with me?"

If I didn't just witness him struggle so hard with it and I wasn't so struck by everything he said before he got to the question, I would have used the dead air around us right now to laugh at him. He might be two years older and he might even have a whole lot more experience with dating then I do, since I have none at all, but even someone like me could have taken less time to ask someone out.

"Please say something." He says and all I do is smile at him. The smile, I do it for two reasons. It's the only thing keeping me from cracking up at him, but it's also supposed to offer him some security because right now, he looks scared.

There is just something so wrong about the quarterback of the football team scared. It's just something that should never happen considering he gets knocked on his butt by some pretty big looking guys every time he plays.

"Yes."

"Yes, you'll go out with me?"

I can take going out two different ways. He could be asking me to be his girlfriend or he could be more literal with it and asking me out on a date so that he can see if I'm girlfriend material. No matter what way he's asking, the answer isn't going to change, though I'm starting to get now why he said that he didn't tell my mom the truth.

I'm not sure her understanding of Dillon and her willingness to give him a chance extends to him being with me in any other way then friendship. This is definitely not going to go over good when she finds out.

"I'm already out with you Dillon."

"Really Caddy? You're gonna choose now to be a smartass?" he asks, struggling to keep his face straight and failing as he starts to laugh.

"I stopped being one?" I ask playfully and as he laughs again, his head dips down to our hands, both still resting together, wrapped in each other, but not quite linked. I see his lips move but I can't make out what he's saying and by the time he looks up again, I'm pouting and his eyes scrunch in.

"Shit. I screwed up already?"

"I wanted to hear what you said but I couldn't read."

Understanding crosses his eyes and he leans back a little but not enough to break away from the way our legs and hands are still touching, which comforts me. How quickly he jumped to the conclusion that he somehow did something wrong worries me. Even if he's not asking me to be his girlfriend and he just wants the chance to take me out, I can't have him questioning every step. It's not right.

"I said that you never really stopped being a smartass and that I'm really glad you said yes."

Here's my chance to get answers. I need to know what I'm saying yes to, even if my answer doesn't change. I want to know if when I go back to school today, I'm going back the same Cadence I was when I left or if I'm going back as Cadence, Dillon Murphy's girlfriend. It might not seem like a big deal, but I'm no stranger to the way the world works, especially in high school. It matters a lot. It's going to change everything.

"What am I saying yes to?"

Now it's his turn to tip his head sideways in confusion and watching as he does it, it seems we're pretty similar that way too. What started out as the same eye and hair color has now morphed into our movements being the same. It's strange but cool at the same time.

"You don't know what you said yes to?" he asks, again using his free hand and running it through his hair. "If you didn't know, why did you say yes at all?"

"Because it's yes no matter what."

"For real?"

I nod and his hand falls from his hair and the smile is again lighting up his face. Right now, the way he's sitting here, his lips lifted, his eyes shining, I'm pretty sure he's giving the sun a run for its money. Not because he's brighter than it or something cheesy like that, but because the way he looks right now rivals it in how important it is to me.

I spend a lot of time outside just watching and the best time to do that is during spring and summer when the sun is so high and bright in the sky that it just lights up everything around it. It's kind of the same thing Dillon's doing right now. He's so bright that he's lighting up everything around him, including me.

Maybe it's cheesy after all.

"Will you be with me Caddy?"

Answering my question with one of his own, he's given me exactly what I need. He doesn't just want to go on a date with me, he wants to be with me. Gone is the awkwardness from before, even though the words he said still linger with me, and in its place is the confidence I've come to recognize as distinctly Dillon.

"Yes."

His hand moves then, releasing mine and for a split second, my heart drops in my chest. Distance, even something as small as him moving his hand away doesn't feel right. It's only when both of his hands make their way around my back and my body moves forward that I realize what he's doing.

He's hugging me.

As the seconds pass wrapped tightly in his arms, the distance between us on the bench lessened considerably with the move, I enjoy the way it feels being this close to him. The scent of his sweat mixed with a cologne I can't place wrapping itself around me as easily as his arms just had until the only thing I can sense in any way is him.

Pulling back just a little, he brings his hand to my face and running his finger in a small trail from my ear, all the way across my cheek, he comes to rest at my lips and looking up, I can see that his eyes are locked on the place where his finger lies and I find myself wondering what he's thinking. Before I can open my mouth and ask him though, he leans down and presses his lips to mine and all thoughts, all questions fade away until all I can feel, taste and smell is him.

I place my hand on his chest, feeling the same vibration I did the first time we kissed this way and I ache to be able to hear what it sounds like. The intensity of all of my other senses, joining together the way they are as I kiss him back, quickly squashes it until it becomes more than enough. For the first time in my life, even though I can't hear, everything is completely right.

I'm a completely normal girl; one who's in serious danger of falling in love with this angry, beautiful boy.

My boyfriend.

Dillon

There's one thing I'm sure of in my life and with the way everything happened at lunch, the natural high that I found myself on after it was over, I should have seen it coming, but I didn't.

Nothing that means anything ever comes easy. Any time I've been happy in the last eighteen years has always come with a price tag attached. In order to get something great, I need to pay dues doing something that's not so great and this time is no different.

Well, that's not exactly true. This time is way different because the thing that makes me happy, the one thing that means something isn't even a thing at all. It's a person. The one person on the entire planet that can look at me and see right through me and my tangled web of bullshit. She's not just a person either, that makes her seem so much less than what she is.

She's everything.

So of course now that she's said yes, I've gotten everything I could possibly want and I'm walking around with the confidant swagger to prove it, it's time for me to pay the piper.

The piper in this case being my father.

I heard my phone going off a couple of times when I was at the ravine, but I ignored it because now that she's agreed to be my girlfriend even knowing what being that means, there was still one more thing I needed to do with her and nothing was going to keep me from it.

The spray paint was a last minute edition. When I planned on asking her to be mine, that never played a part but remembering the rock from the last time we'd been there and how completely devoid of color it was, I thought of a way to change all of that.

Cadence entered my life and in her unique way added color to it so that I no longer felt like the rock that we ended up sitting on. If she can do that for me, then it was my bright idea that we could add color to the rock together. No matter where we went from this point on, whether we stayed together forever or only a few days or weeks didn't matter. Painting this rock, filling it with color, it means that no matter what happened; this, us, it would never be forgotten.

Where I think she wanted to fight against it when she first saw me holding the can, by the time I explained everything to her, she was more on board with it than I was and by the time we walked away from the ravine and headed back to school, the rock was complete with our names and even though it pains me to admit because I'm the one that did it, a gigantic heart.

Nothing leading up to that moment has ever felt so right, at least it never has for me and it's a memory that no matter where I go from here, I never want to lose. Something tells me though that even if I wanted to forget, Cadence wouldn't let me because it means just as much to her.

I saw the messages from my dad when I got in the car, waiting for her to join me to head back to school, but again I ignored them. I can't ignore them anymore because now, right when we're about to head into class, he's not texting; he's calling and I know what's going to happen if I don't answer.

Squeezing Caddy's hand and watching as she looks up at me with a smile, I come to a complete stop and wait for her to do the same. I've gotta take this damn call and the only way I can do that is if I let her know so that she can head to class and let her mom know I'm not reverting back to my old ways.

"My dad's calling. I need to take it. Can you go in and tell your mom?"

She nods and as she slips her hand out of mine and starts to turn, I reach out to her again. There's no way after everything that just happened I'm going to let her walk away like it's any other day. No, this isn't just some random day and we're not just two random friends anymore.

Cadence Taylor is my girlfriend and no matter what the people walking around us think, I'm going to treat her that way.

Pulling her back into my arms, I do the exact thing that a few days before had made me sick just witnessing and I place my lips to her forehead before leaning down and brushing my lips against hers.

"Thank you. I'll be in soon." I say, breaking away and watching as she levels me with one final smile before turning and making her way down and into the class. It's only when the door shuts behind her that I breathe a momentary sigh of relief and look back down at my phone.

I've got three missed notifications, calls from him and now it looks like I've also got a voicemail message too. Deciding against listening to it, choosing instead to just dial him back and pray that he hasn't lost his mind not being able to get ahold of me, I wait with baited breath as the rings go in.

"What did I tell you about not answering my calls!" his voice booms through the phone, getting right to the point, no greeting to warm me up.

"That your time is valuable and it would be in my best interests to answer whenever you choose to call, sir." I say, my voice cold and robotic, the way it always is when dealing with Bruce.

"Remember that for next time. I don't take kindly to having my messages and calls ignored, Dillon. Especially when I know that until about five minutes ago, you were on lunch and not in class."

Well there goes using class as an excuse.

"I had the ringer on silent, from being in class." I lie, knowing that it won't even matter what I say now since I hadn't answered but still hoping to curb some of his anger before it gets worse. "What's so important?"

There's another fight. I already know the answer to my own question and he doesn't disappoint.

"How are those bruises healing?"

"Another couple of days and they'll be gone. Why?"

"This weekend, Brody Garner. Same place as before."

"And if I say no?"

No one says no to Bruce Murphy. Not unless they wanna end up in a hospital room on a ventilator. He's an angry son of a bitch and it's only gotten worse lately. I want nothing more than to say no to this and just hang up the phone, but if I want to enjoy time with Cadence now that I've got her, saying yes to this is the only way to do it. Bruce won't let me live at all if I don't. It's amazing I've lasted this long with his temper.

"Dillon, I don't have time for your jokes."

"What time?" I ask, not even bothering to respond to the way he takes my question, jumping ahead to the acceptance part of the phone call. I can't get out of this, no matter how badly I want to. This is my life and I'm only fooling myself thinking I deserve any other one.

"Six. Unless you've got practice. If you do, text me and let me know and I'll figure it out."

Telling him I had practice would be the right thing to do right now. It would get me out of this fight or at least prolong it for a little longer, which is as good as I can ask for. It's just not what I do, because despite my need to get out of this, especially now, I bend to him.

"I'll let you know."

Pushing end on the call and looking down the hall, I've got a decision to make. With as sick as I feel after the conversation with my dad, the last thing I want to do is go to class and pretend nothing is wrong for the next two and a half hours, but on the other hand, there's a girl in there; one I just asked to be my girlfriend waiting for me to do exactly that. A girl I promised that I would be different for.

As much as I don't want to give her a reason to lose faith in me, the decision is easy to make. Turning around, I start walking, as far and as fast as I can from the class and away from her.

I can pretend all I want that I can be someone different, but the reality is, as long as Bruce is my father and I allow myself to bend, I'll never change. I'll always be what he wants me to be; what I've been for so long that it's hard to imagine even trying to be anything else.

I'll always be the asshole.

Chapter Seventeen

Cadence

When a half hour passes and there's still no sign of Dillon, I know something's wrong.

I don't even try hiding it from my mom when she starts making her way around the room, checking in with the other kids and then making her way over to me. She can see the look on my face, there's no doubt she knows it's about him and with the way her eyes go soft and she motions with her head toward the door, I can see that I'm not the only one concerned.

It's only been four days since his big revelation about starting over fresh, so he could have easily gone back to the way he's always been but I don't believe that. The Dillon that I've seen over the last few days, the one that came by my house even knowing that it probably wasn't the smartest decision, isn't the same guy that slumped himself into the desk a week before. He's different.

Getting out of my seat and leaving my bag behind, I walk out of the class and immediately start scanning the hallway for any sign of him. He had only been about six or seven feet from the door when I'd left him, but with the time that's passed he could be just about anywhere now.

Putting myself in his shoes, trying to figure where he would go if he needed to get away from everything for a while, I'm rewarded. There are only two places I can imagine a guy going. He either went to his car or he went to the locker room.

Having taken tours of the school during my time here this past week, I know exactly where the gym is and moving as fast as I can without completely giving into the frantic way my mind is working, I head down the stairs and don't stop running until I find myself standing right outside the doors.

Knocking lightly, not sure what I'm expecting to be the response but wanting to at least give some kind of heads up to anyone who might be in here and not completely dressed, I wait a couple of seconds before pushing on the door and walking inside. Taking tentative steps forward, I scan the first strip of lockers and finding nothing, make my way even deeper in until I see another row of lockers and the body at the very end.

"Dillon," I call out and he turns at the sound of his name, his eyes coming to rest on me and the fact that I'm only a few feet away from him. The way he looked when he kissed me before I went into class, it's not the way he looks now and the closer I get to him, I see him struggling to change it. He knows how he must look and it hurts knowing that he feels like again he's got to change who he is and what he feels in order to talk to me.

"What are you doing here?" he asks and as I take a seat beside him at the end of the bench, I put my hand on his shoulder, squeezing just a little before giving him his answer.

"Worried about you."

"I'm fine."

"You're lying."

"Oh of course I am because I can't do anything but lie, right?"

I don't have to hear him to know he's angry and now that I'm here, he's got someone to take it out on. It's just too bad that I'm not going to let him. He can be pissed off all he wants, but I'm not going to let him use me as a punching bag.

"I'll leave. I'm sorry." I say as I slide my body off the seat. Now that I know he's here and he's alright, at least physically, going back to class is the only thing I need to do.

His hand comes to rest on my arm and turning back, I watch as he opens his mouth to speak again.

"No, I'm sorry. Don't leave."

Sitting back down, he turns his body into mine and his eyes, they aren't as hard as they were before. Now they're sad.

"Remember what I said at lunch? That something would happen and I'd screw this up?" I nod and he continues. "It's happening and we haven't even been together an hour."

"What happened?" I ask, not even acknowledging what he says. Whatever happened on the call with his dad is what's causing this. He's doubting himself even though he has no reason to. He isn't ruining anything.

"Same old shit, different day."

"Huh?"

"The other day, when I came to school and I could barely move, do you remember what you said to me?"

I nod, unable to forget anything that happened that day even though I want to.

"Right, and I said it was three pretty big trucks. Caddy, I know you know what I meant by that, but you don't know everything."

"Then tell me."

"There's something you don't know about me. I'm scared that when I tell you, I'm going to ruin this; us. I want to be different for you, I want you to know the real me, but this, it's all I've known for six years and I don't know if I'm ever going to escape it, no matter how badly I want to."

"Remember your words at the ravine." I say, not asking him to remember but telling him so that he can focus on that and remember what we said.

When we were spray painting our names on the rock, there was a minute where we stepped back from the fumes and he said something and it's been with me ever since. It matters even more with what he's about to tell me because what he's afraid of, it just isn't going to happen.

There's nothing he can say that would make me run, because I've seen the worst parts of him. I'm still here and here is where I'll always be if he'll let me.

"This is the beginning of something that no matter where we go, will never have an end."

I nod as I watch him repeat his words back to me and despite the seriousness of the moment, I smile. Other than my mom and dad, no one has ever said something like that to me before and no matter how many times I hear it, it will always melt my heart.

"I won't run. Tell me what's wrong."

"I've been fighting for my father since the day I turned twelve. He schedules fights for me; sometimes with people my own age, but most times with adults as old as he is. What he wanted when he called is what he always wants, Caddy. He was calling to tell me that when my bruises heal, he's got another one for me. I never feel right after I talk to him, but this time it's worse because even if I do say no and walk away, he'll find me and the punishment will make me wish I'd just done the stupid fight. After the call, I couldn't face you and even now, I'm not sure I can face you."

The first time I met him I knew there was something in his life that made him the way he is, or at least helped it along and with what he's telling me now, it's the one person on the planet that shouldn't be doing it. Dillon's father making him fight, it's not right.

He's been fighting for his life since he was twelve.

I don't even know what to say.

"Say it. Say you hate me. How could you not hate me?"

"I don't hate you."

"You see it now, right? Why I didn't want to feel anything for you; let you get close to me. I'm going to bring you into this mess and in the end I'm not the one that's going to get hurt. You are."

"You're not hurting me."

"Not yet maybe, but I will. It's all I ever do."

"Not ever, Dillon."

"You don't get it. You're being amazing, but you just don't get it. I can't walk away from this. Saying no to Bruce isn't an option, so unless you plan on being with someone who fights other people almost as much as he bullies the kids he goes to school with, you're going to end up getting hurt worse than I ever could. You need to walk away Caddy; before I drag you down with me."

"I'm not going anywhere."

Dillon

There's nothing left to say. I've laid it all on the line.

The secret that I've been keeping for six years, the one that I didn't want to get out because of what it would mean for my reputation and the way I'm looked at here. It's out now and there's not a damn thing I can do to take it back.

When I finally told Cadence the truth, something happened to me. I felt lighter. Like I've been weighing myself down with this for so long that I adapted to the way it felt and now that I've gotten it out there and who I told it to, the heaviness is gone and I feel like I can breathe again. It's like I'm breathing for the first time and it's all because of her.

She has no idea what she's saying, standing by me like this. I expected her to react this way even though deep down I hoped she would get scared by the truth and run as far and as fast as possible in the other direction. This is not a fight she needs to be a part of, no matter what she sees in me.

Nothing I say gets through to her. She won't leave me and honestly, with the way she almost walked away a few minutes ago, I'm pretty sure I don't want her to even though it's best she does. The closer we get, the more she's going to get pulled into the life I lead and it's not a place someone like her should ever go. The fighting, my anger and the way I release it, it's too dark for her and even now, with her sitting here fighting against me every step of the way, she's proving it.

She's too good for me. I knew that the day I met her, but I was selfish. I liked the way she made me feel, keeping me on my toes and not letting me get one over on her the way everyone else does. So I kept pushing it even knowing that we would get to this point and I'd push her away in an effort to keep her safe. I did what I always do and I chose the selfish road and now that she's taking it with me, I have no idea what to do next.

"Just go, Caddy. Run now, before things get worse."

"No."

Damnit. This girl, she's killing me. This is not the time to be stubborn.

"You're not scared by this at all, are you? Despite everything I just said, you still wanna be with me."

"Yes." She answers as she nods her head, emphasizing her point, which just makes it even more unbelievable.

"Why?"

"Because the fighting isn't what you want; it's just what you do. Because what I said that first day is still true and you admitting everything proves it."

"What does that even mean?"

"I told you that someone turned you into the person you are when you're here and now I know who. He shouldn't be doing that, but now that I know he is, I know what I have to do."

"What's that?"

"Fight back."

Cadence Taylor is the strongest person I know. She's sitting here with me, her eyes never wavering from mine, standing her ground and saying that she's gonna fight my father. If I didn't already believe her to be strong, especially with everything she has to deal with because of her disability, it would be right now where my mind would be changed.

"How do you plan on doing that?"

"When are you supposed to fight?"

"Two days."

"Then I know what I have to do."

"What's that?"

"Talk to my mom. Dillon, you're not gonna fight in two days. In two days, after school or practice, you're coming home with me and you're not leaving."

It's in that moment, when she speaks, every sound she makes like music to my ears, I realize it for the first time. What I think I've known since the day in the bathroom but had been too afraid to say out loud. Her determination to do right by me despite knowing the person I am, standing to her feet the way she is now and holding out her hand to me, wanting me to come with her, it's never been so clear.

I'm falling for her and for the first time, I don't want to catch myself before I fall completely. This time, with this girl, I want to crash and I want to crash hard because when it happens, she's going to be there and she's going to pick me back up.

Chapter Eighteen

Cadence

So much has changed since I got here a week and a half ago and sometimes, like right now, I find myself stepping back and giving myself the chance to take it all in because a lot of it seems so unbelievable that I feel like I'm dreaming.

When I came here, being with someone was the farthest thing from my mind. Sure, I found guys attractive, I even had crushes on them a time or two, but actually stepping out of my comfort zone long enough to act on it was unheard of. It just wasn't something I spent a whole lot of time fussing over. My life is hard enough as it is; adding boys to the mix seems like overkill.

That's the first change because now I'm with someone and it's the last person on the planet I ever would have imagined being with. I attracted a bad boy, the worst really and in the span of a week, what at first appeared bad, has never looked so good.

Dillon, for all of his perceived failings and things about himself he thinks he needs to protect me from, is underneath all of the bravado one of the softest people I know. When you look at him, it's easy to believe that he was born without a heart; especially with all the things he's spent the last four years doing, but I know different. He does have a heart and it's the kindest, most delicate one I've ever come into contact with.

He'll never admit to that of course because despite all the changes he's made, he still believes that showing any form of real emotion makes him weak. It's something that for him, he just can't be, but in the moments when we're alone together or even hanging outside with the others, it's there and it's so powerful that even he has a hard time denying it or pushing it down.

That's another thing that's changed since I got here.

It seems that something's going on with the two football players that's bringing them closer than they've been in months; years really if everything Isabelle tells me when we're hanging out is right. Apparently that day when Amy cornered me, they worked together to find me. It was looking for me that the two of them bonded in some way, at least that's how I see it and now, over the span of a couple of days, we've been hanging out with them and this time, it has nothing to do with some plan Dillon wants to put in motion. This time it's real.

I know all of this because I've talked with Dillon and then when he's off at practice, I've talked to Isabelle. There's no one else alive that knows Kayden the way that she does, so when I talk to her, it's like I can see things through his eyes and it makes understanding him easier.

We're a lot alike, Isabelle and me. We both saw something in these broken boys that we knew the rest of the world needed to witness. We didn't back down even when it was probably the smartest thing to do and now we're reaping the rewards that come with never giving up.

Things are so different that we're even sitting around making plans together. Where Homecoming had been a complete disaster in the fall, this time around, the Senior Prom, it's a chance for yet another fresh start. The havoc Dillon put into motion all those months ago has the ability to be wiped clean and if the way Kayden and Isabelle are responding to our talks of going together, means anything, this might be the night that everything gets set right again.

Where everything becomes what it should have been.

Before I can think about prom though, there's something else that needs my undivided attention.

I made him a promise two days ago. Dillon isn't going to go through with the fight his father has planned for him tonight because I'm going to bring him home with me and make sure that the man doesn't get anywhere near him. I'm not exactly sure why I promised something like that considering I'm maybe a hundred pounds tops and his dad is a whole lot bigger, but I did and now it was time for me to live up to it.

That's another thing I've learned since I've been here. It's really not about the size of the person in the fight, but the size of the heart, the sheer determination of the person in it that decides which way something is going to end. Bruce Murphy might be bigger and stronger than me, but there's one thing he doesn't have and that's heart. A heart that his son stole from me that day at the ravine and the heart I never want him to give back.

It's that heart that's going to get us both through this, no matter what happens along the way. I'm sure of it.

"You're sure your mom's alright with this? I know she's been cool with me lately, letting me slide on some stuff, but I mean, hanging out at your house all night? Isn't that a bit much?"

To be honest, she's not all that pleased about it, but after my attempt at asking her if Dillon could just come over and hang out for a while failed, I had to resort to telling her a half truth. I mentioned his dad, but left the fighting out of it and she seemed to get it. While she wasn't pleased that this boy she still had concerns about would be spending the entire night with her daughter, she understood why it had to happen and why it was so important to me.

"You worry too much. You're gonna get gray hair."

"I've had gray hair since I met you." He laughs softly. "Keeping up with you is enough to give gray hair to a baby."

He might be right about that, but there's no way I'm gonna admit it. He's not used to being with someone like me. I think at first he thought that because I'm deaf, I was going to be like Isabelle or Eric and back down from him at every turn. When he realized I wasn't like that, he struggled to keep up. I'm starting to think that's one of the reasons why we ended up together. I represented something different for him.

Reaching across and smacking him on the arm, he catches my hand the minute it makes contact and brings it down to his leg, wrapping his own around it and smiling. The smile is subtle, not as bright as I've seen him do before, but the tenderness behind it and the entire move itself melts me. That's another way everything's different.

As heightened as my senses are, touch being the biggest, I tend to shy away from a lot of physical interaction. It's too much for me sometimes. I can handle it when it comes from my mom or dad, but for anyone else, it has to be a slow build otherwise I'm just not comfortable. With Dillon though, that all just seemed to get thrown out the window. It's when I'm not touching him that things become harder to deal with and I'm thankful that he seems to feel the same.

For the last two days, the only break we've had from each other is when he's at practice and we're at home and apart during the night. When we're here like we are now, we're both reaching out and bridging the gap between us because the distance is too difficult to take. Aside from watching his lips move and noticing the changes in his eyes when he speaks to me, holding his hand, brushing up against him, any way interacting physically is my favorite part of being with him.

"I thought since we're gonna need to kill a lot of time, I'd bring over some DVD's and we can have a movie marathon or something. I think I might even have a few your mom might like."

"Unless you've got a collection of romantic comedies, I'm pretty sure there's nothing you can bring over that my mom's gonna like."

"That's all she watches?"

I nod and he laughs.

"Maybe if we show her enough cars blowing up, we can change that."

Just as I'm about to answer him, I feel his hand, the one connected to mine start to tense and just as I look up in protest, the squeeze hurting a lot more than I think he's intending, I see the sun get blocked out by a shadow and it all starts to make sense.

He's reacting to whoever it is that's standing there.

It only takes swerving my body a little to see who the person is that's causing him to act this way and where I expected to find Amy or one of the other girls, it's not any of them. It's actually the last person I expect to feel this reaction from.

Tim Bradshaw is here and he's smiling.

Dillon

A couple days ago when I asked Cadence to be my girlfriend, I knew something would happen that would turn everything upside down. I thought at the time, it was my dad because when he called that day and I reacted the way I did, it seemed like he was going to be the thing that ruined everything before it began.

When I caught Tim walking up behind us, that feeling I had when my dad called, it came back again and I realized that this time, it wasn't going to be one singular thing that turned everything I was beginning to feel on its axis. It was going to be two things.

Since the day in the hall when I dumped and walked away from Amy, I haven't spent any time with Tim or the others. I see Tim on the field when we're at practice and even in the locker room, but we haven't said shit to each other and as weird as that is because for the past four years we've been inseparable, I've been enjoying the break.

I used to think that we were friends because of how similar we all were. The way we felt about the people we went to school with, our idea of fun being the same bonded us somehow. I know different now. We didn't hang out because we're alike, we hung out because there was never a better alternative. Tim is nothing like me, he's definitely nothing like Kayden, so why he ended up with us, I don't think I'll ever know, but now that I've taken the steps away from them, I'm not itching to go back.

The new version of me; the better version, wants no part of whatever it is that's bringing him over here. I just wanna sit here under this tree, enjoying the way it feels laughing and joking with my girlfriend and watching the world move on around me. Nothing more, nothing less. It seems that I'm not going to be allowed to have my way.

Story of my life.

"What do you want?" I snap the minute his shadow falls over us. No doubt he's here because Amy sent him over, which if that's true, just makes me wanna deal with it even more. I might be different now, more like the old me than I've ever been before, but that doesn't mean I'm not willing to get in this guy's face if he's over here in an attempt to start something.

"You mind breaking away from the retard for a few so we can talk?"

Retard is a word I used a lot before I met Cadence. I even used it after I met her that first day, but where it was my go-to word before, it's not anymore. Since we started getting closer, I've been going out of my way to erase that word from my vocabulary all together and the last thing I want is to hear anyone else saying it.

Cadence doesn't know this, but when I get home every night, I've been looking a lot of stuff up on the internet. At first, I looked up all I could find about being deaf, but then it changed from that to searching for stories about kids being bullied because they were deaf. Some of the things I read could put what Amy did to her and what I've been doing to people for years to shame, that's how bad it is for them. I saw the words retard and deaf mute thrown around so much, it woke me up pretty quick to the hell I've been putting people through all these years.

I never want to use those words again.

"Don't wanna talk to you; especially if you're gonna call my girl that."

"Are you shitting me right now, D?"

"Nope. Go away, Tim. No one wants you here."

"Amy was right about you."

Of course she was. I've spent enough time with her to know that she's probably said a lot of things about me, made assumptions and tried treating them as facts based on my behavior; all in an effort to get the others to hate on me as much as she did, but the thing is, even knowing that she's done it, I just don't care.

She can say whatever the hell she wants about me because she never really knew me to begin with.

"Yeah, I bet she is. So why don't you run along back and tell her that. I don't wanna hear it and I'm pretty sure Caddy doesn't either."

"From what I've been told, she can't hear shit anyway so I don't think anything I say matters to her."

The tense hold I've had on Caddy's hand since Tim walked up, I finally release it and as I see her start shaking her hand, free of my grip, I slide backwards and jump to my feet. There's no way in hell he's going to say that shit about her. She might not be able to hear it, but I can and that's enough for me.

Fighting in front of the girl that's trying to protect me from it isn't right, but this is a different kind of fight. What I'm about to do to Tim's face, he deserves for saying what he did. No one talks about my girlfriend that way; especially not this moron.

"You wanna repeat that, Tim? I didn't quite hear you the first time." I say as I shove into him, causing him to stumble backwards. Stalking forward, nowhere near done with him, I hear my name from behind me, but it doesn't even matter.

Grabbing Tim by the shirt, I bring him into me and catch sight of his eyes the minute I do. He knows me. He knows where this is about to go and any second now because of the fear he feels, he's going to stammer off a half assed apology so I'll drop him. The thing is, that's not what's gonna happen this time.

"What the fuck has gotten into you man? Since when did you become a mute lover?"

"Since now." I snarl before tightening the grip on his shirt, lifting him off the ground and throwing him forward, watching as he stumbles and falls to the ground. Moving quickly I stand over him, bending down on one knee and grabbing his shirt up into my hands again, yanking him to me, rage boiling over inside me and needing to break free.

Reaching my free arm back, I hit him, his head dipping backward before coming to rest in front of me again. Shoving him down, I start hitting him, first in his face until I see the blood start to drip from his nose, and then moving downward, hitting him once in the throat before making my way down to the stomach and leveling him with as many hits as I can. I continue to assault on him until I feel my body being pulled off. Leaving Caddy behind in order to wail on Tim, I thought for sure she was the one behind me, but with the strength needed to get me off the son of a bitch who called her names, I know it isn't her.

It's only when I'm completely off and away from Tim and I make out Caddy out of the corner of my eye, standing with her arms wrapped around herself, a look of fear on her face that the person that's restraining me speaks.

"You're scaring her. Knock it off. I get what you're doing, but it needs to stop before Daniels catches wind of it."

Kayden.

My ex best friend.

The one that made sure to haunt me at every turn for the last three months, looking for any chance to see me fall, just yanked me away from beating on the guy that until a few days ago, I considered the only friend I had left.

"He needs to pay."

"And he will, but not now. Dillon, you need to chill out."

I see the shadow moving and I turn toward it. Where Cadence had been standing a few seconds ago, there's now a wide open space and following the shadow as it moves farther away, I see it's her and she's running. Kayden telling me to chill out, in my anger I didn't get why he was saying it considering he knew why I was beating on Tim, but the faster she moves away from me, I see it crystal clear.

He's right. I did scare her and now, she's running for her life, but not toward me the way I always pictured her doing if anything ever happened. No, this time she's running away and the further she gets, the more pieces of my heart she takes with her.

Tim wasn't the one to turn everything to shit after all. My father hadn't even been the one to do it. She heard all of that and still chose to stand by me and fight.

The thing that blew all of this apart has been here the entire time.

Me.

Chapter Nineteen

Cadence

I don't know why I'm running, all I know is I can't stop.

The minute his hand gripped mine in a hold so strong that I actually felt my fingers going numb, it should have been an indicator that things were about to take a turn for the worst. That the peaceful easy feeling we had sitting together, joking the way we were was going to come to an end, but I stupidly believed that what I was experiencing would work itself out differently.

Tim standing behind us smiling, I caught his first words to Dillon. The hold on my hand became that much tighter and I knew he was close to the edge. Just because we're together and he's trying to be different doesn't mean that the way he was before is just erased completely. Dillon is still driven by a deep seeded anger and it's that anger that took control the minute Tim said the words.

Calling to him was supposed to stop him. He knows how hard it is for me to say anything out loud, at least when there are other people around. He always reacts to me when I speak but this time, it's like he didn't hear me at all.

Fighting Tim, he was doing it for me even though it's the last thing I want him to do. I'm doing everything I can today so his father can't take him to a fight and here he is attempting to pick another one. Tim's words didn't hurt me, I didn't react to them at all. I've heard the word retard enough that it's lost all meaning to me and deep down I know Dillon knows this.

He thinks he's doing right by me, but he's not.

I hate violence. I would rather just ignore what I saw Tim say then fight with it, physically or verbally. You can't change ignorance by beating a hole into someone's face. Doing that only makes you as ignorant as they are.

Kayden stepping in and pulling Dillon off, it should have put an end to everything, but I could see what no one else could. Dillon's eyes, there was a rage in them, a look I haven't seen since the day that he faced Eric down in the hall and seeing it now, knowing that it was directed at someone he used to call a friend, it turned me inside out. Being with me is not supposed to tear him away from his friends, even if I think the people he hangs out with aren't that great. It's not supposed to change anything at all, other than making us happy.

He's the opposite of happy as he's looking back at the boy he just beat into the ground, this sick twisted smirk on his face, feeling accomplished at having taken down the guy saying things about me. I saw Kayden's lips moving, an obvious attempt to smarten him up and bring him back to reality. I even saw his head move in my direction, which means whatever he was trying to say to get through to Dillon, had my name attached.

That's when I make the decision. I couldn't stay there, seeing him react that way, knowing that it's second nature to him. It's not that way for me and I'm not going to spend my last two days here with that version of him stuck in my head. I want to leave here at the end of the week remembering the Dillon with the soft heart who is nothing but tender and sweet, not the monster he's failing to distance himself from.

Slamming my way through the bathroom door, I head for the sink and turn the tap on. Watching as the water starts pouring down, I cup my hands under the stream and bring it up to my now flushed and overheated face.

This is all wrong. None of this should have happened. I thought being with him was making things better but in reality all it did was mask what was there all along and made everything worse.

Leaning over again, splashing more water on my face, I try to wash away everything I've just spent the last few minutes witnessing, but I can't. All I can see as I stand here, looking in the mirror at my own reflection is Dillon's cold eyes staring back at me and it makes me want to break all over again.

I would rather be bullied than be haunted by those eyes for another second longer.

Backing away from the sink and turning toward the door, I see the pair of shoes come around the corner first, ones I've seen multiple times. Seeing them now causes my heart to seize in my chest until I look up and see that it's not who I thought it was.

It's Kayden.

"He's in the hall, and he's pretty messed up." He explains slowly, reacting to the obvious shock that must be written all over my face at him being the one standing here.

"Don't want to see him."

"I figured that, which is why he's out there and I'm in here."

I've never noticed it before, but when he talks to me now, his lips move slower. There's an ease to them that reminds me of the way my mom is. She takes her time when she speaks because she knows that speeding up means there's going to be a lot that I'm going to miss and it seems he's the same way.

I don't know why I notice it or why I even care, but it's comforting to me. The way he's reacting is putting my mind at ease, which I need since I can't seem to slow it down on my own.

"He's never going to change."

"Cadence, I can't believe I'm gonna say this because I want to agree with you considering everything I've been through with the guy, but that's not true."

"You saw what he did."

"I also know the reason why he did it. Do you know how many times I've wanted to beat on Dillon, Tim and the others for the shit they've said and done to Isabelle, even after I warned them about it? It's a daily thing. I have to focus every bit of energy I have in order to control myself because I swore I was done with the fighting."

The reason Dillon did it was me. He doesn't even have to come right out and say it, but the fact that he's sympathizing with it throws me. I know the two of them were taking steps to understand each other again, getting along a bit, but actually agreeing with each other, that's a shock.

"I didn't want that."

"I know you didn't. You're a lot like Belle. She's so used to hearing shit about her that it rolls off, but Cadence, what you guys don't get is, we can't do that. Dillon and me, despite all the horrible shit in our history; when someone talks shit about someone we care about, we can't walk away and ignore it."

"Why not?"

"Well—we're guys. If you haven't figured it out already, we don't think with our head a lot."

He's making a joke, putting me at ease and I want to laugh but I can't. I know what he's trying to say but it doesn't change anything for me. I can't handle Dillon reacting that way. I'm strong enough to take care of myself when something like this happens. I don't need a knight to come to my rescue. He's taking things too far and just like every other time with us, I can't let him skate by on it because I have feelings for him.

"The Dillon you know and the one you've heard about, they're two different people. He's even different from the way he was when I met him freshman year. Dillon cares, he's just spent so long being told that it's wrong that when he has anything remotely close to an actual feeling, he does whatever he can to sabotage it or make it go away."

"Why are you telling me this?"

"I have no idea. I can still barely stand him most days, but right now I understand him a lot more than I thought I ever would because for once, we're walking the same road."

"What road is that?"

"The one where someone comes into our lives and in the span of a few days turns our entire world on its axis. We question every single thing we've been taught, told or experienced before we met the person until we're so tied up in knots that we don't know from one minute to the next what the hell is even going on. Cadence, the way Dillon is right now, is the way I was a few months ago."

"When you met Isabelle." I whisper, putting together all that he's trying to tell me so that the need for questions stops. This is something I don't need to have him answer because deep down I already know it.

"No, not when I met her. When I fell in love with her."

He can't mean what I think he means. If they're walking the same road and everything Kayden just explained is what Dillon is going through then he thinks Dillon is in love with me and as much as my heart wants to grasp at the words like they're the truth, I don't think I can make my head believe in it.

"He's not in love with me."

"Cadence," Kayden sighs. "I'm not gonna sit here and tell you how to handle this because even though we're pretty similar, he's not me and you're not Isabelle, but I know Dillon. What happened out there, that's not him acting like a dick and getting angry over nothing. It's him trying to do right by a girl he's head over heels for, but not thinking it all the way through first."

Well there's one thing he says I can agree with. Dillon didn't think it through. I don't know how much truth there is to the rest of it, but I do know that much. The only way I'm going to find out the rest is by doing the one thing that when I ran from him, I'd been trying to escape from.

I've got to talk to him.

Dillon

The second Kayden comes out of the bathroom, I'm up off the lockers and heading straight for the door. The guys from the soccer team might have done what he asked of them before he went in but they weren't gonna keep me from her anymore. If Kayden was done, it was my turn.

I needed to know that she's okay. I can take her being upset with me, wanting to kick my ass and even walking away from me again if it means that what she just saw me do out there didn't break her.

It's this exact thing that I was warning her about a couple days ago. I know what I'm like and I know what kind of mindset I get into when it comes to fighting. It doesn't matter who I'm going up against, whether it's someone ten times bigger than me or someone smaller like Tim, it's always the same rage fueled reaction. That's why I told her to run, because I knew if she stayed, there'd be nothing left of her by the time I was done.

She needs to be okay. She doesn't need to turn into me. One Dillon is enough.

"How is she?" I ask the minute he meets me in the middle, my eyes not on his but on the door that's standing between me and the girl I need to fix things with.

"Messed up man. You scared the shit out of her."

"Tell me something I don't know."

"You want the truth?" he asks and I just nod. Now's not the time to sugar coat anything. If what I did to Tim a few minutes ago is gonna be the one thing I can't fix, I need to know before I go in there and try. It won't change what I do, but it will help me in coming up with a way that can turn this around.

"You need to go in there and you need to say goodbye to her. She's leaving in a few days and what she saw today, what you did, I don't think you're gonna be able to fix with a few nice words and there's not a whole lot of time for actions. Let her go, Dillon."

That's not happening. I'm not letting go of the one thing in six years that makes me feel right again. I don't care if it's selfish or not. I won't ever let her go.

"Not happening."

"Dillon, this isn't a game."

"I know that. Now she just needs to know it too."

Moving around him and following the same path he did, I ease my way in and wait until the doors completely shut before reaching out and locking it behind me. Whatever happens now, I don't want an audience for.

Coming around the corner, I see her and the minute the shadow of my body crosses over her place under the bathroom lights, she looks over at me, her head staying level with my chest, making no attempt to go higher.

Seeing her this way, it tears me apart inside. I know how she feels about my fighting. I mean the entire reason I'm supposed to spend the night at her house tonight is because she wants to keep me safe and away from it. She wants to find a better solution then me going toe to toe with some random person my father hand picks to beat on. She wants better for me even though I'm not sure I deserve it.

"Dillon..." she says, and as always, the sound of my name coming from her lips, warms me in a way that I used to despise but now can't get enough of.

Bridging the gap between us, I go to her and lift her head up to meet my eyes, wanting to make sure that whatever I say now, she's able to see because I don't want her to miss any of it.

The only way I'm going to get through to her, the only way to make her stay and not walk away after everything that just happened is for me to go all in. I need to lay everything I feel, everything I think out there for her even if she doesn't believe it. The last time I stood before her like this, I made the decision to let her know the real me and now, I need to stick to that, even if the real me is too much for her to handle.

I don't want to be anything other than completely real with this girl.

"Caddy, I'm sorry. When he said those things about you, I couldn't handle it. It bothered me at first, but when he said it again even worse than the first time, I lost it."

"Why didn't you just yell at him? Why did you have to beat him up?"

There's no answer for this, other than it's all I know and that's not good enough. I'm not sure why I didn't just rip into him and walk away. If I had then none of this would be happening now.

"I don't know. I just lost it."

"Do you lose it a lot?"

I lower my head and nod, her words getting to me more than I want to admit. I do lose my temper a lot and there's never really a good reason for it. Things just set me off and instead of thinking things through rationally, I always just let the anger consume me until there's nothing left but the rage.

"I can't do this anymore."

Reaching out as her eyes lower to the ground, I run my hand across her cheek and bring my other hand up to level her to me again. As painful as it is for me hearing her say that she's giving up, it pains me even more having her look away and I don't even want to start with how it feels inside my chest, the way everything is all torn up because I'm standing here and not even touching her the way I want to.

"You can't do what?"

"I liked you for you, Dillon. The way you were right from the start. I knew that you weren't a nice guy, I knew everything you did to people, but I still saw past all of that and liked you anyway. I didn't want you to be different, but then you decided that you needed to be."

"I did need to be different."

"Why?"

"For you because the person you talked to that first day wasn't someone worthy to even sit near you, let alone talk to you the way I did."

"Dillon, stop it."

"Stop what? Telling you the truth? I'm sorry. I can't do that."

"I need you to hear me!"

It's the first time I've ever heard her shout and even though she sounds the same to me as she always has, there's something completely different about this. Her words, it's like she's punched me in the stomach, that's how powerful they are.

All this time I've been going about things the wrong way. Cadence isn't the one that's deaf. I am. I've been able to hear her speak to me all this time, something that she doesn't have the luxury of doing with me, relying only on the move of my lips for understanding, but I haven't really heard a damn word she's said, despite my claims otherwise.

I've listened to her, been captivated by her, but never actually allowed myself to hear her.

"What do you need me to hear?" I ask but before she can answer, I place my finger to her lips. "I didn't hear you before, but I swear I'll do it now."

"Dillon, you don't need to be anyone else when you're with me. You only need to be you." She stops, taking a breath her eyes not giving any hint of what she's about to say next and I brace myself. "The parts of you that you hate so much, they're parts of you that I love because even though they're not so good, if you lost them completely, you'd lose you. I don't want that. You've been doing it with me a lot, thinking you have to act a certain way, say things differently, being someone other than you." Again she pauses and I wait, afraid to speak until she's done.

"I hate the fighting, the violence, the reactions you have. They scare me, but they're you. I don't want you to stop being you. It's why I can't do this anymore."

"You can't do what?"

"I can't do this. I can't be with you and watch you change because you think it's what I need or want. I can't be the reason you change or even lose yourself."

"But the way I am when I'm with you is better. You think that I'm changing into something I think you deserve and that's true, but for the first time in six years, Caddy, I'm changing into someone I can actually stand being around. I'm changing back into me."

"Dillon—"

"I love you—don't do this."

The way it feels letting those words slip, it's powerful and as much as I didn't want to admit to her, let alone myself, it's the truth. I'm in love with her or at least what I believe love to be. If saying those words is what stops her from doing what I know she's going to do then I'll say them as many times as I need to.

I can't let her walk away.

"I—I have to go. Goodbye Dillon."

She moves so quickly that in the time it takes me to adapt to the change in atmosphere, she's around the corner and I hear the door opening and closing behind her. Coming in here, I thought that if this is where things were going to go, I could stop them. Admitting the truth to her, telling her how I feel even though I know it's fast and it could possibly be too much to take was supposed to put things back together again.

It didn't do that. All it did is leave me facing something that I never wanted to again.

Being alone.

Chapter Twenty

Cadence

Falling back into my old routine, waking up in the morning, making my lunch and waiting for my mom to finish her daily ritual of spending an hour trying to tame her hair so that she could take me to school was easier than I expected it to be.

Sure, those were the parts of the routine that haven't changed with the pipes bursting but where I expected to wake up today and school to be the last place I wanted to go, it wasn't and things fell into a comfortable groove almost immediately.

The four days leading up to it weren't quite so easy.

Thursday, I didn't even bother going with my mom. I couldn't face what happened the day before and the way when I walked out on him, I bailed on the plan of having him spend the night. She knew there was more going on than I was telling her and in her usual way, she didn't let up on me until it all came spilling out.

"Caddy, I know you think that because I'm old, I don't notice things, but I've been watching you and I think there's more going on than you're admitting to."

Sticking to the decision I made, not to speak another word after walking out of the bathroom the day before, I start signing and after her first initial eyebrow raise, she sits down on the bed and waits until I'm finished.

I don't want to talk about it.

"Does it have something to do with Dillon?"

Yes and no.

"Caddy; you like this boy, don't you?"

That's such a silly question. Of course I like the boy. I wouldn't have gone to bat for him so much if I didn't like him. She knows this and since I know it's not what she really wants to know, I just give her the answer she's after.

Until yesterday afternoon I was his girlfriend.

"What happened yesterday afternoon?" she asks and I can tell she wants to say more, but she's giving me the space I need to get it all out on my own. It's her mom and teacher roles combined and I'm the guinea pig she's testing it on.

Tim said some things to Dillon, it set him off and he went after him. I couldn't handle it so I ran and everything blew up after that.

"What did Tim say?"

Not telling you that. You know I hate saying it.

She doesn't say anything for a few minutes and I wonder what she's thinking. She knows how I am about repeating nasty names back to her, how it makes me feel no better than the people who originally said them.

"So you're telling me Dillon defended you?"

I nod, not wanting to sign at all anymore.

"Maybe I was wrong about that boy after all."

Huh? She's the last person in the world to condone violence. She's half the reason I feel as strongly as I do about it and now she's admitting that what he did defending me was right? Since when?

Violence is never right, Mom. You're the one that taught me that. *I sign and she nods her head in agreement.*

"Yes. I'm the one that told you that and as wrong as what he did is and there can be no disputing that it was wrong, defending you will never be wrong to me."

Great, so my mom's on Dillon's side. It makes what I did walking away that much worse.

"Did he do something to you? Is that why the two of you aren't together anymore?"

When I admitted that Dillon and I were dating, I expected her to get mad at me. I know she's not a mean person, but she is my mom and hiding the fact that I'm dating from her, I have to figure she would have had some kind of response to, but so far she hasn't said a word about it. It's like she knew all along.

He didn't do anything to me.

Except tell me he loves me and plead with me not to leave him.

"Well, I'm glad to hear that. So the reason you don't want to go today, it's because of seeing him again?"

I nod weakly and she sighs.

"Is there more going on that you aren't telling me?"

"Can I ask you something?" I say, this time speaking aloud.

"You can ask me anything sweetheart."

"Is it wrong to have someone change for you?"

"I don't believe it's wrong for someone to change, but a person shouldn't do it just to please someone else. I think if they really want to change and be a different person, it has to be for them alone."

"What happens if you like the person just way they are, faults and all? Is that wrong?"

"Caring about someone, it's never easy. Seeing past their imperfections; the things you don't necessarily like, it speaks to the size of your heart and the person you are. That can never be wrong."

"Mom, I think I screwed everything up."

"Do you want to tell me why you think that?"

"Dillon, before I walked away from him, he said some things and I think I should have stayed but I didn't and now I think I messed up."

"What did he say?"

"That he wanted to be someone that could be worthy of me. He wanted to change for me, but at the same time, he wanted to be someone he hasn't been in a long time."

"So he was changing for both of you."

I nod slowly and she smiles, though it's so small it doesn't even look like a real smile at all.

"Dillon cares a great deal about you. You've been a good influence on him and something tells me that what you're feeling, believing you screwed up, he's feeling even more so. With everything you've told me about him since the two of you started hanging out, I think that's his default setting."

"What do you mean?"

"The bullying, fighting, name calling; all of the things he does that no one around him can tolerate, they're all his way of dealing with his life because he hasn't been taught the right way to handle it. Before you came along, I would venture to say that he didn't give much thought to any of that and was just surviving the only way he knew how. When you came along all of that changed. Now he feels as though all of those things are screwing everything up."

"He's not a screw up."

"We know that, but I don't think he's quite there yet."

"Is this where you tell me that he needs someone to show him the way?"

She laughs and I can't help but smile weakly in return.

"No, I'm not going to tell you that. Putting that much pressure on one person isn't right. Dillon has to learn how to do this on his own. He has to realize that not every step he takes is the wrong one in his own time and way."

"Are you going to let me stay home?"

"For today, I think I am, but you know the rules. No leaving the house, no answering the door and I'll be checking in as often as I can."

She wasn't so accommodating for my last day. She woke me up early and we went through the motions of our daily routine, though I was definitely not feeling it as the majority of the time I was slumping along and wanting to just go back and hide under my covers. Not coming back out until all visions of Dillon Murphy were erased from my memory altogether.

Going to class, seeing the seat beside me empty, it just made me want to turn around and run out, until I was as far away from the room and the school as possible.

If I thought staying in class without him was going to be the worst of it, I'd been wrong. Sitting in the middle of the desk was a piece of paper and it didn't take a brain surgeon to know who it was from.

This is the beginning of something that no matter where we go from here, will never have an end.

- D

There were no more notes that day and no matter where I went in the school, even the locker room where I expected to at least catch a glimpse of him in passing while I hid out, he was nowhere to be found. I didn't want to be let down by it but I was. With the way my mom talked to me the day before, making it seem that there wasn't anything in the world that couldn't be fixed, I hoped I would have gotten the chance to do it even though my feelings haven't changed.

I'm still wary of the reason for him changing. I don't want that kind of pressure on either of us and no matter how badly I want to change the way I think so that we could work through this, I know it won't happen.

We're no good for each other and it has nothing to do with him being a fighter and me being deaf. It's the way we look at the world. For all of our similarities, there are things that we won't ever see the same and they're big enough that staying together knowing it would be wrong.

So here I am now, after a weekend spent crying in my room, saying goodbye to something that never really had a chance to be anything, back at my own school and miles away from the school where the troubled boy that has my heart is. Where I should be focusing on my friends, my work and everything that comes with being back here, all I can think about is prom and all the plans that we never got around to making.

Dillon's wrong. What we saw as a beginning that day at the ravine, it wasn't something with no end. It had a very clear end and the way things are now proves it. No matter how much I miss him, how I wish things were different, it has to be this way. We can never go back.

This is our ending.

Dillon

It feels so fucking good to be back.

Walking the halls and seeing people duck away, some of them even turning and running from me, it brings me an immeasurable amount of pleasure. This is where I belong.

I might have gotten sidetracked for a while there, thinking I could be someone different, do better and be a person that would eventually mean something to the world, but not anymore. That craziness left the day that Cadence walked out of Wexfield and with her not planning to return, I didn't have to worry about it coming back.

The first thing I made sure to do the minute I got here this morning was search out Tim and the others and make amends. Kayden tried to stop me when he saw where I was headed, but just like I'm done with Cadence, I'm also done with him. He can go back to his stupid girlfriend and leave me alone. I don't need him. I never did.

Now that I'm square with my friends, we can get back to what's really important. Today that means finding Eric and finally making him pay for what happened two weeks ago, and also for being the reason I'd gotten thrown into the class to begin with.

I can't wait to make that stupid little baby pay.

"So, you and Ames; you back together yet?" Tim asks when I've finally escaped class and made my way into the hall.

"No, not planning on it either. I'm sick of her shit."

"So you're going stag to prom?"

"Not going at all."

"Dude, you gotta go. Coach expects us all to be there. Solidarity and all that."

How could I forget that? He mentioned it during practice last week. With everything that happened at the last dance, he felt that for this one, we needed to show a united front, showing the world and Daniels that even though we hated each other, we were gonna do what was right for business. The only business I even give a damn about—football.

The idea of getting dressed up like a monkey and parading around a dance with a bunch of people I can't stand makes me sick, but there's no way I'm going to go against what Coach wants. If it wasn't for him, I would have been kicked off the team completely last fall and there's no way I'm risking it again.

"It's all about the after party right? I'll suffer through it as long as we're planning on partying hard later."

I've actually got another fight coming up that night, but I'm not about to admit that to Tim. There's only one person in the world besides me and my father that knows anything about my extracurricular activities and with her gone, it's gone back to being buried down deep again.

Maybe the after party will be worth it after all. I'm pretty sure after the fight I'm gonna need to get good and wasted and maybe if I get drunk enough, I can find a girl willing enough to help me banish Cadence and her stupid voice from my brain once and for all.

"Well, I asked Eve to go with me, so if you wanna ride with, you're more than welcome."

"No thanks, man. You've been talking about getting into her pants for a while now. Wouldn't wanna be a buzzkill."

Tim stops and following where he's now pointing, I see why. Standing at the end of the hall is the very person we've been looking for. He wasn't in class this morning so I was beginning to think he wasn't gonna show today, but now that I see him, my day is looking up considerably.

It's time to get a little payback.

"It's about time, I've been waiting to smash that little punk all week." Tim says and I grin. He's not the only one. I might have gotten sidetracked for a while, but I'm definitely back on track now. No more distractions for me. It's time to get back to doing what I do best.

Time to bring another stupid moron to his knees.

"You go that way and corner him. When he tries to run, which we both know he will, I'll come from around the other side. Got it?"

"Yeah man, let's do this shit."

Watching as Tim takes off down the hall exactly the way I told him, I veer off down the opposite hall in order to make my way around. Picking up speed until I'm jogging, I don't stop until I turn and see Eric boxed in against the lockers and Tim hovering over him. It reminds me of the way things went the first time we picked on him, Kayden choosing him in an effort to get Isabelle's attention.

He's wearing the same frightened expression and the sight of it, where before would have made me happy, actually turns my stomach. As much as I want this, want to pound on this kid for all the shit he'd brought down on me just by breathing the same air as me when he shouldn't be, the look on his face, it stops me cold.

This is the guy that Cadence got hurt over, the person she cares about. If I go at him right now, it will hurt her when she finds out. There's something about the idea of her hurting in any way, despite her walking away and ignoring the hell out of me that doesn't sit right with me.

I can't hurt her, even if hurting this kid is exactly what will make me feel better right now. Shit. The girl isn't even here anymore and she's still reaching out and bringing me down.

I've never wanted to hate someone so much in my life.

Shaking off the thought of the brown eyed girl I can't seem to get out of my head, I move forward until I'm standing directly in front of Eric. When he looks up, his eyes blinking rapidly and the sweat from the fear he feels pooling at the top of his hairline, I smile. All thoughts of the girl that left me behind are gone and all that's left is the same old rage that's been there from the start.

I'm definitely going to enjoy this.

At least that's how it is until I land the first punch into his stomach, his body bending with the impact, Tim hitting him with another three in quick succession, bringing the kid to the floor.

The way his hands go to his face in an attempt to block whatever we're about to do next, it stops me from going any further. Right now he looks the way Cadence did the first day when Amy threw her to the floor. A way I never want to see again. Watching Eric, the way he's crumpled on the floor, I should feel great, having done what I set out to do but that's not what's going on at all.

It's not Eric that I'm allowing Tim to beat on anymore. It's not him I just leveled with the punch.

It's her.

Chapter Twenty-One

Cadence

The first thing I notice when I turn off the sidewalk into my driveway is that there's someone sitting on my front step. My heart betraying me like always, skips a beat seeing the form, but moving closer, I see that it's not who I thought and the skip is replaced by nothingness.

Where my heart wanted to believe for a second that the person sitting so comfortably on the step was Dillon, it's not, but it is someone he goes to school with and also the last person I expect to see sitting here. It's not shocking that it's him, but considering that he's never been here before or even interacted with me outside of school, it's definitely unexpected.

Eric Carmen, leaning against the bottom step, his head facing up toward the sky, looking so comfortable it looks like he belongs there.

"Eric?"

Lifting his hand, he waves and despite the emptiness I've been feeling all day, I smile in response. It looks like my plan of heading inside, going to my room and hiding under my covers is shot to hell.

What are you doing here? I sign and he wastes no time coming back with an answer.

"Got bored waiting for my mom to come home, decided to take the bus and come visit."

Does she know you're here?

"Yeah, of course. She'd kill me if I didn't let her know."

The way his lips part and his body shakes, I can tell he's laughing so pasting on the best happy smile I can, I laugh with him though it pains me to do it. I don't want to fake anything and especially not with Eric.

Well come in. Mom had to stay late for some meeting so I'm on my own for dinner.

"Not anymore you aren't." he says and smiles before I turn and he follows me into the house.

I'm not sure I believe his reason for being here. There's something about it that just doesn't seem right. I'm pretty sure there's a million other places that he could have gone if he was bored being home alone, ones much closer. Coming all this way on the bus, it just seems like a total waste of money.

It's that thinking that makes me turn on him the minute we're both in the kitchen and I've passed him a soda from the fridge. Leveling him with a look that I hope says that I want the truth, I get right to the point.

Why are you really here?

"I told you..."

No, what you told me is a lie. Why are you really here?

His eyes fall away until they're resting on the table in front of him, his lips completely out of my view. Just as I'm about to ask him to lift his head so I'll be able to see his answer, he lifts his hands and starts signing. It's messy and I'm not entirely sure what he's saying is actually what he means to say, but I get the basic gist.

You wanted to talk to me about something?

"Ask you something." He signs again, this time getting the words right.

Why didn't you just tell me that before?

He signs his response again, this time shaking his hands nervously.

Whatever he's got to ask me makes him nervous enough that he's willing to lie about it. I'm not sure how I feel about that. I'm the last one he should feel the need to lie to.

He signs again and though I get the point, for the first time since the bathroom with Dillon, I want to rely more on speaking then I do signing.

"Can you look up?"

He does as I ask and repeats the words he signed to me, letting me know that he's nervous because he's never done what he's about to do before.

"What do you want to ask me?"

His answer despite his nervousness, evident with the way he's picking at his fingers yet still looking straight at me, is immediate and definitely not what I'd been expecting when he said he had something he wanted to ask.

"Will you go to prom with me?"

"Aren't you a junior?"

He nods and I'm thankful that I remembered what my mom told me. With all of them being in the same class and it being different than it is at my school, I sometimes forget that he's younger than some of the others.

"Why do you want to go the prom?"

"Because I've never done it before and I can't hide forever."

He's got a point about that. He can't hide forever even though Dillon and his friends sure go out of their way to make sure that's exactly what he does. Well, they did before Dillon broke away from them. Hating the fact that I'm thinking about Dillon when there's a guy standing in front of me asking me to be his date to prom, I shake the thoughts away and focus my attention back on Eric.

"I don't go to your school. Why don't you ask someone there?"

"No one wants to go with a person like me. You're all I've got."

His eyes as he admits this, they lower again, but his head stays level, as if he's afraid to look at me but not bothered enough to turn away. Something that right now I'm thankful for because turning away would completely ruin what he's here to do.

It hurts me inside that people treat him the way they do. If they could only see the kind of person he is, the soft heart he has and his willingness to help anyone, maybe he would be able to get a date to his prom with someone that actually goes to his school and not have to reach outside for one.

"There's one person that wants to go with a person like you." When his eyes raise, I smile and move toward him. Leaning across the table, I bop my finger on his nose and laugh. "I do. Looks like you've got a date to prom buddy."

"Really?"

"Yes really."

The awkwardness that I'd seen earlier, the picking at the corners of his fingers, the way his hand came up to his mouth and he started nibbling on his nails, it's all gone now and all that's left is a smile. Despite the fact that I'm not sure going to prom is the smartest move considering who's sure to be there, I'm not taking it back. If me going to prom with him makes him this happy, then the reservations I've got about it don't matter.

Eric being happy is what matters. I can always talk myself into it later when he goes home. Surely having a couple of days to come to terms with going back there, to the place where my life was turned upside down would take all of the worries I have right now away.

Right?

Dillon

The last thing I want to do after getting out of practice is stop and talk to anyone, but no sooner do I make my way across the field and to the parking lot then I hear my name being called. The quick getaway I had planned the minute Coach said we could leave falls apart around me, leaving me even more pissed off than I was earlier.

After Tim leveled him with another couple punches, I put an end to it. I can tell it confused the hell out of him considering what I said about dealing with Eric personally, but I didn't care. After looking down at Eric on the ground and seeing Cadence's face, I'd seen more than enough.

It left me in a sour mood for the rest of the day. Where I saw her instead of Eric, it happened at other random times too, which did nothing for my already dwindling mood. I wanted to forget about her and everything that came along with our short time together, but it seems that my head doesn't want to let me.

It's my heart that doesn't want to let me and I know it, but since I'm trying to go back to appearing as though I have no heart; that's the last thing I'm gonna admit to.

Hearing my name again and this time unable to ignore it as it's closer, I turn and come face to face with the last person I expected to see.

Ms. Taylor is walking toward me and where I expect to see an angry expression on her face after everything that went down with her daughter and me, there isn't one. She's not smiling at me or anything, but wearing no real expression at all is better than the alternative.

"What's up Ms. T?"

"I came by the locker room to see you but your coach told me you didn't head in with the others. I was hoping to get a couple minutes of your time to talk about something."

If she wants to talk to me about Cadence, I don't want any part of it. With the girl haunting me around every corner all day, the last thing I want is to bring her up willingly. She'd managed to stay out of my head the entire time I was on the field. I want to keep it that way.

"What's up?"

"I know that you probably don't want to talk to me about it, but it's about Cadence."

Yep, she's right. I don't want to talk and definitely not with her mom of all people. Up until a week ago this woman despised me as much as the rest of the faculty. It's what I want her to go back to doing now. The way her eyes look remind me of her daughter and I've had enough of it. I don't want another Taylor woman looking through me.

I don't open my mouth and tell her any of this though. I do the one thing I'm fighting so hard against. I open myself up to talking.

"What about her?"

"Despite trying to appear otherwise, it's obvious that she's not acting like herself. I was wondering if you could shed some light on it."

"I haven't talked to her since Wednesday afternoon, so I'm not sure there's a whole lot I can tell you."

"Why don't you let me be the judge of that?"

Great. Now I'm going to have to rehash everything that happened with Caddy and watch her expression change from the one she's now giving me to one of hate. There's no way she can hear everything that happened with us and not be pissed as hell at me. I asked her daughter out without going through her first and then I went ahead and acted like a total asshole, ruining it and her in the process.

I've got enough hate for everything that happened and my fault in it all on my own. I don't need hers too.

"What exactly do you want me to say?"

"You can start by telling me when you decided that you wanted to be with her."

The answer to that question is easy for me, but I'm not sure telling her the truth is the way to go, so I lie.

"The day I asked her out."

She turns toward the school, not even acknowledging my answer and I start to think she got what she came for and she's finally gonna let me leave, at least until she turns back and smiles.

Looks like I'm not getting out of here anytime soon.

"Come with me. If we're gonna talk, I think its best that we do it inside and not out in the middle of a parking lot."

Doing as she says, I follow behind her until we've walked around to the front and into the office. A place I know a lot better than I should.

"Everyone's gone home for the night, so I don't think using Principal Daniels office will be a problem." She says as she heads down the hall and disappears into the room.

The right thing to do would be to follow her and get this over with, but I'm sick of doing the right thing. The few times I tried, it's always come back and bit me in the ass. I'm not looking to make a repeat performance.

"Are you coming?" she calls out and I know its decision time. I can walk out of here now, not looking back until I'm in my car and halfway down the road away from this entire situation, or I can go into the room and get this over with even though just the thought of opening myself up and talking about Cadence is enough to make me wanna throw up.

Heading toward the office, remembering the last time I'd been here, three days before she walked into my world and turned it upside down, I want to kick myself for choosing the wrong thing and I'm about to literally do it when she speaks again.

"Dillon, I know everything."

Wasn't expecting that.

"What do you mean?"

"Cadence told me about what happened between the two of you before she left. Well, as much as I could yank out of her anyway."

"If you already know, why are you talking to me? Like I said, if she's different, it's got nothing to do with me. Maybe something else happened the last two days she was here or over the weekend."

"Can I tell you something?"

"Do I have a choice?"

"You always have a choice, but something tells me if you didn't want to hear what I have to say, you wouldn't be standing in the room right now."

She's got me there. I want to know every single thing she's willing to tell me and I don't care if it makes me look like a gigantic pussy or not. When it comes to this girl, I'd be willing to be just about anything for a scrap of information about her.

"What do you wanna tell me?" I ask, finally throwing myself down into the chair across from her.

"My daughter spent the majority of the weekend locked in her room. She doesn't think I'm aware because I didn't go out of my way to call attention to it, but she was crying. Her heart is hurting Dillon and while I'm pretty sure that right now you're thinking I'm about to lay a guilt trip on you, I'm going to do the opposite."

Cadence crying is wrong. Knowing she spent the weekend doing it because of what happened with us is even worse. I know there's nothing else that happened to her that could have caused her to cry. I made sure of it. I warned every person away from her those last two days because I didn't want her to have to feel any more broken then I already made her.

"I don't follow."

"Cadence wasn't crying because of something you did to her, Dillon. She was crying because of what she thinks she did to you."

Huh—what? She's got to be joking. Cadence doing anything to hurt me is crazy. Sure, I asked her not to go, telling her I loved her, but she had every right to do what she did and leave. I knew the way she felt about things and I completely disregarded it to act like an imbecile.

"She didn't do anything to me."

"I figured that would be your answer."

"Ms. T; what happened that day, it's on me. I went after Tim knowing I was going to scare her. I knew she hated fighting and with everything she tried to do to help with my dad and what he's got me doing, it should have been enough to stop me, but it wasn't. I couldn't see anything but making him pay for the things he said."

"Can you tell me exactly what it was that he said?"

"She didn't tell you?"

She laughs and I'm confused. How there is anything funny right now is beyond me.

"Cadence hates admitting when people call her names. There's something about repeating the words that make her feel that she's as bad as the people saying it. As if repeating it somehow means she believes it. So, no, she didn't tell me."

"When he showed up, he asked if I minded walking away from the retard so he could talk to me. I reacted to that one, but that's not what got me in his face. It didn't make me attack him."

"What else was said?"

"I told him that we, Caddy and me, didn't wanna hear what he said to say and he ripped on her for being deaf. I couldn't handle it after that. I lost it."

"Thank you. I'm sure it wasn't easy, considering your friendship with the guy in question."

My friendship with the guy. That's a joke. There's no friendship with him and that was obvious today with the way I reacted to what we did to Eric. I'm over doing that now, despite wanting to be the way I used to be and the only thing between Tim and me now is familiarity.

As long as he's with me, I don't have to be alone.

"Can I be honest with you and have it stay between us?"

"If there is something you want to speak to me about in confidence, of course. I will never speak of it, not even with my daughter. That is who you want me to keep it from right?"

"No, I want it kept from everyone else. I think Caddy already knows it anyway."

"Well what is it?"

"The other day, Kayden said something to me. At the time I didn't pay much attention to it because well, your daughter was there and when she's around, I don't really pay attention the way I should. Anyway, he said something about realizing the day in the parking lot with Isabelle that he was tired of the way things were. When I got here today, I thought things were going to go back to the way they were before. I even tried to make them the way they used to be, but I can't do it."

"Because what Kayden experienced is now what you're facing?"

"Exactly. I get what he was talking about now. I knew it last week, but again, I ignored and buried it because it just didn't seem important at the time. The truth is, I haven't been right for a while. What happened at Homecoming, it was up to me to see it through and there was a second there where I almost didn't do it."

"Why didn't you follow through on it?"

"Because it's not what I do. I'm not the good guy, Ms. T. I'm pretty sure you know that; especially now."

"Here's what I know. You're a misguided boy who when faced with the right decision backs down because doing the right thing is harder than going through with the wrong one. You've spent the majority of your life having excuses made for you and your behavior and it's made you entitled. For whatever reason, you're starting to see it yourself and for a while even wanted to change it."

"Except I didn't change anything."

"But you did. You changed. I know what happened to Eric today. He told me about it after class, when he was sure you and Tim were not in the vicinity. Where you would have been the one hurting him before, that's not at all what happened. Tim will be dealt with, but it was your behavior that stood out."

"Did he tell you that too?"

"As a matter of fact he did. He said that you're the reason he was able to get up and walk away. You may have gone into it with a different outcome in mind, but something stopped you and you want to know what that something is?"

"Your daughter haunting me?" I answer, realizing too late that I just gave away the real reason the stuff with Eric ended up the way it did. She laughs and I just shake my head. Now that it's out there it's not like I can take it back. If she finds it funny there's not a whole lot I can do to stop her.

"No, though I can see that happening. It's you, Dillon. Your desire to do the right thing. As hard as you try to bottle it, it's not letting you anymore and it has nothing at all to do with how you feel about my daughter or the impact she may have made on your life. It's all on you. You were ready for the change."

"That's not right at all."

"She was right about you. She told me what you said to her the last time you spoke. That you wanted to change for her because you want to be worthy of her. What you need to realize is you were worthy of her the whole time. You just couldn't see it because you've buried yourself so deep in self-hatred and the way you think things should be that it's impossible to see much else."

"Even if what you're saying is the truth, what does it matter now?"

"Before I answer your question, can you answer one for me?"

"If I can."

"How did it feel today, walking away from Eric the way you did?"

"Pretty damn good."

"Then you've answered your own question. It matters because despite her being gone, the two of you having no contact, you're staying true to what you told her from the start. You're becoming the person you've always been, the one that's been buried for six years under a weight no child should ever have to carry."

I don't want to admit it, but she's right. I told Cadence the reason for me changing was her, but it wasn't. I made it about her, putting the weight of it on her but it was me the entire time. I'm just like Kayden. I got tired of being someone I couldn't stand looking at in the mirror every morning and was just looking for the right motivation to change it. I found it in her and I've been changing ever since, even though my reason is no longer there.

"Her not being here, I'm not okay with it. I'm not okay with the way we left things." I confess, not sure where it comes from but needing to get it out before it eats me alive.

"Well, if you're not happy with the way things are, you know what you have to do, don't you?"

Yeah I do. I need to fix it. I need to go to her and I need to make her understand everything that I've learned here today, what I've been learning since before she even left four days ago. I can't do it though. I ran out of chances.

"I can't fix it this time, Ms. T. I tried that day to make her see the truth, the way I felt about her and it wasn't enough to make her stay."

"You want to know a secret? A little bit of information I've picked up over the years?"

"Sure."

"Love isn't about trying, failing and giving up because it didn't work out the way you wanted it too. It's continuing to try despite it."

Chapter Twenty-Two

Dillon

I'm not the guy that tries. If it doesn't come easy to me there's just never been a point. That's probably because I've been handed everything for so long that trying never entered into the equation.

Two weeks.

Fourteen days.

One girl.

That's all it took for everything I've spent the last six years believing and feeling secure in, to change. I'm not sure from one second to the next if I'm moving up or down, forward or backward, but what I do know is that everything I've been through these last two weeks, I wouldn't change for the world.

It started out so simple. Spy the new girl in the special needs class, get her to talk to me, bring her as close as possible to me and then completely destroy her for my own amusement. That's not what ended up happening at all. If anything, she brought me in as close as she could and been the one to destroy me.

Who knew that being destroyed could feel so good?

After talking with her mom, putting everything out there and being on the receiving end of support and understanding for the first time in my life, I'm clear on what I've got to do now. I need to do what Ms. T said and I've got to try.

Cadence walking away from me can't be the end of this. I can't let it be the end of me or of us. I might not be all that familiar with the way I feel about her, never feeling like this about any girl I've ever been involved with, but I know enough not to turn away from it just because for the first time in years, I don't have all the control.

That's what it's been about all this time. I need to be in control. When I'm in a fight, whether one of the ones my father plans or the ones at school, I control it. Even that day in the parking lot with Kayden, even though he took me down, I was still in control because I didn't let it end there. When I pick on kids, especially ones like Isabelle and Eric, I feed off the control I have over their fate.

When I'm in control, I'm strong and that's what I've been holding on to for six years. It ends now. If it means that I have to appear weak for the first time in my life, then so be it. I care about this girl, more than I've ever cared about anyone in my pathetic existence and I'm willing to give it all up to prove it. Not only to her, but to me too.

The ride over here, I tried to work out what I would say when I saw her again. How I wanted to start things off and even how I would react to her response. I even had the entire way it would end mapped out. I wouldn't settle for anything less than her being in my arms again.

Pulling up into her driveway, thankful that I managed to beat her mom home even though we left at the same time, I put the car in park and watch as the door opens and two bodies walk out on to the steps. One I expect to see, I mean it's her that I'm here to see, but the other one surprises me. The knot in my stomach seeing them together gets even worse as I watch her wrap her arms around him in a hug.

The doubt creeps in as I wonder if I've been deluding myself all along. Eric is the one standing on her front step with his arms around her and I'm the chump sitting in the car staring them down, wanting nothing more than to get out of the car and slam his face off the side of the house.

Am I too late? Did Cadence not feel the same as I did during our time together and Eric is the one she's wanted this whole time?

There's no denying that he would be a better fit for her. He understands her in a way that despite wanting to, I don't think I ever will. I've seen him signing to her before, which means he knows enough about her to want to make things easier. If I really want to be with this girl, learning all that I could about her disability and ways I can make it easier on her should have been the first step.

Instead I'd been the idiot and jumped ahead fifty steps. Yeah, Eric is definitely a better fit for her even though I can't stand the thought of it. She's mine and no matter what happens now, she's always going to be mine. I need her. She makes me want to be a better person. She makes me want to be me again.

When they separate, I see her eyes lock on the car and her forehead creases. She's spotted me. Now not only do I look like a stalker, sitting here watching them the way I have been, but I'm also bothering her.

I want to turn the key in the ignition and leave. She may have caught me in her driveway, but since we haven't spoken and she's not making a move to come closer, I can still pull out and take off. I don't do that though. Instead, I keep her mom's words running through my head and open the door and get out, not stopping until I'm directly behind them.

It's time to face this head on. Even if the way I pictured it going in my head isn't the way it turns out.

Looking up, seeing her eyes on me, I smile, hoping that with the small action, I can somehow put her at ease. I didn't exactly want an audience doing this, but now that he's here, I know he won't leave until he knows she's safe.

"Can we talk?"

Her hands start moving and it takes me no time at all to see what she's doing. Her lips are frozen in the straightest line and she's making no move to separate them, which means whatever she's signing, it's not meant for me. She knows I don't know how to sign. It only makes me wanna kick myself more for not even attempting to learn.

It's only when Eric turns and faces me that it all becomes clear.

"She has nothing to say to you."

"Well, I've got some things to say to her."

"Dillon, you really want me to tell her that?"

"If she can read lips, she already knows."

Eric turns back to her and I watch them as they silently carry on a conversation. It bugs me. It's like watching two people speaking in a different language and wondering if they're saying something bad about you. I know I said I don't care what people think of me, but Cadence is different. I actually give a shit what she thinks and I hate the idea of her saying anything right now that might be bad.

"Can you please just say this out loud?" I ask, no longer willing to sit here and watch the two of them go back and forth.

Eric turns back to me and takes the final two stairs down until he's on the ground beside me.

"I was just telling her goodbye and to be careful with you. I don't know what you're doing here, but I don't feel right leaving her alone with you."

"I'm not going to hurt her."

"You've done that enough already don't ya think?" he asks and it takes every bit of restraint I have not to punch him. He has no idea what's going on with me and Cadence so he needs to butt out and keep his opinions to himself.

"None of your business. You don't know anything."

"So you didn't single her out a couple weeks ago?"

His words make my blood run cold. How the hell does he know about the plan? The only people that knew what I wanted to do in the beginning were Tim, Amy and the others and I'm damn sure they didn't go out of their way to tell Eric about it.

"You not arguing means I'm right. You did single her out. You wanted to hurt her."

"Does she know?" I ask, thankful that Eric is facing toward me more than her so she isn't able to see what he's saying. If she doesn't know, I don't want her to know. It will ruin everything.

"No. Seeing how screwed up she is over what happened with you, I figured it was smarter to keep it to myself."

I want to breathe a sigh of relief so bad I can taste it, but I don't. As thankful as I am that he didn't tell her, I know it's only a matter of time before it does come out. It means I need to be the one to tell her the truth, even if it screws up the entire way I had this planned in my head. I won't try to fix this by keeping things from her.

She was a game to me in the beginning, but that didn't last long once I got to know her. She pulled me to her in a completely different way and now that she has, I never want to look at her like a game ever again.

"How long have you been playing her?"

"A day or two at most. I tried to do it and couldn't. I don't expect you to believe me, but this is about more than a game now."

His eyes lift, surprised with my answer, but his body tells a different story altogether. He doesn't trust me even though for the first time since I've known him, I'm telling the truth.

"She said she'd be fine with you, so I'm gonna get out of here, but Dillon, don't hurt her. She's had enough of the stuff you and your friends do. You wanna pick on me, go ahead, but don't do it to her."

He walks away before I can respond and my eyes instantly make their way back up to where she's standing on the step waiting. When our eyes meet, she motions behind her into the house and I make my way up and inside, not moving once I'm inside. Hearing the click of the door behind me, I turn and again flash a tiny smile her way.

I need to break the ice and I need to do it quick.

She moves and before I know it, she's going around the corner into the kitchen and I'm jogging to catch up with her. When I see that she's seated at the table, a paper in front of her, I follow her lead and sit down to her right. It's only when I'm completely seated and comfortable that she slides the paper over to me and I read what's on the page.

What are you doing here?

"We need to talk." I say, passing the paper back to her and waiting as she starts writing across the page. I know that I've earned her doing things this way again, but I really hate that she's not speaking to me, especially with the way I feel about the sound of her voice. Right now I need to hear it. Hearing her will make me right again.

What do we need to talk about?

Here goes nothing.

"I attacked Eric today. With you gone, I thought it would be easy sliding back into my old routine, so I went after him. Landing the first hit on him, it didn't make me feel right at all. It felt wrong. All I could see when I hit him was you."

Is that supposed to make me feel good? You saw me when you were beating up my friend?

"No Caddy, it's not supposed to make you feel good. It's supposed to make you hate me. Make you see that what you saw in me weeks ago, it was wrong from the start. I really am the asshole everyone makes me out to be. The way I make myself out to be."

That's a lie and an excuse.

I can't argue with that. She's right. I'm on my default setting right now and I need to stop. No more excuses.

"I thought in the beginning that me changing, it was because of you. I had to change in order to be good enough for you. The thing is, you were right. I didn't have to change for you, it was just easier throwing it all on you. I didn't think at all about what that kind of pressure would do to someone. What it would do to you."

And you know now?

"Yeah I do. I wasn't always an asshole. I think I might've been a pretty decent guy before, but I let things and people change me. I used you as my excuse to be better, but I wanted to be better all on my own."

If that's true, why did you attack Eric today?

"To feel something again, even if it was the wrong something. To deny what I just told you."

Okay.

Her response isn't much and seeing the one word on the paper should just make me quit while I'm ahead, but I can't do that. I made a plan to come here and try to make things right, walking away wouldn't solve anything but put us right back where we were before.

"Caddy, I miss you. I don't want to miss you. I want to just go back to school and forget you exist, but I can't do it. You're there in my head, in the school. Every damn corner I take, there you are, your words on repeat. I can't escape you. I don't want to escape you. Not anymore."

What do you want me to say?

"I want you to tell me the truth. Can I fix this? If I walk out right now, am I ever going to be able to come back? After everything that's happened, can we be friends the way I wanted to be in the beginning?"

She sits completely still, her head facing down toward the paper, the pen dangling in her hand, no intent to write in sight. It physically hurts watching her like this. The silence is deafening. I just want her to say something, write anything so this torture can end.

After minutes pass and I come to terms with the fact that she's never going to answer me, I try one more thing. So far, everything I've told her is the truth, but there's still one thing she doesn't know and even though it might mean she'll be done with me forever, I need to make sure she knows it.

I need to be able to leave her, no matter what the outcome knowing that I left nothing unspoken.

Sliding the paper out from under her hand, not wanting to reach out and touch her so she can read my lips, I reach across and slide the pen out of her limp fingers and start writing, not looking up once until it's all out there.

When I walked into your mom's class the first day and saw you, after I got over how good looking I thought you were, I focused on just what was wrong with you that made you end up in the class. I decided that day to talk to you, get you to open up to me, even make you like me so that I could screw with you in the end. You were a game to me. I didn't know at the time how I was gonna do it, like what I would do to you to end it, but I wanted you to hurt.

I see her face drop the minute she reads the words and I know I've put the final nail in my coffin. Any hope of getting her to forgive me for all the shit I did that final week is now blown to shit because of the way it all began. I did the right thing telling her the truth, but that right thing didn't give me the calm I wanted.

Doing the right thing this time, knowing that I hurt her—again, it made me sick inside.

Whoever said that the truth will set you free was full of shit.

Cadence

His words, what he wrote to me, I already knew all of this. No one had to tell me, it's just something I knew all on my own. I've heard my mom talk about Dillon, the way he is, the things he does, so him seeing me that first day and choosing to play a game to keep himself entertained, it's not surprising.

With the way I feel about him, there's no way his words won't get to me. They hurt, because like I told him when we got into it a couple of weeks ago, I think there's more to him buried underneath, but not enough to change anything.

I should probably hate him, but I can't. He's standing here admitting to things that are probably better left quiet. Picking on Eric, playing a game with me, wanting me to hurt the same way he does, you don't admit to those things unless you've got nothing left to lose. I believe everything he's telling me despite the nagging voice inside that wants me to think this is just another game.

So after a few minutes of complete quiet, where I process everything he's said and done since he showed up in my driveway earlier, I do the only thing left to do. If he's gonna stand here now, putting everything on the line in order to tell me the truth, it's time I do the same.

Picking the pen up off the table and flipping the sheet over so that I've got a free space to write, I let the words pour out of me. I don't know what he's going to think, but this, what I'm writing to him now, good or bad has to be the end of it. Walking away from him should have done it, but it didn't. This has to be it now.

I'm deaf, Dillon. Not blind. I know what you thought about me the first day. I show up in a class full of special needs kids, it's obvious that I would have been one of them. It must have felt like Christmas for you that day. You had someone new to pick on.

I get it. It hurts hearing it, but I get it.

I miss you too. You're not the only one that's haunted. It should have been easy to get back to my life here, going back to school and hanging out with my friends, but I haven't been able to separate myself from the last two weeks and I'm not sure I'm ever gonna be able to.

You're not the only one that changed during those two weeks together. I did too. I don't know if we can fix this, but the only way that this is your last visit here is if you let it be. The same thing goes for the friend thing. It only changes if you want it to change.

There's so much that I want to put on the paper, but the words won't come, at least not yet, so I just slide it across the table to him. It's going to have to be enough for now.

When his eyes finish scanning over the paper, he slides his hand across the table until his fingers are barely resting on top of mine. As I look up his lips start moving and just like every other time he's spoken to me, I'm locked in place watching, completely unable to look away.

"You mean it?"

Nodding, I watch as his lips lift in a smile.

"Will you go to prom with me?"

I shake my head slowly and using my free hand I reach for the paper, knowing that he's going to take this the wrong way and needing to explain before things get out of hand. Dillon might be different, but things just don't change overnight and with one misunderstanding already happening between us because of something I said, I'm not eager to repeat it with another one.

I can't go with you because Eric asked me and I said yes. I want to do this for him. He deserves it.

He sighs, pulling his hand away from mine and raking it through his hair.

"You know he likes you right? He asked you because he has a thing for you."

I shake my head the second he says the words. He couldn't be more wrong. Eric doesn't have a thing for me other than wanting to be my friend. I don't know where he gets his information, but this is most definitely wrong.

"Shit. I sound like Amy right now."

Now he's lost me. What this has to do with Amy, I don't get but I hate anything remotely attached to me being compared to her.

What does that mean?

"When we were together, all I did was ride her about her jealousy. I hated the way she always thought every girl on the planet wanted to get in my pants. Pissed me off huge." As I nod my head, he continues. "Your mom told me that Eric likes you, so I swear it's not jealousy. Well, it is a little, but it's more than that. Caddy, you can't go with him."

I want to know how my mom knows that Eric likes me, but since she's not here to ask and I'm pretty sure she didn't share that much with Dillon, it looks like I'm gonna have to wait until she's home later and ask her. Right now though, it looks like I've got to deal with the rest of it.

I already said yes to him. I'm not backing out. I'm sorry.

"Do you want to be with me?" he asks as he reads what I wrote. Reaching out to take the paper from him, more than ready to give him an answer, he pulls it away from me. "No more writing. Just say it."

The way the muscles in his cheek twitch make me think there's an edge to his voice and I'm thankful I can't hear it. When he asked, my answer, it was so easy. Now though, I'm not so sure. He knows how I feel about speaking, no matter how comfortable I feel around him. I might be able to do what he says and say it out loud easily enough, but forcing me to do it, it's not going to work out well for him.

If I can accept him for the way he is, then he needs to do the same for me or this, whatever it is going on with us, won't go anywhere.

"No."

"No?" he asks and my heart sinks with the surprise and hurt I see in his eyes. I can't go back though. It doesn't matter how I feel about him. If he can't understand even the simplest thing about me, than he's never going to be able to be with me in the way I want him to be.

I was right before. We're just not right for each other no matter how much I wish it were different. Reaching across and grabbing the paper that's now loosely hanging in his hands, I start writing.

No Dillon. I don't want to be with you.

"You're lying. I see your words, but your face..." he says, his lips closing before he finishes his thought.

I'm not lying.

"Yes you are! You said you missed me! You said that things would only change if I let them. I don't want them to change. It's the whole reason I'm here. This isn't a game to me anymore, Cadence. I want to start over. I want to be with you!"

With as worked up as he is, his hands dangerously close to ripping what's left of his hair from his head, my next words, I know what they're gonna do. It doesn't make them any less true. What he said to me just brings it all back around again.

We've always been a game, Dillon. The game's over. You lose.

Chapter Twenty-Three

Dillon

This is much better. I don't know why I was so against it. I've never felt more alive.

Watching all the people making their way in through the barn doors, walking off to different corners of the room where my dad's got a ton of metal chairs lined up, I shake off the remainder of the shit with Caddy from my mind and focus my attention on the beast standing in front of me.

Stripping off my shirt and throwing it toward a group of girls that are huddled in the far corner of the back row, flashing them a grin as one of them catches it, I turn back just in time to see Frank step forward and nod his head at both of us. Stepping closer, more than ready to get the show on the road, I see my father standing a few feet behind my opponent for the night.

I've known about this fight for a few days now. With me hiding out and bailing on the last one, driving as far out of Wexfield as the gas in my car would take me, Bruce set this one up as a way for me to pay him back. Where I figured I'd just take off out of town again, after everything that went down with Cadence a few hours ago, a fight sounded pretty damn good.

Thinking about her can't happen. I owe Bruce a fair fight. One where my head's completely in it and I take this asshole down exactly the way he taught me years ago. Not thinking about her is impossible though so as I stand here, waiting for Ricky to make his way toward me, his mammoth size alone proving this is going to be as far from a fair fight as it gets, I let my mind go over it all again.

"We've always been a game, Dillon."

Maybe in the beginning that's exactly what we were because that's how I looked at her, but from about the second day in, it stopped being about that. The way I felt when Amy threw her down proves that. I couldn't handle that it was happening to her. I might have fought against the truth for a while after, but Kayden dropping the truth in my lap, it woke me up.

Telling her I loved her the day she walked away from me, back then, I think I still might have been fighting against what I was feeling, but now, I'm positive. I don't have the first clue what love feels like, I've avoided it for as long as I can remember, but if the way I was with her has anything to do with it, than I know I did love her.

I still love her even if she doesn't believe a word of it.

She pissed me off calling us a game. It was that anger that drove me here now. It's what is gonna drive me to win this fight. I'm gonna take this son of a bitch down or die trying because no matter what I do, I can't get some stupid deaf girl to believe in me.

Shit. I don't mean that. She's not stupid. She's not even some girl. Cadence is *the* girl.

When I asked her if she wanted to be with me, she wanted to say yes. I don't give a shit what came out of her mouth after it, she wanted to say yes, but something stopped her. Maybe it was how I reacted to her going to prom with Eric, or it was when I took the paper away from her, forcing her to speak to me. Whatever it is, I know it's my fault she said no.

That's another reason I'm fighting now. I fought myself in order to be with this girl that even I admit I don't know the first thing about and I lost. Standing here now, I know I can't lose. This is the kind of fight I was born to win.

"You know what you gotta do now, don't ya son?"

Shaking off the chill I get hearing him speak, I nod my head. I do know what I have to do now. I've gotta wait for Frank to start this thing and do whatever's necessary to bring this big guy to his knees.

The same way that Cadence brought me to mine.

"Good, because I got a lot of money riding on this fight and a loss is unacceptable."

God, I've never wanted to turn around and level him so much in my life. Even if he didn't have money riding on this, a loss would still be unacceptable. He's half the reason the slash over my eye was as deep as it was. He took what they did to me and made it worse. Bruce hates to lose.

"Ya, I got it. Let's just get this over with."

Putting my focus back where it belongs, I stare Ricky down. He's at least 6'4 which isn't a whole lot taller than me but enough that I'm gonna have to work harder to win this than if it was against one of the guys from the other day.

"You ready?" Frank asks me and I nod. His eyes before he turns to ask the same of my opponent surprise me. He's been in a ton of fights since I started doing this and never once has he looked at me like that. If I didn't know any better I'd say he looked concerned.

Hearing Ricky's grunted reply, I turn, just in time to duck to the right avoiding the first punch and sensing what his next move is about to be, I dodge before his left hand can land the uppercut he so obviously wants to on my jaw. Reacting I bring my left arm up with an uppercut of my own, landing it square in his stomach as he's reeling from his missed attempts.

Watching as he stumbles backwards, I run at him, throwing the full weight of my body into his until I've tacked him to the ground. Once Ricky falls, his back hitting the floor with a crack so loud it reminds me of the day Cadence fell in the hall, I jump up and stomp on him with my legs, one after the other until his body is still.

Leaning down until my knees are level with the ground, I start pummeling him, not letting up for a second, landing shot after shot on his face, the rage inside of me now at an all-time high. It's not Ricky's face I see anymore. First I see Kayden and what I should have done to him that day in the parking lot and again at the dance, and then it quickly turns to Eric, my anger at Cadence accepting his prom invitation, the jealousy so strong I feel like my heads gonna explode.

His face is bleeding now, I can feel the wetness on my hands but I don't stop, knowing that nothing is gonna please Bruce more than for him to see me decimate Ricky, leaving him within an inch of his life.

That's what no one gets. I could have easily taken down my best friend months ago, but I deserved to be hit so I let it happen. It's exactly why I love beating on the weak babies at school too. They deserve to be beat on as much as I did and maybe even do now.

I want them to hate me as much as I hate myself.

Backing away, catching my breath, it gives Ricky enough time to get his bearings and before I know it, he's shoving his arms into me, making me stumble until I lose balance and fall to the floor across from him. In the time it takes me to blink, he's hovering over me and this time, he's the one leveling me with his fists, putting my arms up to block coming two seconds too late and it's the final punch that does me in.

The minute I feel it connect with my jaw, my head snaps to the side and my body completely goes limp. The shooting pain rising to the surface and making me want to scream from the sheer agony of it. In a weak attempt to keep him off me, I raise my hand up to swing, but it falls flat as it barely rubs his shoulder.

The room around me is spinning now and I know it's not going to be long before I pass out, essentially pissing Bruce off even more and losing him a shit ton of money. Forcing my eyes to stay open as Ricky prepares to level me with his final blow, I dodge out of the way at the last second and crawling across the floor, attempting to find anything I can lift myself up with, that's when I hear it.

First the scream and then my name from a familiar voice, a voice that I would think would be the last person to show up to one of these things. Since I never told him about any of it, what he's doing here at all makes no sense.

I feel myself being grabbed from behind before I can look up or even respond to the sounds I'm hearing and it's not long before I'm being swung through the air and slammed hard and fast down on to the floor below, the hay doing nothing to soften the blow. I feel my legs go numb and even though I can still hear the voices around me, one stronger than all the others, it starts fading as my eyes start clouding over with dark spots.

The last thing I hear before I completely pass out is the most beautiful music in the world. The sound of my name being said by the only person in the entire world I ever want to hear it from.

Cadence.

Cadence

When Dillon left after I pretty much ripped his heart out, my mom came home. I'm not sure if it's because I didn't wipe away the tears that she noticed something was wrong or if it's because the minute she came in the door I bolted for my room, but whatever the case, she caught on and prevented me from hiding away.

After signing it all out to her in excruciating detail, so much so that by the end my hands physically hurt from the constant movement, she stood up and went to the front door after telling me to hold on. I watched as she opened her briefcase, slipped out a legal sized notepad and a couple of pens before turning and making her way back to the sofa.

When he left here, how did he appear to you?

How do you think? He was upset. He thinks I don't want to be with him.

That is what you told him, Caddy.

I sigh before focusing my mind on the paper, trying again to make her understand everything I'd just spent the last thirty minutes signing to her.

I know what I told him, Mom. You weren't here. The way he told me to speak to him instead of writing and the way he reacted when he heard Eric asked me to Prom, it was too much. I can't be with someone who doesn't

understand what it's like to be me. No matter how I feel about them.

When I hand her the pad and she makes no motion to write back to everything I've said, I take a chance and look at her. It's only when she meets my eyes that I see why she's not writing. She's disappointed in me.

"Oh, Caddy." She sighs, her eyes falling to the pad and my words and then coming up to meet mine again. "He doesn't understand you because you aren't giving him the chance to."

Do you ever think that we're just not compatible? I sign to her before stopping completely and thinking out what I need to say next. **You're the one that told me he was bad news remember?**

"I know what I said and I also know when to admit I'm wrong. I've been teaching a group of kids and for years I've preached to them how wrong it is to judge a book by its cover. How can I expect my students or even my own daughter to listen to my advice when I don't even take it myself?"

Unsure of what to say in response to her admission, I lower my head to my hands and just stare at them resting on my leg. She had a change of heart and a lot of that had to do with me, she didn't have to come out and say it. I'm the one that went at her so hard about Dillon in the beginning and now it's like the roles are reversed.

After a few minutes of neither one of us making a move, I reach out to the pad and pull it into my lap. I don't know how much good it'll do, but maybe with as much information as she has, not only about me and the kids she teaches but the stuff she's learned about Dillon in the short time he's been present in our lives, maybe she can tell me what I'm supposed to do now.

How am I supposed to feel, Mom? How am I supposed to react to him? I don't want to change him but the way he is, it's hard to handle. I get that he might be upset that I said yes to Eric, but we weren't together when he asked me. I said yes because I want to do right by Eric and if Dillon really wanted to get to know the real me the way he

claims to, he should understand that and want me to go through with it too.

Her response is immediate the minute her eyes scan the page.

Dillon can't let you go through with this because he's in love with you, Cadence. I know you don't have a lot of experience with that outside of the way I feel about you, but one look in the boy's eyes and you can't deny it. A boy or even a man in love is not going to handle his girlfriend being with another guy in any way that's smart or right.

Dillon's in love with me? I know what he said to me before I came back to school, but I just figured he said it to try and get me to stay. It's not like he went out of his way to tell me earlier or give me a clue that he felt it.

My mom's right. I have no idea what being in love is even like. No one's ever cared enough to want to try with me and the feelings been mutual. At least it was until Dillon.

Caddy, what does Dillon do when he's upset? You've heard me speak about him more than enough times over the last year and now you've interacted with him yourself. When he gets upset or gets thrown into a situation that doesn't turn out the way he expects, what does he do?

He hurts people.

In other words, he fights.

I nod my head and that's when I figure it out. What she was asking me first, how he reacted to everything that happened between us, she was making a point, one I didn't catch.

Dillon's default setting when he's mad is to find someone to take it out on. He will bully anyone he believes to be weak at school or worse, he'll go looking for it elsewhere when he doesn't have the school option. Knowing what I do about his father and what the man puts him through, everything makes perfect sense now.

"You think he left here and went to fight don't you?"

She nods slowly, but before I can say anything more, her lips move first.

"I most definitely do and knowing Bruce Murphy, I wouldn't put it past him to help his son out if he got a call asking for it."

Would Dillon really call his dad and ask him to set up a fight? Would what happened with us really push him to that point? I saw him that day in the locker room when he told me his secret, what he's been holding onto since he was twelve. He doesn't like it, doesn't want to be a part of it and was so afraid to get close to me because he didn't want to drag me into it. I can't believe that the way he was that day would change with what happened tonight.

It's obvious from the look on my mom's face though that she doesn't think the same way. She can definitely see it and it's that look, the fear I see in her eyes as she stands from the sofa and makes her way into the kitchen that drives me forward.

Following her into the kitchen, she motions to the phone. "Did Dillon ever tell you where these fights were held?"

"A farm." I say and armed with my answer she picks up the phone and starts dialing.

"Who are you calling?"

"Kayden. If there's anyone that would know where this farm is, it'd be him."

Sliding into a seat at the table, I wait and watch as she starts speaking. She's moving so quickly that right now I know it's impossible to keep up, but with the way her mouth curves up and down the entire time she's on the phone, there's no doubt that whatever she's heard it's bad.

"What did you find out?" I ask nervously, not sure I want to know with the way she's reacting.

"Jim Brown before he died had a farm. It's on the outskirts of Wexfield, which is why I didn't know about it. Kayden says it's been abandoned for years but if there was a place in town that people would use for underground fighting, it would be there."

"So what do we do now?"

"Kayden is on his way over. He's going to come with me and we're going to the farm to check it out."

"I'm coming with you." If she thinks she's gonna keep me away from this, especially since I'm the reason for him doing it at all, she's mistaken.

"Caddy, you have no idea what you'll be walking into if this is what I think it is."

You don't need to protect me from this. Dillon told me how bad it is. He also told that he hates doing it. I know it's not going to be pretty. I sign to her, not trusting my voice anymore to get the words out.

So many different scenarios are running through my head right now that it's hard to keep up, but the one thing I'm able to focus on is my need to be there with them. If Dillon is there, no matter what shape he's in or even if he doesn't want to see me, there's nowhere else I need to be.

Mom's right. I never gave him the chance to get to know me.

I just hope by the time I get to him, it's not too late to start.

Chapter Twenty-Four

Cadence

The minute I step out of the car when Kayden pulls up in front of the barn, I'm met with an overwhelming smell of manure, which with how abandoned the place looks, doesn't add up to me. Putting my fingers to my nose, attempting to block out the smell, I start moving toward the barn door, not wanting to waste any time finding out what I'm going to see on the other side.

There are cars parked around the side of the building which means my mom was right making the call earlier. When I told her that Dillon fought in a barn, I knew deep down this is where he would be, but I'd been holding out hope for a better result. If she hadn't jumped on it and we ignored it then god only knows what would be happening now.

I had to put a stop to whatever waited for me on the other side of the door. Unfortunately, it looks like Kayden and my mom have other plans.

I feel the strong grip on my shoulder before I'm pulled back and even though it's not a touch I recognize, it's easy to see its Kayden. When I'm pulled back far enough, his hold on my shoulders never breaking, he comes around to face me and the grim expression on his face tells me everything that his words can't.

"Caddy, I know you wanna run in and get him, but we gotta do it together."

As right as he is, I still want no part of it. What does Kayden know anyway? He hasn't spent real time with Dillon in months. He probably doesn't even wanna help him out right now.

As my mom makes her way up to stand beside Kayden, nodding her head as she does, agreeing with what he said, I resign myself to the fact that I'm going to have to do this the way they want. As much as I want to rush in there, find him and drag him out even if he hates me, I know it's not smart. I might not be going in blind, but being unable to hear anything going around me could spell disaster. As stubborn as I am, even I can't deny that.

Taking my hand and leading me slowly toward the door, my mom right on our heels, Kayden wraps his hand around the handle and pulls on it slowly. It's only when the door is cracked wide enough for me to see around it that I catch all the people sitting around on chairs, some jumping up out of them, their mouths wide open, probably yelling at what's taking place directly in front of them.

Making our way inside, we let the door close easily behind us and take in what's going on. It's following everyone's eyes to the center of the room that I see what all the fuss is about. Why people are jumping up, obscenities flying, at least the ones I can catch with as fast as everything is moving.

There's a big guy, giant looking from where I'm standing and he's on top of another guy, his arms moving up and down every few seconds as he hits the guy hard, one punch after another until the guy on the grounds face turns to the side.

My ability to see, how sharp my senses are because of not being able to hear, show me exactly who the person on the ground is the minute his head lops to the side. It's Dillon and not only do his eyes look like they're rolling back in his head, but there's blood, a lot of it, on his eyes, his mouth and at the top of his head.

It's seeing him like this, my breath catching in my throat, heart beating out of my chest that my lips part and I'm screaming. I feel the rumble in my throat, the force I'm using even though I can't hear the sound. At first it's just a scream, but the minute I try to move toward him, being pulled back by Kayden, it stops being a scream and it's his name, over and over.

I need to get to him. I need to get this big giant guy off him and we need to get out of here. He shouldn't be here like this. Looking at him now, how still his body is, I'm already scared I've gotten here too late and he's already lost to me.

Kayden releases the hold he has on me, turning toward my mom and saying something I can't quite make out before turning back and making his way forward. When he moves, even though I'm sure he's not expecting it, I move with him, not willing to let him get within a foot of his old friend without me by his side.

Turning to me, his eyes blazing with an anger I never got to see during my time at school, he levels them on me and speaks slowly, making sure I catch every single word he says because he's warning me.

"Go back with your mom, Caddy. I'm gonna get him out of there, but not if you're with me. I don't want you getting hurt."

If he thinks for a second that I care about what could possibly happen to me, he's lost his mind. I know what he's trying to do and it's sweet but there's no way he's doing this alone. I'm going to help him get Dillon out of there if it's the last thing I do. I don't care what happens to me.

I'm the reason he's like this to begin with. It's only fair that considering I caused it, I be the one to fix it. Dillon's not the only one that struggles with their need to fix things. I do too and right now I need to help him so I can figure out after how I'm gonna fix the situation I put us in.

"No." I sign and as expected, he turns his head toward my mom, not understanding what I'm saying. It's in that split second when he turns that I make my way forward and before I know it, I'm hitting the big guy with as much force as I've got.

I know I'm not gonna be able to stop someone like him but I'm gonna try.

When the big guy turns around, his focus off the broken body on the ground in front of him, I start shoving at him again, this time balling my fists and hitting him. The smile that appears when I land my first hit makes me furious so I hit harder and faster, wanting nothing more than to wipe the smug look off his face.

It's only when his hand comes out in front of him that I realize what's about to happen and moving in an attempt to stay out of his grip, I trip over Dillon's leg and where I expect to feel the ground below as I fall, all I feel is air. Looking up, I see that the guy's got a grip on my jacket and he's yanking me up.

Getting involved, just like Kayden said, was a bad move and now that I've done it, there's no way out. I'm trapped and my attempt to get Dillon out safe is gonna fail, just like everything else has with us from the start.

His hold begins to loosen on me before he can make his next move and wondering why, I search around me. It's when I make out the side of Kayden's head behind the guy that I realize what's happening. Kayden's coming to the rescue, attempting to take the guy down so that I don't end up the same way as his old friend.

Bending over from the impact of whatever it is Kayden did, the guy drops me and I hit the ground hard. Wanting to react to the pain but needing to check on Dillon more, I turn my head and what I see, it turns my stomach. His chest is moving up and down, but it's weak. His eyes are shut tight, having been knocked out from the repeated blows to the head I watched him take and it takes everything in me not to scream again.

He's not supposed to be like this. It wasn't supposed to happen this way. I was supposed to protect him from this so that he would never have to do it again. He's doing this because I pushed him away.

Even though it hurts, I inch my body slowly over to where he's passed out and bringing my lips to his cheek, I press them into it, kissing him, wanting him to at least know that he's not going through this alone.

My body aching and my head pounding, I rest my body beside his, bringing my head down on his shoulder as close as I can be and finally allowing my body to rest. Kayden, I can see out of the corner of my eye is still going at the guy that did all of this and I can even make out another older man, attempting to pull him away. Unable to take any more of what I've seen and the way I'm feeling, I completely shut them out and focus on the feel of Dillon's heart as it beats into my hand, becoming weaker with each passing second.

My last thought as my eyes close and I allow my body to succumb to the pain it's in is simple.

Someone needs to stop this. Dillon, if he makes it out of here can't be forced to go through this again. I can't let him go through another second of this and it's because of one simple fact.

I love him.

Dillon

When my eyes opened the first time, my last memory of Ricky over me wailing away on my face, I expected to see clouds, bright light and a whole lot of angel wings. Ha, who am I kidding, the only thing I expected was a whole lot of darkness and maybe even a face to face showdown with the devil himself.

It's what I deserve.

The way things went down was nothing like that. I woke up in a hospital room, an IV line running straight up my arm, and a whole lot of pain running through every single part of my body. If this is what hell is, it seems fitting.

Even with my blurry vision, a byproduct of the beating my face took no doubt, I can see the room is empty. At least it looked empty until I shift my aching body in the bed and hear the grunt from the other side of the room.

"Wondered when you were gonna wake the hell up." The voice says and it's only when he steps forward and throws his body down into the chair beside me that I see who it is.

Kayden.

My memories, they're hazy after the last shot I took when Ricky slammed me down onto the ground, but I do remember seeing him for a split second before everything went dark. I remember thinking that Kayden being there was wrong, since he had no idea about any of it. Now that he's here, I suppose I can get answers.

Well I could if I my damn throat wasn't so dry. Even pulling my lips apart hurts.

"Looks like you're the one that needs the paper and pen now, huh?" Kayden laughs and I feel like forcing myself up just so I can hit him. Thing is, he's right. Talking right now is obviously not gonna happen so if I wanna get answers, I'm gonna need another way.

It's not lost on me how everything seems to have turned around and I'm the one that's mute. It makes all those names I called Isabelle, Eric and the countless others I've picked on over the years hurt even more than I already am physically. The way I was is physically turning my own stomach.

I'm such an asshole.

"Here," Kayden says, putting the pad and pen on my chest. "I still think you're a total douche, but right now you're a pretty screwed up one. You need all the help you can get."

The first thing I want to ask him the minute I lift up my hand and grab the pen, wanting to know why he was there to begin with, it fades away as an even more important one rises to the surface. There was someone else there with him and right now, she's what I care about.

Cadence was with you. Where is she?

"She's in a room down the hall. Apparently one look at you and she lost her fucking mind." He says and my stomach turns over again. He can't possibly mean what I think he means, right?

Lost her mind how? What happened to her? Why is she in a room down the hall?

Seeing my questions and somehow sensing my desperation, he places a hand on my shoulder and takes a deep breath.

"Slow down, man. Seeing you the way she did, she went after Ricky. I got involved, he dropped her, but she hit her back and legs pretty hard when she fell. They're checking her out. It's nothing too serious."

Cadence, the girl that earlier in the night told me she didn't want to be with me, got involved and was hurt trying to protect me. It's exactly what I warned her about that day in the locker room. I did end up hurting her with everything I told her even if I wasn't the one that literally did the hurting.

Shit.

This is all my fault.

You think you can get a wheelchair in here? I need you to take me to her.

"I'm not taking you anywhere, Dill. Your body is fucking destroyed. I get why you wanna do it, but man, seeing you like this, it's not going to help her. Think about what you're doing."

He's right. Of course he is. He knows about this better than anyone. He doesn't realize it, but that story he threw around last fall when he was out for three days after the dance, I knew it was bullshit. He thought he was hiding stuff so well but I knew better. Dean has been knocking him around for years, even if he didn't talk to me about it and it was because of him that Kayden was out.

It was pretty easy to put together when Dean ended up locked away and word spread all over town. Wexfield is nothing if not the hub for gossip and shit talking. The adults were even worse than the kids with it.

I'm pretty sure that he wouldn't want Isabelle seeing him after what happened so I know what he's getting at about me showing up in front of her with the way I look. I don't exactly know how bad it ended up being, but if the way he's looking me over is any indication, it's gotta be pretty damn gross.

How bad is it?

"Her or you?"

Me. You said that it wasn't bad with her.

"You've got two black eyes, a slash through your right eyebrow that's pretty damn deep. They gave you stitches for it. When we brought you in, your arm was dislocated, but it looks like they put it back together nicely since it doesn't look like a limp noodle anymore. They're gonna take you for x-rays on your back soon, there's some concern about your spine. A few other things going on with your face, but I think that's about it."

I shouldn't have been all that surprised with everything he told me but I am. I know I slammed down on the ground pretty hard when he dropped me but them being worried about spinal damage, that's surprising.

"Now you see why I said you can't go see her right now." He says, catching the surprised look on my face with the list of injuries he's given me.

Cadence. Tell me everything.

"Dill," he says with a tight laugh. "I don't know what the hell's going on with the two of you, but if Isabelle ever did what Cadence did, I'd never let her out of my sight again. The girl went crazy. I warned her not to get involved and even though she saw what I said, she still took off at him. She wouldn't stop hitting him even though the dude didn't even flinch. She fell down, crawled to you and passed out on your shoulder."

There's a part of me that wants to feel proud that she did all of that for me, but the part of me that's able to see how screwed up this entire situation is won't let me. She never should have been there, let alone throwing herself in the middle of it. Cadence was never meant to see any of that.

She's better than what I do.

What was she even doing there? How did she know?

His answer is immediate and this time, all traces of the smile he'd been wearing when he explained what Cadence did is gone and he's all business.

"Ms. T figured it out. She asked Caddy what she knew about where you go to fight. What you do when shit goes down you don't like and she called me for the rest. From the way the two of them were going at each other in the car, signing and stuff, I get the feeling that her mom wanted her to stay home and she wasn't having any of it."

That's definitely Cadence. I expect nothing less from her. I don't know her as well as I want to but the one thing that was clear right from the first day is that she's stubborn and didn't see things the way everyone else did. If her mom wanted her to stay home safe, no matter who it was about, she wouldn't have done it.

Yeah she's like that. Are you sure she's okay?

"She'll be bruised for a while, but that's about it. She's only being checked over right now. I'm pretty sure they're gonna let her go soon and she'll be home by the end of the night."

I feel better knowing that nothing that happened tonight will stay with her physically, that she got lucky and Kayden had been there to stop anything worse from happening, but I can't shake the feeling that if she hadn't spoken to me that first day, none of this would be happening now. Her liking me, believing in me, almost got her killed.

Fighting this way for my dad, it might seem dramatic saying that she could have died, but it's not. Every time I went into a fight, I went in knowing that one wrong shot, falling a certain way could end things forever. It's half the reason I hated it so much. I didn't fight because I was suicidal, I did it because it was better than the alternative. An alternative that Kayden lived with and knows a whole lot about.

If I didn't fight, I would have been Bruce's punching bag and in some way, these fights seemed like the lesser of two evils.

Please tell her mom I'm sorry. She never should've been there or been a part of any of this. I'll stay away from her.

Kayden laughs under his breath and again I feel my blood pressure rising. I didn't think any of what I just wrote is funny, in fact it's as serious as I think I've ever been. I meant every word of it, just like I did earlier when I told her how I felt.

What's so funny?

"Man, you know our history. Most of it is pretty bad. Sitting here like this with you, I never thought in a million years I'd be doing it, but what you just said, it's something else I never expected to see."

Well that didn't help. Now I'm even more lost than I was before he started talking.

You gonna explain that or just keep me in suspense?

"Doing the right thing. I never thought I'd see it. It's also kind of hilarious seeing you in love too."

Screw you.

"You're actually gonna sit here all busted up and broken and deny it? Dillon, the reason we were such good friends for so long is because we're exactly alike. You don't wanna admit it because you're this macho fucking asshole, just like I was, but you can't deny this. You went into the fight because of what happened with her, she explained that much to me when we got here. You don't willingly throw yourself into a fight like that unless you've been driven bat shit crazy over a girl."

This where you tell me you know that because you went through it with Belle?

Instead of answering right away he nods and grins at me and for the first time in months, despite the pain it causes me the minute I attempt to do it, I smirk back at him. We are alike, no matter how much we try to run from or deny it and what he's saying, it's all true. If there's someone out there that might just know me better than I do myself, it's him.

"You know how many times I went at Dean over Belle? He called her shit and it just drove me to a point where all I wanted to see was him dead. I was that pissed off. I used to get into it with my brother over a lot of different things, but never over a girl. It's how I know what's going on with you, because you did the same damn thing. You wanted to have someone beat the feelings out of you because it's easier not feeling at all."

None of that matters now. After what happened tonight, it proves she's better off without me. She probably wants nothing to do with me.

He laughs again but this time instead of pissing me off, it just makes me curious. He's laughing like he knows something I don't.

"We could barely get her off you when the paramedics showed up, Dill. Somehow I doubt that the girl wants nothing to do with you. I'm in here because it was the only way to keep her calm."

Listening to him, taking in everything she did tonight in an effort to protect me, wanting to believe what he's telling me about the way I feel and me wanting to do the right thing, it's almost too much to take. As much as I believe I'm wrong for her, she'd be better off without me, I know that won't ever work for me. I won't be able to let this girl go; especially now and there's no sense trying.

If Kayden's right and she feels the same way about me as I do about her and I'm pretty damn positive that's the case after the conversation we had earlier, then there's only one thing left for me to do.

It's time for me to get her back and this time, make sure she never leaves again.

Putting the paper on the side of the bed, despite the pain in my jaw and the way my lips seem to be super glued together, I clear my throat and force them to open. If I'm going to do this then I'm gonna do it without the pen and paper.

"I need your help."

Chapter Twenty-Five

Cadence

I don't know whose bright idea it was to turn the prom into a masquerade ball, but whoever it was, I'm going to kick them in the balls for it.

After spending the last four days holed up in my bed, milking my bruised back with my mom in an effort to get me out of the date with Eric, this is the last place I want to be.

My mom saw through every pathetic attempt I made to avoid being here and forced my hand the night before when she walked in with the mask and told me exactly what the theme would be. She listed all of the reasons why it wasn't a good idea to bail despite my desperate need to do otherwise and well now I'm here, feeling as awkward and out of place as ever.

Everything she said is right and I do still want to see this through for Eric, but being here especially after what happened at the beginning of the week, doesn't feel right. I saw the way he looked at me when he picked me up tonight, how weird he was acting standing by my front door. He was fidgeting and sweating and his smile, it was different.

The way he feels about me, the things Dillon told me, they're all true and being here with him now, it's wrong. He might have asked me to this so he didn't have to go alone the way he told me, but there was more behind it and knowing that is only going to make this end badly for everyone.

He doesn't realize it because I played it off earlier when he asked, but I left my heart with the broken brown eyed boy in the hospital. It doesn't matter how much time passes, I'll never be able to give it to another person even though if I could, Eric would be someone I would want to give it to.

When the doctor gave me the all clear, explaining to me that the only thing wrong with me was something a good night's sleep would cure, my mom went to find Kayden so she could take me home. She doesn't realize it, but when I told her I wanted to use the restroom before leaving, that wasn't where I ended up.

Despite her warning that what he endured would be too hard for me to see, I still had to do it. So when they rounded the corner and out of my sight, I went to the nurse's station, writing Dillon's name on a piece of paper and passing it to her and within a couple of minutes she lead the way to his room. When I went in, he was sleeping but I saw just how bad it really was. Leaving, even though I knew I had to do it was hard but staying would have been worse.

The way he looked in the barn before I closed my eyes, it was bad but that was worse. Seeing things hooked to his chest, the machines lighting up with every breath he took, the IV sticking out of his hand and running up his arm, it was horrible. He never should have been in that barn to begin with.

Guilt never really goes away whether you're entirely at fault or not and standing here now, in this gym full of people I don't even know, it's eating me alive. I'm guilty for pushing Dillon to fight, I'm guilty for leading Eric on even though it wasn't intentional. It's all my fault.

My mom told me this morning that he'd been released from the hospital and sent home with his mom and it should have made me feel better, but all it did was tie the knot in my stomach up worse. The last place he needs to be is with a mother that has no clue what he's really going through. I'm thankful he didn't end up with his dad, Bruce being picked up, along with some others for running a fight club, but his mother wasn't any better.

I had no idea where he should have been, but home wasn't it.

She asked me if I wanted to go by to see him and I did, but after the things I said, calling us a game, telling him it was over, I figured that I would be the last person he would want to see.

It didn't matter how much I love him, what I said, the things I did, it meant I had to stay away.

Admitting how I feel or what I believe my feelings to be, it's easier now and despite how wrong we seem to be for each other, what I feel isn't. He was right that day at the ravine. What's between us, no matter where we go, is a beginning with no end. The way I feel about him, it won't ever end.

I'm going to carry a little piece of Dillon with me for the rest of my life.

Sensing the touch before it comes, I look up and see Eric standing in front of me, a clear plastic cup extended out in front of him, a smile his way of greeting. Taking it and bringing it to my lips, blocking all thoughts of Dillon and what happened four days ago from my head I smile in return before drinking the entire cup down in one swallow.

"You didn't ask if it was spiked." He says and I smile. "I could have been trying to get you drunk."

I'm so thirsty, I'll take it, spiked or not. I sign out to him, my eyes falling away and back to the room around me.

Brushing me with his hand, he waits until I'm looking directly at him and speaks again.

"Do you feel like dancing?"

If I had my way, I would spend the rest of the night standing right where I am now, at least I would until he finally got bored and took me home, but with my mom chaperoning the event, there's no way she'd let me. I've already spied her eyes on me a total of ten times already and I'm afraid to push it and see what other looks she'd level me with.

Nodding slowly, I place my hand in his and let him lead me to the dance floor. Even with the mask on my face, the eye holes a little too small for my liking, I can see the looks people are giving us as we start to dance. It's pretty obvious I'm the deaf girl and they're all trying to figure out how I can dance when I can't hear the music.

I don't need to hear the music to know how to move. When you have a partner like Eric, who understands and can take the lead, I can dance so flawlessly it will appear like there's nothing wrong with me at all. I'm just another average girl out in the middle of the gym, dancing with a beautiful guy.

After spinning me around a few times, bringing me in close and me pulling away, his demeanor changes. The last time he spun me around, he'd done it with a smile and now, his face is empty. Pulling me to him and turning me around, the other couples continuing to dance around us, I see why there was a change.

Dillon's here.

Time seems to stop as we just stare at each other, his eyes I'm sure mirroring the look in my own. As shocked as I am to see him here with the list of injuries Kayden told me he had, I'm determined not to let him see it.

"Can I cut in?" he says and turning back to Eric he nods his head, giving his okay, leaving the choice of whether or not Dillon dances with me completely in my hands.

With the voice inside me screaming to accept and Eric now backing away and making his way to the other side of the room, I nod and watch as he moves forward and slides his one arm around my back, taking his other hand and bringing mine up into it.

The minute his body makes contact with mine, it takes everything I have in me not to melt from the way it feels. With the way he brings me into him, my eyes are level with his neck and I'm afraid to look up. Staring at him before he asked to cut in, I noticed the damage the fight had done but avoided breaking from the pain of it. Now, I'm afraid to look up and see it again because the last thing I want him to feel being here like this is that I feel bad for him.

Moving me around the floor, his movements are slow and deliberate and I start to wonder what kind of song is playing, as the other people around us are all still moving at the same pace. The way he's moving, it's as if he's doing it to his own music, a slower song and one that only he can hear.

I've never wanted to hear something so much in my life.

After we've moved in a complete circle, he looks down at me and his eyes, dark as always, are tender, glowing a little as we continue to move under the lights above us. Where the mask covers my entire face, his is wide open and it's relaxed, almost as if he's feeling the same thing in this moment as I am.

Seeing his lips part, knowing he's about to speak, I lift my finger up and place it to his lips. I can't let him talk until he answers something for me first.

"What are you doing here?"

"You saved my life. There's nowhere else I need to be."

I always wondered what it would feel like to be a completely solid being one second and suddenly turn into a puddle on the floor and with what he said, I'm experiencing it firsthand. My legs feel rubbery, relying on him even more to keep me moving around the room and my head feels lightheaded.

"How many trucks this time? I ask, attempting to lighten the mood in order to call attention away from the way every part of me seems to be falling apart and he smiles before answering.

"One very big truck. From what I hear, you got run over too."

There's nothing funny about what we experienced, but him smiling at me, there's no way I can ignore it. When I asked the question this had been the reaction I'd been looking for and I'm so glad he didn't disappoint.

"I didn't think I'd see you tonight."

"I refer you to the answer I gave to your first question. Nowhere else I need to be, Caddy."

His body tenses and despite how close we already are, he brings me even closer and trying to turn in order to see what's causing this reaction, he leans back down, turning my face into his so I'm able to see not only his eyes but his lips too.

"Tim and Amy."

I nod and cease all movement, choosing instead to focus on him, the way he smells, that same mixture of sweat and talcum powder I smelled the first day and the way it feels being held by him. Following along with his lips as they move, I see that he's not happy that they're here and it doesn't take me long to find out why.

They're here for me.

Dillon

The minute I found out Cadence would be coming to prom with Eric, I expected something like this to happen, especially with what happened the last time we were here. Where I'd been the ringleader of it before though, this time it was going to be different.

This time it wasn't going to go off the way they expect.

When I called Kayden a few hours ago, making sure everything I asked him for in the hospital was put in motion and ready to go, I bugged him for one more thing. Whatever his feelings are toward me now, he agreed. It's only when I got in his car, trying to situate myself right so I didn't aggravate the injuries any more than I already had since getting home that he filled me in on everything I've missed.

It seems that passing by my friends on Wednesday, he caught wind of a plan and even though no one was named, there was only one girl that Amy would want to get revenge on so bad that she's go out of her way to make it happen. Cadence.

I have no idea why they planned the damn thing in the hallway, having learned nothing from me over the years, but they did and he was able to catch all of it. Apparently, the idea was to rig the prom queen event the same way we did with Homecoming and make Cadence win it. This is where everything changed from the original plan.

Tim, having access to the locker room and the ice bath we take sometimes after a game, was going to take a bunch of the water and ice and go up into the rafters above the stage and release it on her.

There was a time where a plan like that would have sparked interest in me, but those days are over. It's because of that and who they were going to do it to that I made sure the minute I got in the gym I went right for her. No one was going to repeat Homecoming tonight, not when I've been doing everything in my power to make what happened then right again.

It didn't even have to be Cadence they were targeting. If they decided Isabelle needed to be the target, I would have done the same thing. The way things used to be, it doesn't work anymore and even though it took me too damn long to realize it, I'm putting an end to it all now.

These two, despite who they've been to me for the last four years mean absolutely nothing now. They never knew me to begin with, they just knew the person I wanted them to see.

"So Dill, when did you become a retard lover? Oh wait, that's right. She's not retarded, she's deaf, which is even worse. At least Isabelle can hear the shit we say to her."

No matter what they say, I need to keep calm. I refuse to repeat the same mistake I did over a week ago. Cadence is not going to witness me losing my shit on these two even though it's exactly what I want to do.

"Nice one Tim, you think that up on your own or are you just recycling my old lines again?"

Content that I've shut him up the minute his mouth wires shut, I turn my attention to the person beside him. The girl that up until a few weeks ago I'd been dating. The girl I claimed to care about, before I knew what real caring was.

"I know what you're gonna do and it's not happening. Next time you wanna destroy someone, try not planning the whole damn thing in a public hallway where anyone can hear."

Looking down at Cadence, sliding my hand into hers, I motion toward the door and start walking. Standing there, exactly where I need him to be is Daniels and for the first time since the meeting with my mom, he's wearing a different look then the normal disdain I'm used to whenever I'm around.

"What can I do for you Mr. Murphy?" he asks the minute I stop in front of him and just like I did the day he walked me to class, I resist the urge to say something about what he called me, focusing instead on the very real threat my old friends have planned for the girl whose hand I'm gripping tightly in my own.

"Remember what happened last fall? I didn't do the right thing that night and we both know it, but tonight, I am. Amy, Tim, Charlotte and Eve, they're planning on doing something when you announce the prom court. I'm letting you know so you can stop it."

He looks me over like he doesn't believe a word I'm saying and while I know for a fact that Cadence won't be stepping on that stage tonight, there's no stopping whoever does take her spot and I don't want it happening to anyone else. I need to make him believe me.

"Get someone up in the rafters. You'll see a bucket of ice water. They're planning on dumping it on the queen's head. I know I've screwed up a lot and you don't believe shit that comes out my mouth, but you're gonna want to believe this."

Giving him the facts seems to be all it takes. He nods his head and right before my eyes, he walks away, heading not only for Coach on the other side of the room, but also to where Cadence's mom is standing. When she looks across the room, catching my eye, she nods her head and smiles and that's all I need.

She's letting me know that even though she doesn't know what's going on, she knows I did the right thing this time.

There's only one thing left to do now.

It's time to go back to the beginning and this time, do it right. It's time to make Cadence Taylor mine.

Epilogue

Cadence

When he asked me to dance, the way it felt in his arms, even though I couldn't hear the music and he was the one leading me, holding me as close as possible as we swayed around the gym, it was pivotal. It was a turning point for us; at least I thought it was.

The dancing is over, the prom court about to be announced and I'm on the sidelines, Dillon nowhere to be found. It's obvious that the moment I thought we shared, the way it felt being in his arms again was all in my head. Nothing's changed. We're right back where we were on Monday.

Feeling a body brush against mine, I turn, looking up and hoping to see a particular pair of brown eyes looking back at me, disappointed when I see that it's a pair of dark eyes alright, but not the ones I'd been desperate for.

It's Eric and despite the smile on his face, I still feel destroyed inside. After everything I've been through with Dillon, knowing what his life is like and the darkness that surrounds him, I should be with someone like the boy standing beside me now. I should be allowing myself to fall for that smile, the softness in his eyes and instead I'm standing here missing someone that's his complete opposite.

He reaches into his suit jacket and pulls out a tiny envelope and looking at me, his smile never wavering, he passes it to me and takes a step back. Whatever this is that he's handed me now, it's obviously not from him or he wouldn't feel the need to step back and give me privacy to read it.

My heart jumps at the thought of what is waiting for me on the inside of the envelope. As I slide the paper out and look at the scrawl on the note card, my heart drops again. It's not from him, I'd be able to tell his writing anywhere.

Take a walk with me?

Looking back over at Eric, again being hit with a smile that seems somehow brighter than before, I smile weakly and motion toward the door, giving him my answer at the same time.

It's only when we've made our way out of the school and down through the trees that will take me back to the one spot that means something to me that I stop. I'm pretty sure he has no idea what the place he's taking me means, but I think before he does it I should tell him. I'm not sure how right I feel about going to the ravine knowing it's the place I had my first kiss and gained my first boyfriend.

Going here with Eric now would be unfair to him and also to Dillon. I can't do it.

Shaking my head and pointing toward the ravine, I take a step back, fully prepared to turn back and head inside again.

Before I can turn, he reaches out to me and pulls me back toward him and the place that I really don't want to go. Pulling another envelope from his pocket, he hands it over to me and just like before, I slip the small card out and read it, completely confused as to what's going on. He can talk to me, so using note cards is throwing me off.

Trust me. I swear it's not what you think.

There's a happy face emoticon at the end of the sentence and for some reason, the same way it did when Isabelle sent them to me, it lightens the mood. I do trust Eric and I know he would never do something that would hurt me. He just doesn't realize what the ravine means to me.

I can't go there. I sign to him, hoping that he'll get the hint so I can stop whatever is about to come next.

"Yes you can, Caddy. You need to."

What does he mean I need to? I don't need to do anything. Right now he's reminding me of the way Dillon was in my kitchen. I don't like being told what I need to do.

"Eric—"

"Just come, Caddy." He says and not giving me a chance to reply, he drags me by the hand, and pulls me the rest of the way through the trees until we make it completely through to the other side. The water comes into view automatically, and seeing it this way, at night, it warms me.

It's beautiful. The way it looks during the day, seeing the water all brown and murky, with discarded garbage lining the sides, is enough to turn anyone's stomach, but right now, none of that is visible, and all I can see is the lights from the street reflected as the water slowly moves in waves.

Looking up at Eric and watching as he points down the bike path, I follow his hand and that's when I see the real reason I'm here. It wasn't Eric wanting to bring me here at all.

Standing about fifteen feet away from me, at the rock that we sat on the first day we came here is Dillon and surrounding the area, in the trees above him and resting all around the rock are lights, so many of them that he's completely lit up and glowing.

I've never seen a more beautiful sight in my life.

Turning back to Eric, expecting to see a look of disappointment on his face, especially after what my mom told me, all I see is his familiar smile.

"What is this?"

He opens his jacket one more time, again passing along another envelope and as I take it, he bends in and with a small squeeze of my shoulder and a kiss on my cheek he points toward Dillon.

"It's time to go, Caddy."

Turning away and walking back the way he came, I turn my attention back to the note in my hand and slip it out of the envelope, my heart starting to pump faster in anticipation and fear at the same time. This time, the handwriting is familiar and as I read the words and slip it back into the envelope, I turn toward the writer and make my way forward.

Hi. My name is Dillon.

Dillon

I swear to god with the amount of work I put into this, it better go down the way I want it to.

When Kayden suggested bringing Eric into it, having done the same thing when he wanted to reach out to Isabelle, I was completely against it. I know the way the guy feels about Cadence, letting him be involved in what I wanted to do for her, it would only cause more shit than I was prepared to deal with.

Despite it, Isabelle brought him in and considering what she was doing for me after what I did to her, I wasn't about to argue it. She didn't have to help me at all and I knew it, which means that Eric being involved in this was the way things had to be.

Thankfully the only thing she tasked him with was making sure Cadence showed up when I texted Kayden to let him know I was ready. Standing here and waiting for him to show up with her though, I start wondering if he bailed out at the last minute and just took off somewhere so he could be alone with her.

I swore to myself when I put this in motion that I wouldn't doubt myself or my worthiness anymore. For whatever reason, Cadence Taylor saw something in me that for the longest time I'd been denying and it's for her that I would see this through. Armed with the information Kayden dropped on me at the hospital, it was the only thing left for me to do. Nothing else mattered.

Seeing her as she came through the trees behind Eric, the way she turned to him as he passed her what looked to be the last envelope, my heart stilled for the first time since I started putting this all together. He had come through and delivered her just the way he promised and watching him walk away and her even from this distance, reading my words, I'm more than ready for what's about to come next.

My note to her, the one I left her the day before she left, it's what has to happen now. What happened between us at school, it was preparing us for this moment right here. This is where we have our beginning with no end.

Right here, in this moment right now. This is our forever.

Coming to a stop in front of me, her eyes never breaking from mine, I slip an envelope out of my pocket and pass it across to her. This was a last minute decision, but one I'm feeling pretty damn confident about. I could have easily said all of this to her, but there's a lot of it and writing was a lot easier than trying to remember everything I wanted to say.

Watching her eyes go wide as she pulls out the lined sheet of paper, I can't help but smile. It's obvious she was expecting another note card. It's too bad for her that everything I want to say to her couldn't fit on twelve of them, let alone one. When her eyes stop flicking over the lines on the page, she folds the note back up with her free hand and passes it out toward me.

Our hands touch as I take it from her and put it back in my pocket and the jolt I experience, it makes all of this perfect. After spending the last three weeks attempting to navigate through the sea of confusion I felt when I walked into Ms. Taylor's class that first day, wanting nothing more than to do the right thing by this girl that just got to me in ways no one else had been able to, I've been dying for things to be this right.

"Do you mean it?" she asks, my heart jumping at the sound.

"Every word of it."

"What is all of this?" she asks motioning up toward the trees and the ground around the rock that I still think of as ours. It's only when her eyes seem to lock on what's resting on top of the rock that they go wide. "More spray paint?"

Despite the seriousness of the moment, the way she questions me about the spray paint reminds me of the first time we came here and she eyed the can suspiciously. Unable to hold back, I laugh and her head swivels back toward me, her eyes lighting up, catching me in the act though I'm pretty she didn't hear me.

"Yes, more spray paint, but we'll get to that. First, I need to say something and I really need you to hear me."

Her eyes lower, but before she can take my words the wrong way, I reach out, resting my fingers against her chin which makes her lift them back up to me. There is nothing wrong about what I said and I'm about to show her why.

"I love you Cadence." I say, but at the same time even though I'm painstakingly slow at it, I make my hands repeat the words. It's only when she catches on to what I'm doing, her eyes darting from my lips down to where my hands are signing the words to her that I know I've hit my mark.

As the tears begin to pool in the corner of her eyes, I silently thank Isabelle and whatever god I can for being able to have this moment right now. Her reaction to the small attempt I've made at understanding her, adapting to her needs, it's everything.

"Why didn't you just sign the words?"

When I decided that learning how to sign was going to be my first step in starting over with her, Isabelle asked me the same thing. I insisted on learning the individual letters and at the time, I never gave her an explanation for it because it wasn't any of her business. The only one the explanation matters for is the girl standing here now.

"Coach told me once, when I was too busy screwing around to pay attention that the only way he could get through to me, make me hear him was to spell everything out. I wanted you to hear me."

If I thought the growing pool of water in her eyes couldn't get worse, I was in for a rude awakening. No sooner do I say the words then I notice the tears begin to fall from her eyes. Before I can reach out to her, make them stop she puts her hand up between us.

"Happy tears."

Nodding, I step toward her, fully prepared to push her hand out of the way if I need to if it means I can have this girl in my arms. It feels like forever since I've touched her even though it's only been a few minutes and if I don't do something soon to end it, I'm going to go out of my mind.

"All this time I wanted you to hear me, but it was me that wasn't listening. You've heard me this entire time because you heard me here." She says as she reaches out and rests her hand over my heart. "Thank you for hearing me."

This girl—she's exactly the way Kayden says she is. She's the one that helped me, the one that made me realize that I'm better than the way I've been for the last six years and she's here now, thanking me when the reality is she has nothing to thank me for.

Moving my hands again and watching as her eyes lock on them, I spell the same words out again, for no other reason than I don't want to spend another second of this moment together not letting her know how I feel. I ran from it, denied it, fought like hell against it for three weeks and I'm done.

I'm head over heels for Cadence Taylor and I'll repeat it as many times as I have to so that she never spends another second doubting it. I'm the person I am now, the one standing here signing because of her believing in me. I might have thought I was the strong one, the fighter, but the truth is, it was never me at all.

It's always been her. She's the real fighter.

"It's my turn." She says slowly, focusing my attention back on her and whatever she's about to say next. This is the moment of truth, this is where everything changes, this time for keeps.

Her hands move first and even though it's short, I'm pretty sure I know what she said. It's now that what she said earlier, about me hearing her in my heart becomes true. It's the three words she signs to me before I grab her and pull her into my arms that make every single bit of what we've gone through worth it.

"What was that last word?" I ask, remembering the full sign for I love you from my research on the internet and knowing that it wasn't a part of it.

"Your name means loyal so—"

"So that means..."

She smiles at me and I'm completely undone at the sight of it. The way she looks right now, her eyes shining under the lights above us, I wanna freeze time and keep her this way forever. Her hands lift and her lips part at the same time and just like before, she stops my heart as she signs her feelings to me, loud and clear.

"It means I love you, Dillon."

Cadence

When Dillon signed to me, my heart, I'm pretty sure it stopped beating in my chest. It kicks in again and releasing the hitched breath I'd been holding, I steady myself from the impact that small gesture has on me and then it happens again.

Explaining to me why he signed out the letters, his memory of what his coach told him; the impact the words had in bringing him to the moment we're in now, I'm completely altered by it. To some people, it might not have been the most romantic thing to say, but for him, knowing him the way I do, other than the way it felt seeing him sign I love you, there is nothing in the world that has ever sounded sweeter.

I don't need to hear the sound of his voice, his tone or even the words that he says because no matter what he says, I can feel them. The way his heart seems to have been hearing me all this time, it seems like mine has been doing the same and it's something that I never want to lose.

The way I felt on the dance floor when he had his arms around me, I feel as he wraps them around me again, his head resting on the side of mine, the feel of his even breaths on my ear. Being with Dillon Murphy, I'm starting to learn, is a full body experience. He's given me the ability to hear him because of all the ways I can feel him, the most important being the effect he has on my heart.

Pulling back just enough to be able to bring my face up in perfect unison to his, he leans in and his lips brush against mine and in that moment, the world around us, the lights in the trees, the blowing of the breeze, the dance taking place only a few minutes away, it all fades away and the only thing left is us and the all-consuming feeling that comes along with being so completely owned by another person.

It's only when we break away from the kiss that I remember the only other thing left that he needs to explain.

"Spray paint?"

He smiles and points to the bike trail that spans out for a distance both behind and in front of us.

"We might end up getting in trouble for this one because it's a bit bigger than the rock, but do you remember what I said to you the day I asked you out?" When I nod, he continues. "Well, we're gonna leave our mark on the trail. A variation of those words for the world to see."

"You want the world to know?"

"Yes, Caddy. I want the world to know how I feel about you, but I'm not doing this for everyone else. I'm doing it for the only person that I want to be a part of my world."

"Me?"

"Yes, you."

An hour later, my dress filled with as much of the paint as the ground in front of me, Dillon's jacket having been ditched for the same reason, that's exactly what happens. Before us now, are the only words left to say. Words that we want the entire world to hear.

This is the beginning of something that has no end
<3

(Read on for Dillon's letter to Cadence)

Dillon's Letter

Cadence,

I never got the chance during our time together to really start from the beginning, so I'm going to write all of this to you now so that when you show up tonight, we can really start again.

I wasn't always such a mess. I didn't always pick on people I thought were weaker than me and I definitely wasn't always so angry and full of hate.

Until you came into my life three weeks ago, I can only remember loving one person and she passed away a long time ago. I used to think that my dad and the fighting turned me into the person you've heard about and seen, but it wasn't. The day my grandma died, the way I used to be, I turned it off. I was eight years old and the one person in the entire world that I gave a damn about was taken from me.

She died naturally in her sleep, but all I could see back then was that when you love someone, they're destined to be ripped away from you. I shut my feelings off then, thinking that as long as I didn't feel nothing could get to me and when my family imploded a couple years later, taking me down with it, I just rode the wave and became the person you met when you showed up at Wexfield.

I'm the one that made the decision to change after she died and then, when my dad started hounding me about the weak versus strong stuff, I accepted it as fact because it made the most sense. Only the weak feel things; cry, care and love. It became my mission from that point on to make sure that every single one of them I came across, I put the fear of god into. I wanted them to know that the way they were, timid and weak was wrong and that the way I am, it was the way to be.

Cadence, I was so wrong. I hurt so many people and no matter what I do now, where I go, I'm never going to completely make up for any of it, but I swear to you, I'm not going to stop trying to. Hurting people, no matter if they have disabilities or not is wrong. The way I've been living for the last ten years, it needs to stop and this is my last ditch attempt at doing something about it. Changing it and fixing it.

You didn't change me. I put too much pressure on you when I said that I wanted to be better for you, but you did play a big part in me wanting to change. You showed me just in being you that the way I've been doing things is wrong and that the way my life was going, isn't right for me. You didn't make me change, I did that all on my own, but you did shine a light on something I've spent way too much time running from.

Your mom told me the other day that when you care about someone, you don't give up. You don't stop trying and even though I said this is my last ditch attempt at changing it, I lied. No matter where we go, ours is a beginning that will never have an end because I won't give up no matter how many times you turn me away. I will keep trying because that's what love is.

Love, it's about more than just the times when things are picture perfect. It's about continuing to do it when they aren't. It's continuing to fight when there doesn't seem to be anything left to fight for.

For all the time I've spent fighting, I've never done it for the right reasons. I want to do that now. I want to fight and this time, fight for the one thing that matters the most to me. I want to fight for the light when things get dark; for the smile when all I want to do is cry. I want to stand my ground and for the first time since my grandma died, fight for what's right.

I want to fight for you, for us and most of all, for love.

You're not the only one that's spent their life living in a world with no sound. The difference is, the reason it happened to me is because nothing until now has been worth hearing. That all changed the day I walked into your mom's class. Now my world is filled with sound and it's the best sound. It's a sound I never want to lose now that I've found it.

If you look up at me now, you'll see it.

You're the only sound I hear and you always will be.

Dillon

The End

Hear Me Now Playlist

Just Like You by Three Days Grace

Echo by Trapt

Tears by The Tragic Thrills

Pain by Three Days Grace

Second Chance by Shinedown

Hear Me Now by Framing Hanley

Great Divide by Nick Carter

With Me by Sum 41

That's My Goal by Shayne Ward

Fever by The Tragic Thrills

Bleed by Hot Chelle Rae

Hurricane by Parachute

How Love Should Be by Tyler Hilton

Help Me by Nick Carter

Run To Me by Nick Lachey

On The Way Down by Ryan Cabrera

Dreams by The Red Jumpsuit Apparatus

For The Nights I Can't Remember by Hedley

Anthem For The Underdog by 12 Stones

Sorry by Daughtry

Sick Of It by Skillet

Simon by Lifehouse

Your Arms Feel Like Home by Three Doors Down

The Story Of Me And You by Evan Taubenfeld

Acknowledgements

Caleb, Noah, Raine and Isabella. You are my light when it gets dark, my smile when all I want to do is cry and the reason this amazing dream of mine even exists. For the rest of my days, your sound is the only one I ever want to hear because in it, everything is beautiful. I love you.

Daddy. You told me when I wrote Count On Me that you wanted to see it do something, move people and it's because of that faith and the love you have in me that every book I have ever written exists and why this one is about to be introduced into the world. You are the strongest, most amazing man I know and I'm so thankful I'm your daughter.

Theresa. Count On Me wouldn't be the book it is without your help and guidance and I wouldn't be half the person I am without your friendship and support. We started out as writing companions and in the span of a few months it became so much more. I am truly blessed to call you a friend.

Lisa. Without you I'm pretty sure there would be no me. On a daily basis you push me, make me better and for that I will forever be thankful. Your faith in me, your love of the words that I string together into books, its life altering in its intensity. So thank you for that and so much more.

Pamela Sparkman. I am inspired by you daily, whether it be your friendly disposition, your writing or just the amazing human being you are. I am honored to know you and as I've told you before, I love you to the moon and back. From Cooper to Kayden...the next bestseller right?

Ryan and Jenn, the two beautiful angels that took a chance on an unknown and never looked back. This, all of it is because of you. Thank you for being who you are. You inspire me daily.

Joey. This book above all others; it's ours. Remember that always.

To all my readers. I do this in every book and I will always do it. I could sit here and write stories all day every day for the rest of my life and they wouldn't mean anything without all of you out there reading them and supporting me. You will never truly know what your comments to me, your reviews, even your ratings mean. I take you with me always. You are the stars here, I'm just merely shining in your presence.

About The Author

Melyssa Winchester is a mother of four from Toronto, Ontario, Canada. When she's not knee deep in adolescent awesomeness, she's falling in love, one book boyfriend and girlfriend at a time. She is a lover of all things romance and will forever believe in a real and true happily ever after.

When she's not off being a mom or writing you can find her doing one of two things. Reading or buried under the covers watching Supernatural, Sons of Anarchy or Veronica Mars.

Melyssa is currently working on Before The Light Book #2: Absence Of Light (Ryan's story) that follows the lives of the characters from the Love United Series before they came together. She is also hard at work on a standalone title Shades of Blue and working on All My Heart (Kayden and Isabelle's continuing story from Count On Me.

You can find her on the web, either at her personal site, Facebook (which she just might have an obsession with) or Twitter (@WinchesterBooks) where she talks incessantly about her kids, her writing and all things book boyfriend related.

Excerpt from: STOLEN BREATHS by Pamela Sparkman

Available Now

One

Going Home Again

Sometimes people drift into our lives like a feather blowing in the wind, landing right in our laps. There's really not a clear explanation for it other than maybe fate; at least that's what my daddy used to say. He was always writing poetry and more often than not he would have that faraway look in his eyes, almost as if he'd discovered a secret but just couldn't put it into words. I caught him staring out the kitchen window one night. He was still, almost too still, like he had gone someplace else, someplace in his memories. Some place I couldn't go. It was a place that he only shared with my mother. I'd watched him from a distance, afraid to make a sound for fear that it would startle him. He deserved to be happy, even if it was only through imagined what-ifs. I was very careful not to disturb his happy place.

My daddy was my heart when I was growing up. I didn't really remember my mother, she died was I was very young. I saw a woman in my dreams, though, with brown hair and brown eyes, like me, and she was always wearing a smile. I think it was a memory of my mom. It was what I liked to believe anyway. I was only three years old when she died. I know it was hard on my daddy. He truly loved her, and it was because of my daddy that I'd always held on to the idea of love. I mean, real, unconditional love. He still wrote my mother poems even though she had passed away twenty-three years before. I wanted a love like that. I wanted a love that completely transported me from my kitchen to wherever my love was, just by whispering their name over my lips or drinking in a sweet memory. I wanted it, but I was also scared to death to get it. That kind of love completely enveloped you and it was rare, so it also scared me to think sometimes that it could never happen to me. What a tragedy that would be. I just continued waiting, hoping, and praying that true love found me.

****

"Are you okay? You seem like you have a lot on your mind."

My thoughts were interrupted by the kind older lady sitting next to me on the plane. I had barely noticed her at all since I apparently had been staring out the window since takeoff.

"Oh, yes, I'm fine. Thank you. I guess I do have a lot on my mind. I'm sorry I didn't mean to be rude."

"It's okay, dear, you weren't being rude. I just wanted to make sure everything was all right with you." She smiled warmly.

"Thank you, but I'm fine." Her eyes were soft and a light blue. Her gray hair was fixed neatly in a bun. She wore glasses and seemed to be knitting a scarf, or maybe it was socks? No, wait, did people knit socks? Okay, so I couldn't tell what she was knitting but it was nice having someone ask me if I was okay, even if it was a total stranger. But the truth was, I lied. I was not okay. I was dying inside, but I absolutely would not break down in front of a bunch of strangers. I'd wait until I got back home - my childhood home. I could fall apart there.

Ever since I got the call about my daddy's accident, I found myself thinking about the things he used to say to me. I guess

I'd been trying to bottle up my memories of him and keep them as fresh in my mind as possible, allowing myself to be consumed by his words, trying desperately to remember some the poems he used to write.

If you see her
Tell her we're ok
Tell her she's everything I am
She's everything I say
If you see her
Tell her I'll make her proud
Tell her I'm no longer lost
I'm no longer under a cloud
If you see her
Tell her she's still mine
Tell her I'll love her forever
And one day we'll be better than fine
If you see her
Tell her that even though we are apart
Tell her I love her so
And that she is still my heart

I memorized it when I was very young. My daddy would say those words out loud like a prayer, kneeling beside the bed every night as far back as I could remember.

A bit of turbulence shook me out of my thoughts once again and the kind lady was still looking over at me. I casually looked out the window again. I was alone. I am alone.

Oh my God, I'll be all alone from now on.

For some reason, I chose that moment to realize that I was absolutely and completely alone now. Tears began streaming down my face and I wiped my tears with my sleeve. Then, the kind lady offered me a tissue.

"Here, dear." She patted me on my shoulder. "Whatever it is, I'm sure it'll be okay. Do you want to talk about it?"

I couldn't hold it in anymore and words started pouring out of my mouth. "My daddy died in a car accident and I'm going home to bury him. He was my only family and I'm all alone." I was sobbing now, and the fattest tears I'd ever cried streamed down my face almost like a faucet had been turned on with no way of shutting off.

"Oh, hon, I'm so sorry to hear that." She pulled me over and held me, rubbing her hands up and down my back to try and comfort me. "There there, let it all out." She even began moving in a sort of rocking motion.

I was trying to be so strong before, holding it all in until I could be alone. But I felt like my heart would burst and tears would spill over.

I cried on her shoulder for another minute or so, and then sat back up.

"I'm so sorry; I didn't mean to do that. You don't even know me."

"It's okay, dear. Really. I'm glad that I could be here for you. My name is Ms. Sophie. What's yours?"

Sniffing, I said, "Lily. Lily Grayson."

"Well we know each other now. Where are you from?" She was the grandmotherly type. She seemed so natural at caring about people.

"Nashville."

"Why, we're practically neighbors, hon. That's where we live – or I guess I should say where I live. My husband died two years ago." She looked sad for a brief moment, then perked back up. "I tell you, sweetheart, I believe it's fate that we met on this plane. Do you believe in fate, Lily?"

"My daddy did." I smiled faintly and was about to say something about me personally, not knowing if I believed in fate or not when she interrupted my thoughts.

"Seems like your daddy knew a thing or two."

"Yes, ma'am, I suppose he did." I decided I would just leave it at that.

"Where will you be staying?"

"Home. I mean the house I grew up in, for now. It's really too big for just one person, but I haven't decided what I plan to do with it."

I still had a lot to sort out when I got back to town. I left my job in Colorado when that call came in. Nothing seemed important anymore. My corporate ladder climb to the top seemed so inconsequential suddenly, and all I wanted to do was go back home and be in the place that I had the fondest memories and be near my daddy. I needed to be near him and I didn't feel like I could be near him if I stayed in Colorado. I walked right into Mr. Levin's office and told him I had to go. He didn't realize I meant permanently. I don't really know myself if I even realized I meant permanently when I said it. The further I got away from my office, however, the more I realized I would not be going back.

"My daddy had always hoped that I would move back. I want to honor his wishes."

"I'm giving you my number and I want you to call me when you get settled. I feel like we were meant to meet each other, Lily. I understand you have no family, so when you find out the funeral arrangements you call me. I would like to be there. Will you do that?"

"You're so sweet, Ms. Sophie. Thank you. You really don't have to—"

"Oh now stop. I want to. You seem like a sweet girl. Let me do this."

She was looking at me in such a motherly way, I consented. "Okay."

The plane landed and Ms. Sophie and I got off and waited for our luggage together at baggage claim.

"My grandson is picking me up. Let us give you a ride. It won't be any trouble, and in fact, I won't take no for an answer. You will come." She smiled warmly, making it hard to refuse her kind offer. Normally, I would never do this – get into a car with strangers — but she didn't feel like a stranger somehow.

"Thank you very much. You've been so kind to me. I want you to know I appreciate it."

"I know you do, dear."

It wasn't long before her grandson pulled up to get us in a sporty little black car. I couldn't really see him through the tinted windows. He got out and walked around behind the car to open the trunk, and I think my heart may have skipped a beat or two. I don't think I'd ever seen anyone who looked like him. He was muscular, but not in a body builder kind of way, more like an athlete, lean. I could tell that by the t-shirt he was wearing and the way his muscles stretched taut behind the fabric. It hugged his body, almost revealing what was underneath. He had dark brown hair that had sort of a messy I don't care look, but he could totally pull it off and still strangely look professional. His eyes were dark, and with his tanned skin, it was almost like looking at a work of art. His strong jaw and soft lips worked beautifully together to form the most amazing smile, showcasing one dimple on his left cheek. He was unbelievably gorgeous, and not in some Hollywood pretty boy sense, but in a real world masculine, boy next door sense.

"Cooper, this is Lily. We met on the plane and we got to talking. Turns out we live close to each other. I told her it wouldn't be a problem if she rode with us and we could take her home." She wasn't asking, really, simply letting her grandson know what the new plan was going to be. Then she turned to me, "Lily, this is my grandson, Cooper Hudson."

He looked at me and smiled. For a moment I thought I was standing in quicksand. I must have looked like an idiot just standing there staring.

Get a grip, Lil! I practically willed myself to step forward to say something, anything.

"Hello, (clearing my throat), it's nice to meet you." I flashed a weak smile and quickly looked away.

His smile transformed into a playful grin, perhaps amused by my reaction. "Hello, Lily. It's nice to meet you too. You must have made a huge impression on my grandmother. She doesn't normally give people she doesn't know rides anywhere."

He glanced over to his grandmother and gave her a quizzical look. She raised her eyebrow and shot him a look of her own. Obviously they had these non-verbal conversations mastered. I was starting to feel uncomfortable. There seemed to be an awkward silence between them, and I was thinking maybe this wasn't such a good idea. I started to ponder if I should go back inside and rent a car, but then Cooper moved towards me, grabbed my bags, and put them in the trunk.

After stowing our bags he looked at his grandmother and then shot a look over to me, "Ladies, shall we go?"

Cooper motioned for me to come to his side of the car, and after he moved the seat up, I climbed into the back seat.

"Do you have enough room back there?"

"Yes, I'm fine. Thank you."

Ms. Sophie got in the front passenger seat and closed the door, and then Cooper pushed his seat back and climbed in, readjusting his rearview mirror. I looked up and saw his eyes and quickly looked back down.

Crap! Why was I feeling so self-conscious around this man? Jeez. I could have sworn I heard him chuckling. Great, he's laughing at me. That's just icing on the cake.

On the way home I tried not making eye contact with Cooper's reflection anymore. I started thinking about my daddy again and how empty the house was going to feel when I got there, and a lump in my throat started to form. I started to feel pressure on my chest again and before I could do anything about it tears pricked my eyes. I felt a single tear roll down my cheek. Trying not to turn into a bawl bag in front of people again, I quickly wiped my tear away.

"Lily, are you going to be okay by yourself tonight?" Ms. Sophie asked, seemingly genuinely concerned for me.

"Yes ma'am. I'll be fine. Really." I gave her a reassuring smile and she seemed to accept my answer.

"You have my number, so you call me if you need anything."

"Thank you, but it won't be necessary. I can do this."

She looked at me in the warmest way possible. "I have no doubt in your ability to cope, but there is no point in doing something hard alone if you don't have to."

Cooper was quiet after he got in the car but I felt his eyes on me the whole time. The last thing I wanted to do was look up to verify my sixth sense, so I kept my head down unless I was speaking to Ms. Sophie. Other than Cooper asking me directions to my house, we really didn't say anything to each other.

We pulled up into my old driveway and Cooper put the car in park and got out. He pushed the seat forward and extended his hand out to help me. The moment we touched I felt something. Call it an electrical current, a bolt, a surge of heat, a rush of charged particles— call it whatever you want, because it was all of those things— but it was something else too, something more. I tried to play it off and hoped he didn't notice my odd reaction, but my immediate response was to pull away. I know that must have seemed odd, so I took his hand again and tried not to act like some stupid teenage girl. I prayed that I could just get inside the house without falling on my face. I was not having the best day. In fact, this entire week had been one giant nightmare that I couldn't wake up from.

I climbed out of the car and he stared at me with a puzzled look. I sighed internally and walked towards the trunk so I could get my bags and they could be on their way. I'd inconvenienced them enough. He slowly followed me, popped the trunk, and carried my bags to the door, waiting for me to find the key my daddy always hid on the porch so I could let myself in.

Ms. Sophie called out to me from the car. "Remember, Lily, call me when you get settled."

I gave her a nod and waved goodbye. I opened the front door and Cooper set my bags down inside the entryway.

"Thank you for the ride home and for your help, I... I appreciate it. You and your grandmother are very kind." I forced myself to look him in the eye.

"You're welcome, Lily. It was a pleasure." His face was warm and his voice compassionate. He held out his hand again for me to shake and I panicked. Not wanting to seem rude I extended my hand out and shook his. Just like before, I felt it.

That foreign feeling invaded my senses and was completely outside my realm of understanding, and it terrified me. He had a strange look on his face and I just wanted to disappear. I pulled away again and shoved my hands in my front pockets.

"Well, I'd best be going." The look on his face was unreadable and I tried to imagine what he might have been thinking. He shoved his hands in his front pockets as well and walked back to his car, glancing back towards me before getting in. He paused for a few seconds, then climbed back into his car and they drove away.